MISBEHAVING WITH MINOTAURS

HAVEN EVER AFTER - BOOK EIGHT

HAZEL MACK

COPYRIGHT

Editing - Krista Venero at Mountains Wanted

Cover - Anna Fury Author

Cover Art - Linda Noeran (@linda.noeran)

❀ Formatted with Vellum

AUTHORS ARE NOW FACING AN UNPRECEDENTED CHALLENGE - ARTIFICIAL INTELLIGENCE (AI).

AI-based "books", which are computer written, rather than human, are flooding the market and reducing our ability to earn a living wage writing books for you, our amazing readers.

The problem with AI as it stands today? It's not capable of thinking on its own. It ingests data and mimics someone else's style, often plagiarizing art and books without the original creator or author's consent.

There's a very real chance human authors will be forced out of the market as AI-written works take over. Yet your favorite authors bring magical worlds, experiences and emotions to life in a way that a computer can't. If you want to save that, then we need your help.

LEARN MORE ABOUT THE HARMFUL EFFECTS OF AI-WRITTEN BOOKS AND AI-GENERATED ART ON MY WEBSITE AT WWW.ANNAFURY.COM/AI

SYNOPSIS

Catherine

When celebrity skyball star Manorin Longhorn arrives in Ever to interview for our coaching position, I have one rule—don't engage. He's my ex from centuries past, a brash male whose heart I shattered when I walked away, and it would be completely inappropriate for me to date a prospective employee.

But the moment I see Nor again, the chemistry is undeniable, and I'm in big trouble since he's staying at the Annabelle Inn right under my nose. When he offers me a sexy no-strings arrangement, telling me I deserve a little fun, I know he's right. We settle on just one rule—all fun, no feelings.

Those horns still make the perfect handlebars, and the way Nor bends me over his desk proves some things never change. But this older, more experienced version of him doesn't just take— he commands with quiet dominance and devastating control, and I'm helpless to resist the delicious surrender.

Lingering looks and stolen trysts quickly turn into something that feels dangerously close to true romance. This isn't the reckless male I once knew; this Nor is older, more confident, and everything a succubus could want in a partner. Our arrangement was only supposed to be a filthy secret for a few weeks while he's in town, but tender moments and the way he supports me threaten to undo everything I've built to protect my heart.

Time is running out. Ever's not the only haven courting Nor for a coaching position, and every scorching night together brings us closer to goodbye. When it becomes clear that our fling is so much more than just a dirty little secret, Nor asks for a chance to win my heart again.

But so much hangs in the balance if our love fails. He says sometimes second chances are worth the risk, but if I surrender completely and he leaves, will there be anything left of me to salvage?

Misbehaving with Minotaurs is a spicy MF later in life, second chance monster romance

GET THE FREEBIES

CONTENT NOTICE

While this book is very sweet and lighthearted, there are a couple heavy themes to mention. Death of a former mate (off page but referenced), assholishness of a former mate (off page but referenced), the dreaded words 'we should talk', thrall attacks, dominance play and beguilement (with consent).

If you have any particular questions, feel free to reach out to me at author@annafury.com!

DEDICATION

For Mr. Fury-Mack, who didn't laugh at me when I said I wanted to start a monster romcom series with the title 'Getting It On With Gargoyles'. You've been there every smutty step of the way.

For my readers, without whom I wouldn't be blessed to do this crazy author thing full time (starting in August, anyhow). You are the cream to my cheese LOL.

THANK YOU!

CHAPTER ONE

CATHERINE

"Annabelle," I admonish as the black cat kitchen timer swivels on its base and meows at me.

The countertop ripples, slinging the salt shaker toward the pan of vegetables I just started sautéing. Rolling my eyes upward, I chuckle as the inn's ceiling tiles pop playfully, clacking like piano keys.

"No more salt." I grab the shaker and shove it in the cabinet above the stove. "Guests can add it as needed, but there's no need for us to go salt crazy."

The timer spins to face away from me as the ceiling tiles still, the kitchen going utterly silent except for the sound of the vegetables in the pan.

"Don't be irritated, my love." Reaching out, I rub the tiles behind the stovetop.

One of the kitchen windows opens and slams angrily shut.

Sighing, I open the cabinet, withdraw the salt, and toss a dash on the vegetables.

For whatever reason, my home has a very strong preference on salt content, and this is not the hill I want to die on today. Last time I disagreed with her about salting the breakfast foods, she locked my bedroom door for twenty minutes until I apologized profusely.

It's funny what topics Annabelle feels strongly about. She and I are usually in lock step about *everything*, but occasionally she surprises me in her vehement preferences.

The salt, for instance.

And her refusal to let me touch up the white paint on her shutters even though it's chipping.

The tiny cat timer executes a darling series of flips along the countertop, leaping onto the back of the stove, its kitty features curling into a smile.

We fall into an easy silence as I finish the vegetables for the breakfast buffet. All of our rooms are full but one, and I'm expecting a guest any mo—

The ding of a bell echoes down the hallway, interrupting my thoughts. Annabelle ripples the backsplash tile to warn me that there's someone up front. I laugh and stroke the tile again.

"Thank you, my darling."

The cat timer meows as the front bell dings a second time.

Leaving the kitchen, I hurry along the skinny hallway to find a handsome young pixie male standing in the inn's front entryway. He holds a suitcase in one hand, a long garment draped over his other forearm. Translucent blue wings flutter lightly at his back, the tips of his pointed ears twitching slightly.

"Welcome to the Annabelle Inn." I slide behind the tall wooden check-in desk and smile. "You must be Gilbert Sintjan?"

His blue lips pull into a half smile. "That's me. I presume you're Catherine, the Annabelle Inn's famous proprietress?"

I laugh. "I do believe you made up that word, Gilbert, but, yes, that's me."

The edges of his lips turn down. "You don't happen to still have breakfast available, do you? I had heard the Galloping Green Bean diner makes a to-die-for burger, and I was actually going to have that for breakfast, but they were *quite* busy."

When I give him a surprised look, he laughs.

"I know, it's odd. I don't like breakfast food. But anyhow, the line was out the door, and the very terse centaur hostess told me in no uncertain terms that it would be at least two hours before she could seat me."

I sigh, shooting him an understanding look. "Alba is direct on the best of days, but you're right that the burger is absolutely fantastic there. You're in luck, though; I was just about to replenish the breakfast buffet. It runs from eight to ten a.m. each morning except on the weekends."

He winks. "You don't happen to have burgers, do you?"

We laugh together as I shake my head. "No burgers, but I was just sautéing vegetables, and there's plenty of variety. I'm so busy these days, it's easier to justify a wide selection of offerings." I return his wink. "And don't worry, it's not all traditional breakfast food."

I take Gilbert's credit card and hand him a key for his room —the mermaid-themed room upstairs. We head for the second floor, where I drop him off at his door and offer to give him a tour of Ever at any point, if he'd like one.

Remembering the vegetables, I rush back to the kitchen. The pan swirls slowly on the stove, the veggies sizzling and snapping.

"Thank you, Annabelle." I grab the pan and toss the perfectly cooked veggies in a bowl. The black cat timer turns to watch me as I carry the bowl through a small butler's pantry and into the formal dining room. My guests are beginning to arrive, and I greet each monster, answering a few questions as they begin to dig into the buffet.

The breakfast hours are a blur while I constantly refill the buffet and clean up as my guests make a bit of a mess. It's not until the last guest leaves that I return to the kitchen and sit at the island for a moment.

Around me, the Annabelle feels happy. I sense her the way I

always have—she's like a warm hug, constantly there, a friend by my side. I've often wondered if this is how shifter mate bonds feel, that innate and deep sense of *knowing* about another being. Because I swear I can think something, and Annabelle seems to know.

I glance up at the beautiful coffered ceiling. "I'm headed to a meeting with town leadership, darling. Arkan thinks it's time to expand Downtown Ever. Most of the businesses are stretched past capacity, as are we. Wouldn't you agree?"

Annabelle groans her assent, the floorboards creaking beneath my feet.

I rise and go to the fridge, grabbing a filtered water bottle. "I suppose we'd have to expand into the rose garden because I don't really want to stack a bunch more stories on top of you."

Around me, she stills. The only sound is the steady tick-tock of the wall clock. I look around the kitchen while Annabelle thinks. We'd need to bump out this space to give it more indus- trial size, and we'd cut into the rose garden a bit. But it's an easy enough fix. Now, if we wanted more rooms, we'd have to add on another story, because there's not enough space in my back- yard to expand that way. Although, to be honest, I'm already a bit busier than I'd like to be. If anything, I want fewer rooms, not more.

Just last night, I was sitting in the front living room reading when a stream of guests came in asking for help with various things. I never did get back to my book after taking care of them. Silence is a blessed gift these days, and I find myself craving it more and more. Considering room expansion makes my nose scrunch in dismay.

The cat timer hops around the back of the stove and to the far end of the countertop. Scrunching down, it executes a leap onto the window ledge, spinning to face the backyard rose garden. Like always, it's a perfect sixty-five degrees outside—a weather pattern I chose when I helped design Ever all those centuries ago—and the rose bushes sway gently, their blooms beautifully vibrant year-round.

The timer spins slowly to face me as the window behind it opens, allowing the breeze in. It brushes over my face, rustling pale gray waves over my eyes. Shoving my hair out of the way, I stare at the gorgeous rose garden behind the inn, musing about what it would be like to finally grow the Annabelle Inn…and if I even want that.

Realistically, Annabelle might be my heart building and best friend, but she was always meant to be my retirement hobby. It's turned into nights and weekends and the need for a helper I just can't bring myself to hire. It's never felt right to add another monster to our mix, but as two separate guests appear in the kitchen doorway, I consider that it might be time now.

Smiling broadly, I greet them.

No rest for the weary.

$\sim$

"So, thrall attacks and warlocks and revenants don't seem to be deterring anyone from moving to Ever. Have you all noticed?"

Town Hall clacks her ceiling tiles in agreement with Ever's Keeper, Arkan. The big centaur crosses his muscular arms over his chest as he swishes his tail lazily against his black-coated sides. He looks around at us with glittering blue eyes. The rest of us are seated, but the handsome young centaur prefers to remain standing during haven leadership meetings. He walks circles around our table sometimes, and it's very distracting to me, but he's an excellent Keeper. Much like a human mayor, if monsters had such a thing.

Alo Rygold, one of two gargoyles from the town's protector team, leans back with a wry look on his handsome, angular features. "Hopefully, Ever's many *charms* are the main draw?

Although, to be honest, having a blue witch living in town is probably pulling monsters here too. There's not a single other blue witch living within the haven system, and Lou is so damn strong. Ever's gotta be the safest possible place in the entire world for a monster to live at this point."

Arkan nods, making eye contact with each of us in turn. I'd almost laugh at how focused he is—young people can be so intense—but we need that excitement.

"Since the opening of the Grand Portal Station at Hearth HQ haven, we're drawing in an average of twenty new residents per month. The wraith motel and Annabelle Inn are constantly full. Homes keep popping up to accommodate the new Evertons. I've got five requests to call humans here from the outside world via the town map. And our businesses are...well..." He glances at Ohken Stonesmith, the troll owner of our singular general store and Fleur, the flower shop. "Ohken, you're busy. Too busy. Tell me I'm wrong."

Ohken sighs around the big tusks that stick up from his lower jaw. "I never thought the day would come when I'd need more help or have to consider expanding the General Store, but I am. Wren and I talked about hiring an architect to design a second floor, but I haven't bitten the bullet yet. I'm not getting nearly enough time at home with her, and that's a problem for me."

I smile. I had the privilege of watching him fall in love with Wren Hector. And I watched her triplet sisters and their young aunt, the blue witch, all fall in love, too. Ever's been awash with love stories in these last few months.

That almost makes my smile fall. I've been working on my own love story.

It's not going well.

I risk a glance at Arkan's father, Vikand, who rests comfortably on a long centaur bench by his son's side. Like always, the brilliant centaur appears lost in thought, arms crossed over his broad chest and pale eyes glazed. Arkan says something, but Vikand looks across the table at me. A soft smile tips his black lips upward.

Even from here, my succubus senses are strong enough to pick up a wash of pheromones from him. He's always found me attractive, but he's quiet, shy, bookish to the extreme. I've been pursuing him slowly, certain he'll never make the first move. I return the half smile. After this meeting, I'm asking him out.

When he glances away from me and up at his son, who's still talking, I shove that thought away. I need to focus because this meeting is important to Ever's future.

Arkan barrels on, thankfully oblivious to my temporary inattention.

"I want to get ahead of the growth because I believe what we've seen so far is just a trickle. Now that it's easier to come to Ever, I predict our tourism will grow by leaps and bounds. We need more restaurants and inns. Actually..." his voice trails off as he sinks down onto his forelegs, pointing at a rolled-up tube of paper on the giant round table in front of us.

"This is a set of old plans from a very long time ago when Ever was created. It wasn't the final design, obviously, but some elements could be reused now. Town Hall provided these to me when I spoke with her about potential expansion." He looks around the table with a smile. "She's on board, by the way, excited even."

I've seen these plans. I know what he's going to show us before he unrolls them. I was there when the various options were originally designed. But it's still fun when he rolls the paper flat and sets paperweights at each corner.

"There," he says, pointing to a street at the far end of Main, just before the Historical Society and Town Hall. "The reason there's currently the grassy area between the last shops on either side of Main and Town Hall is because there was always meant to be another cross street there. We need it now. And I need to be courting business folks from other havens to open locations here. Restaurants, coffee shops, gift shops." He glances at me. "Probably inns, too."

"Let's take a step back for a second. Do we *want* to grow Ever?" Alpha Richard, a handsome shifter male with white-flecked black hair, stands and points at the edge of town. "I'm not saying we don't; I'm just asking if we're all in agreement that we *do*. All the new homes springing up are beginning to encroach on Shifter Hollow territory, and my people are getting antsy. Which again, is fine if that's what we want. But we'll need to expand Shifter Hollow too. The shifters, centaur and pegasi need more space." He stares at the old plans before looking up at Arkan. "My population is growing."

Arkan nods. "Don't I know it. These old plans don't account for that, but I think it'd be easy enough to expand the ward and grow Shifter Hollow's surface area too." He glances over at me. "Can you see any complications with that, Catherine?"

It sounds like he's just asking my opinion as a member of Ever's leadership team, but he and I know the question goes deeper than that. I'm involved in haven creation in a way few monsters know about. Not even everyone in this room is aware. But Ohken looks over at me, his expression neutral. He's been there when I've used my unique power. He's seen what I'm capable of.

I smile up at Arkan. "We're not close to any human towns. There's only forest around us for a hundred miles in every direction...plenty of space to expand into. It's wise to think about this growth now."

I look around to the gathered monsters, wonderful beings I've known, some for centuries. "Our growth rate is only going to increase, and as Arkan mentioned, tourism is on the rise thanks to the new portal station. We never had much tourism before since it was such a pain to travel between havens, but now?" I run my fingers over the slightly curled old plans. "We thought this might happen one day; that's how these plans came to be. I'm in agreement that we need to have these conversations sooner than later."

Arkan barks out a laugh. "Oh, I'm not done with my suggestions either." He opens his hands wide, grinning at the gathered group. "We have a shiny new skyball stadium and a team that never practices. Even so, we almost won last year's skyball championship. I want to put a bigger focus on our team. I'd like to attract regular games and court some rising stars. There's big money in skyball, and we don't get a piece of that pie now."

Ohken lets out an uncharacteristic growl. "I don't want to take *more* time away from Wren, even though I'm technically on the Ever team. You know most of us who play are part-time at best. I assume you'd want regular practices? We don't do that now, and I don't want to start."

"I know we don't." Arkan crosses his arms again. "But we should. Again, with the new portal station, it's a rock-solid investment for us to do this. It'll bring tourism, and tourism will be good for everyone in this room." He shoots Ohken a pointed look. "I'm not suggesting you have to become a full-time skyball player, friend, just that we should consider investing in a professional team."

"He's right," I offer.

"Catherine, care to expand on that thought?" Shepherd, Alo's younger brother, smiles at me from across the table. "Ever's got such a wonderful small-town feel. Are we talking about losing that if we truly bring professional skyball here?"

I toss my long gray waves over my shoulder as I pull my thoughts quickly together. "During last year's skyball tournament, Ever was packed and busy, but it was the best weekend on record for sales at many of our shops and restaurants. Money doesn't buy happiness, but it can buy freedom. I'm in favor of creating that opportunity for our friends and neighbors."

9

I look around at the group of monsters I've come to admire so highly. "I have friends I haven't seen in years because inter-haven travel was previously such a pain. That's already changing because of the new Grand Portal Station. Getting busier is going to happen whether we're ready for it or not. The pinch we're feeling now is nothing compared to what's coming. I'm in favor of being ready. If we do it thoughtfully, Ever won't lose the community feel."

"Exactly," Arkan says, looking around the room as the others chat quietly. "We need more infrastructure to support the growth. And, selfishly, I'd like to see us get a skyball coach, seeing as how we've never had one. I have two candidates in mind, and I'd love to bring them both to Ever on a trial basis."

"Moving fast, aren't you?" Alo lashes his long tail from side to side as he frowns at Arkan from his spot across the table.

Arkan stills. "Part of the reason I came to Ever was to usher in an era of growth. This haven hasn't grown meaningfully in about two centuries. That was fine for a time. But Catherine's point about it happening either way is spot on. We can be ready for it and provide everyone with a good experience. Or we can ignore it and deal with the pains that'll bring."

Ohken sinks back into his chair with a sigh, scratching at his stubble with the fingers of one big green hand. After a long moment, he nods. "I'm in favor of exploring this. At the end of the day, I want more time with my mate. Let's keep Ever func-tioning like a well-oiled machine."

Arkan beams, white teeth flashing in the fluorescent light from Town Hall's auditorium ceiling. "I'm glad you're all in agreement, because I have a call with Manorin Longhorn tomorrow about coming to Ever for a trial period."

Oh my gods.

Manorin Longhorn.

I clasp my hands in my lap as I try to gather the thoughts that dash around my mind at that name.

Alo snorts. "Manorin Longhorn? Are you shitting me? He's a fucking skyball legend."

Arkan's smile grows impossibly broad, stretching across his handsome face. "He coached me when I was going through the Protector Academy. I tried to recruit him for my last haven, but he had no interest in leaving Hearth Headquarters or the Hellions. He agreed to take my call tomorrow, though, so I'm hopeful things are changing for him. I'll keep you posted."

He sighs. "I know it seems like I'm suggesting we move quickly, but if we can get Manorin Longhorn to come here and build a team, wow. That would really be something. And I don't see why we can't do that and plan expansion all at the same time. The stadium's just sitting there unused..." His voice drifts off as he looks around the table.

I glance at Vikand, curious to see what he thinks. To my surprise, he's holding a tiny book in one hand, glasses perched on the tip of his nose as he reads. He's not listening. At all.

A delicious scent curls across my consciousness, and my nostrils flare to pull in more of that delectable smell.

Across the table from me, Vikand glances up from his book, appearing lost in thought. I'd bet a million dollars he's thinking about something sensual, because he smells so damn good, like fresh hay and pine needles. My sensual nature rises as I watch him cock his head to one side. After a moment, he looks back down at the book, shifting on his bench.

I'd pay good money to know his actual thoughts.

Arkan closes the meeting, and when Vikand rises from the centaur bench, I round the table and approach him, marveling at how much taller he is than me. Not that that would be a problem between us. I'm a succubus. I can handle literally anything in *that* department.

Vikand's dark coat shines with health, his form still fit despite his age. He's got to be nearly as old as I am—many, many centuries—and I love that.

"Hello, Vikand." I smile brightly up at the handsome centaur.

He jolts slightly, having been lost in thought. Just as quickly, he tucks the tiny book into a pocket in his vest and smiles down at me, adjusting the glasses perched on the tip of his nose. He and Arkan could be twins, with the same dark skin and long braided hair, but Vikand's age is evident in the creased lines at the edges of his eyes and mouth. Gods above, he's handsome with those high cheekbones and brilliant blue eyes.

"H-hello, Catherine." He clears his throat, slipping a thumb into the pocket of his fitted navy vest. "You look lovely this evening."

I glance down at the figure-hugging emerald wrap dress I picked out. I've always had a full, buxom figure—most succubi do—but this particular dress really shows off my curves.

"Thank you." I beam up at him. "Listen, would you like to have a picnic with me one afternoon next week? There's a great little spot I know; I think you'd enjoy it."

Vikand stares for a long moment, then clears his throat again as bright pheromones saturate the air between us. My power means I can read everyone's scent. It's an ability that helps me understand those around me more easily. It's how I always know which monsters will end up together, because I can literally smell attraction the moment I see them together.

It's how I know *now* that Vikand is sincere in his compliment. I take another step forward, knowing my proximity's having an effect on him as the scent of pine needles takes on a tart, lemony edge. His mouth drops slightly open, his nostrils flaring as his pupils blow wide.

"I...yes, sure. I'd like that. Just let me know when and where."

I knew I'd have to make the first move. Vikand is many, many enticing things, but forward in the romance department is not one of them. And honestly? I'm good with that. I was once mated to a male who could charm the pants off of anyone, and it ended poorly. I've had enough of that sort of monster to last a million lifetimes.

"How about next Wednesday? Pick me up at the Annabelle, and we'll walk together, alright?" I reach up and rest a hand on his upper stomach, curling my fingers gently into the fabric of his vest.

He shudders and shifts from one foot to the other, his voice quiet when he speaks. "Alright, Catherine. Would lunchtime work for you?"

I try to shove disappointment away. Lunchtime feels like a business meeting. But still…it's a start.

"Lunchtime sounds lovely, Vikand. I'll pack us a picnic."

"I'm not a picky eater," he says with a smile.

Errr…okay.

Dropping my hand, I wink at him as I turn and flip my hair over my shoulder. "See you Wednesday for lunch, Vikand."

I sashay toward the exit. My neighbor Alo stands at the door, a wry smile on his face.

"Not a word," I chirp as he holds his elbow out for me.

Alo snorts out a laugh. "Oh, my gorgeous friend, you already know my thoughts on this topic."

"So I do." I wave those thoughts away as I slip a hand through his elbow. "Remember how you ignored me for five years while I suggested you ask Miriam out? I'm going to ignore you like you did me, and it's going to be just fine. Now, can we talk about something more fun on the way back home, or are you going to give me love advice?"

He rests his free hand over mine as he guides me along the long hall to the exit.

"I don't need to give advice that'll fall on deaf ears, Cath. You're a grown-ass woman. Do what you want. For the record, I did eventually ask her out."

I grin up at him. "I will, thank you. And I'm glad it only took you five years to realize your best friend was your soulmate. Despite my weekly needling."

He smiles down at me. "Point taken. Moving on. What do you make of this Manorin Longhorn news? I'm excited about that, although I don't wanna play full-time either. I'd do part-time though."

Something deep inside me heats at Manorin's name.

"I dated him back in the day," I whisper, not willing that secret to go any further than Alo's ears.

"Get the hells outta here." He scoffs, dark horns flexing as his amethyst eyes go wide. "Seriously?"

I nod. "It was pretty serious at the time, but we were younger. It was before he coached skyball at the headquarters haven. And before you-know-who."

Alo waggles both black brows at me. "Well, Catherine. I must say, this is an interesting development."

"Is it?" I feign innocence, then I scowl up at one of my favorite monsters in Ever. "Keep that to yourself. At this point, Manorin and I are nothing but old friends."

Alo snorts. "This news would sure give him a leg up in the coach search."

I shake my head. "No. Our ancient history will have absolutely no bearing on that. You know I love skyball, so I'm fully on board with Arkan's plan to bring it here. I want the best coach we can possibly get. If we all decide that's Manorin, fab!"

"Mhm, okay." Alo's tone is agreeable, but I suspect it's not the last I'll hear on this subject. Just like he keeps promising not to insert himself into my pursuit of Vikand the centaur. Yet, even so, Alo's regular and loud with his opinions on the topic.

It's like he read my mind, because he smirks. "Speaking of males, I heard you ask Vikand out."

I blush despite myself, looking up to smile at my friend. "I'm ready, Alo. Ready to begin dating. I don't want to rush anything, so I'm taking this slowly, but...I want to."

He grins. "And that's the guy, huh?"

I swat his arm again.

He shuffles his big, leathery wings behind us, the curved points hanging above our heads. "What?! I'm just surprised at your choice, that's all…"

"Well," I say, "don't trouble yourself over it another minute, old friend. It's all working out perfectly."

"If you say so," he murmurs, moving my hand from his arm and jogging ahead to open the front door. As I sail through, it's obvious he's barely holding back an opinion on the topic— again.

Not that the opinion matters. I will do whatever, and whoever, the hells I want.

CHAPTER TWO
MANORIN

I glance out of the window in my first-floor office, admiring how peaceful and quiet the skyball field looks this early in the morning. In a half hour, the perfectly manicured field will be bustling with the Protector Academy *and* pro skyball teams—finals practice starts today.

A reminder pings from the blue leather watch strapped around my wrist. I've got an important call starting in two minutes. I've been working at my computer for hours, planning the primary and secondary lineups for the upcoming season, and my back hurts from hunching so far over the desk. Standing, I roll my broad shoulders, grimacing at how my long horns scrape the ceiling if I stand up too straight.

This office wasn't made for a minotaur of my size, much less a longhorn minotaur. I've been the head coach of the Hearth HQ Hellions for a very long time. The coach before me was a gargoyle.

A lot shorter.

And a lot less strict with his players, if the old stories are to be believed.

I probably should've had the office renovated, but it never seemed to be top of mind.

The Hearth HQ skyball team was a damn mess when I came on, but I've whipped them into shape over the last two centuries. Many seasons' worth of players have come and gone during that time, but I've turned out a solid string of superstars, many of whom have gone on to have long, illustrious pro careers. Glancing out the door of my office, I smile at the paintings of famous skyball players lining the hallway. Ninety percent of those were cultivated during my tenure here.

I smile bigger as I consider that. A ping breaks through the thought, the communication disk on my wall flashing blue. A name hologram rises above the tech's circular surface.

Ever Keeper.

Of course, I always knew him as Arkan Canterbury, a centaur who was a star player while studying at the academy. Now he goes by his title—Keeper of the hidden monster haven of Ever, in America.

Massachusetts state, as I recall.

I grab the comm disk and set it carefully on my desk, directing it to answer Arkan's call. A life-sized hologram figure rises up from the disk, and my former player smiles, the grin splitting his handsome dark features.

I cross my arms over my chest. "You don't look a day older, Arkan. Or should I say Keeper?"

He waves away the comment. "The Evertons call me both. It was hard for me to give up my name for the title, even though that's traditional for the role."

I consider that for a moment. I could no sooner give up the Longhorn name than chop off an arm. It's a point of pride for other longhorn minotaurs to cherish our shared last name.

"So," Arkan says, "I'll get straight to the point. I wanted to recruit you in my last haven, but it wasn't the right time for that community or you. I'm pretty sure you know why I'm calling this time, and you took the call, so what's changed?"

I suck at my front fangs as I think about his question. What *has* changed in the decades since Arkan last tried to steal me from my position as head coach?

"To be honest," I say, "I've accomplished a lot for the Hellions. I've run this program for almost two hundred years. My brain keeps going into build mode, but the Hellions are a well-oiled machine at this point." I shrug and glance out the window at the skyball pitch again. After a moment, I return my focus to the black-coated centaur male. "I'm looking for something messy that I can fix up and make shine."

Arkan grins and crosses his arms, matching my stance. "Well, Coach, it just so happens that the Ever team is messy as hells, full of part-timers with no coach at *all*. In fact, one of my players threatened to quit last night if I made him attend a *practice*. The team made it all the way to the finals last year, as you know, despite that. But there's zero recruiting and literally no program to speak of. We have an empty stadium that I don't think anyone's set foot in since the finals. Ever wouldn't just be something messy; it would be starting from the basement and working from the ground up. How does that sound?"

Part of me aches as he talks. That's exactly what I want. But another part of me longs for the open ranges and clear skies of my home haven, Pine Gulch. My dream job would take me there. Unfortunately for me, the Pine Gulch coach has held his role for six centuries with no signs of slowing down. I don't think that job'll ever open up, not unless the gods and goddesses themselves descend to drag Rip Shorthorn outta that job.

"I need more information." I uncross my arms and tuck my hands into the pockets of my too-tight jeans. "I'm interested, though. What's your evaluation process look like? Who else are you looking at? What are next steps?"

Arkan grins. "I hoped you'd say that, Manorin. I'm also

looking at a newer coach from a remote haven in Brazil...Gil Stoneswallow. As for eval, I'd like you to come here for a trial period once your finals prep ends and before the season starts. Gil will be doing the same thing, although you won't overlap. You've got a couple weeks off coming up, if memory serves?" He winks. I may technically have that time off, but he knows I've never taken it once in my entire career.

"I'll manage," I grit out. This is important. It's time for me to consider moving on.

"I'll start making arrangements," Arkan says with a huge smile. "Would you prefer to stay at our local wraith motel or up at the Annabelle Inn? The inn's closer to downtown and the skyball stadium. The wraith motel is like most others—opulent beyond belief with an incredible kitchen."

A smile turns my lips upward, the ring in my nose shimmying. "Does Catherine Evrien still run the Annabelle Inn?"

Arkan returns my feral look. "She does."

"Book me there, then. She and I are old friends."

Friends isn't the right word, but I don't need to get into that with Arkan.

"Done," Arkan says. "I'll email you later with all the details. I'm crazy excited about this, Manorin. I've got the one other candidate because I promised the haven leadership team that I'd do my due diligence. But the reality is that if you'll have us, I want you for Ever."

"You always were my favorite, but don't be a suck-up," I say with a snort.

He beams and tosses long black braids over his shoulder. "My mate is calling me for dinner, but I'll email those details soon. Goodbye, old friend."

I swat at his hologram, and he ducks out of the way. "It's still Coach to you, kid."

He laughs and signs off.

For a long time after he's gone, I stare at the communication disk. Eventually, I set it back on the wall as I consider our conversation. Am I really pursuing this? A team with no coach and no program to speak of? It's something I haven't done yet. The Hellions were a mess when I took them over, but there was the semblance of a program, and there *was* a head coach before me, even if he was shitty.

Ever's a blank slate, but I think I love that for me.

Voices drift up the hall, followed by the thwap of wings and clip-clop of hooves. The academy players are arriving for practice. Turning to the locker in my office, I unbutton my shirt along one shoulder and down one side so I can pull it off without yanking it up over my horns. Tossing it aside, I check out my reflection in the mirror. I might be approaching my eighth century—minotaurs are long-lived—but I'm still built like most of my players. The only hint that I'm older is a bit of salt dusting the oaky-brown fur at my temples.

I grab a Hellions jersey and button it over my broad chest. Kicking my way out of my jeans, I grab a pair of red and black athletic shorts. When I pull them up, they hug my thighs and sack, accentuating the bulge between my legs. I used to think it was ridiculous that athletic shorts aren't made in sizes that fit athletes. Then I realized that's on purpose.

The industry *wants* to tease its fans and onlookers with our bodies. Hot players in tight shirts and dick-hugging shorts are what the fans want. Cock outlines sell tickets. Actual erections are even better.

Adjusting tight fabric around my sheath, I mutter about the shorts issue and grab my whistle. I unclip it and reclip it around my neck. I'm so broad, it hangs down just far enough for me to wrangle it into my mouth. Maybe it's time for a longer string.

When I leave my office, a shorthorn minotaur jogs up the hallway and stops in front of me with a big smile. "You ready for practice, Coach? We're gonna kick some ass out there today!"

"Hells yeah we are," I say, my tone pure gravel. "Those pro

assholes won't know what hit 'em, right, player?" It's all bluster, I coach both Hearth's academy and pro teams, but we're split right now to prep for finals.

"Fuck yes," he hisses, clapping me on the shoulder. "I'm ready, Coach."

Good. I am too.

Ready to kick ass, take names, and maybe start something new.

~

The following Wednesday morning, I walk across the new Grand Portal Station, locating the glowing green portal that'll take me from Hearth HQ to Ever, all the way across the world. To the left of the Ever portal is a fabulous coffee shop called Higher Grounds. I consider stopping in for a latte, but it's actually their second location. The original is in downtown Ever, according to my research.

I'd prefer to try the location I'd regularly go to if this move works out. Smiling, I sling my duffel bag over my shoulder and step through the portal into a short hallway filled with luminescent green light. When I reach the end, the portal opens into Ever's portal station, a cavernous tiled room with a view of the forest beyond.

My goal for today is to get to the stadium as quickly as possible. I'm due to meet Arkan there in an hour, but I'd like to see it alone first...without outside perspective. It's Arkan's job to sell me on this haven and the team, but I like to form my own opinions irrespective of the sales pitch.

Only a few monsters sit on benches inside the station—a big shifter male with two children, and a centaur female resting on a long, curved bench. They glance up at me as I make my way out of the portal itself.

When I stalk across the big open portal station building

toward the door, whispers follow. My size is enough to garner attention on a good day, but couple that with my reputation as a skyball coach, and you've got a recipe for lots of attention.

Not that I mind. I *live* for the attention. But I told no one at HQ about this trip, and I don't plan to make a big fuss out of my presence here. For all the Evertons know, I'm here on vacation for now.

Grinning, I sail through the door and into a beautifully forested area. A singular road leads toward the main drag, according to the map I studied before my trip. It's crisp here. Ever's one of a few havens with the same weather pattern year-round. I'm sure on the one hand, that's nice, but it makes me think of how Pine Gulch simply follows Montana's natural weather patterns. I fucking love the Gulch's snowy, frigid winters.

It's a quarter-hour walk through beautiful quiet forest to downtown Ever. The first business I see, apart from a doctor's cottage, is the original Higher Grounds location, a two-story brick thing with a cute red-and-white-striped awning. I'm desperate for a latte, so I stop in. It's packed full, coffee dripping and popping and machines sputtering as the vampires behind the bar craft their famous monster-specific concoctions.

It takes nearly another quarter hour to order, and a few minutes after that to get my simple order. Twenty minutes to get a coffee is absurd.

Arkan mentioned that Ever's growing, and it's easy to see it's true. The vampires behind the counter hustled the entire time I was there. It's obviously bustling here. Hearth HQ has faced similar growing pains since the portal station opened, although not to the degree of other havens.

I consider the line out the door a good sign, actually. Smaller havens don't usually opt into the skyball program because it requires a certain amount of investment, and Ever's on the smaller size for a monster haven. Growth brings money, and money makes developing a skyball program a whole lot easier.

Heading for the door, I take my first sip of the Azuro dark roast and groan in satisfaction. There's nothing like Azuro coffee beans, and these are roasted to perfection. Even though the shop's busy, whispers follow me here, too. A few furtive glances and finger points later and I'm pretty sure I'm gonna end up signing at least one autograph before I get out the door.

Coffee in one hand and my bag in the other, I shoulder my way out of the shop without being stopped and head up the cross street, Sycamore, toward the skyball stadium. The Community Garden is on my left as I walk, and Catherine's beautiful Annabelle Inn sits across from it.

The Annabelle's pink siding and ornate gingerbread trim make me think of her owner. Memories from my younger years flood back. Cath and I dated pretty seriously for a while. It came to an unfortunate end—she was the one who got away—but it's been a long time since that.

She was the hottest sex of my life, if I'm honest, and I've taken plenty of lovers since then.

My cock hardens in my sheath, threatening to make an inappropriate display as I rein in my errant thoughts. Now isn't the time to think about the succubus who stole my heart and shattered it when she moved on. No, that was a long time ago.

I sip my latte as I continue up Sycamore and past rows of adorable cottages. Ever really is quaint to the max—the polar opposite of the cold, dark, and snowy haven that's been my home these last few centuries.

Rounding a corner, I find the skyball stadium off in the distance across a giant field. I'm guessing the field is for parking. Ever hosted the skyball finals last year, but hasn't hosted a game since. As I walk across the field, it's clear no one has parked here in a long time as grass is growing in the tire tracks. It's a missed opportunity. Hosted games mean money and advertising, both of which are good for local businesses, assuming the haven wants to grow.

Of course, not every haven wants that. Many don't even have a skyball team. There are twenty-four teams at this point, though, so a solid half of the monster haven system has opted into the skyball program. But again, it takes money and commitment from haven leadership to produce a skyball program that's any good. Not to mention the haven itself has to be well designed to attract and keep star players.

That could be a problem in Ever. The downtown's pretty small, and there aren't a ton of businesses to accommodate a large population of monsters. Not all superstar players want the quiet, slow pace of life that Ever seems to offer.

The stadium soars high above me, all dark stone with giant curved archway entries every twenty feet or so. Green-and-gold flags announce the home team as the Ever Misfits. I leave my bag by one of the doors and head into the stadium's interior.

It's brand-new, built last year for the finals. It's got a troll's touch in the way the stone seems hewn directly out of a mountainside. I'd wager a troll worked with this haven's former Keeper to build this place. I run my fingers along the beautiful stone as I walk around the outer hallway where most of the concessions usually are.

By the time I reach the far side, I've got to give it to this stadium's designer. It's gorgeous and well-thought-out. There's plenty of access to the concession locations, and the hallway itself is nice and wide and tall—which is important for winged monsters who often prefer to fly versus walk.

The clip-clop of hooves announces Arkan's arrival. I turn to find the tall centaur walking up the hallway toward me. He grins as he reaches a hand out to shake mine.

His colorful shirt catches my eye. I squint to read it, then snort with laughter as I shake his hand.

He grabs at the shirt and holds the fabric wide as if to help me see it better. "'*I'm a Fucking Delight.*' Wren Hector, our resident green witch, gave this to me and said it suited my cheerful disposition." He winks. "Imagine if she'd met me before I became Ever's Keeper."

My smile goes softer at that. It's well known that haven keeper training strips keepers of most of their emotion, leaving them with an intense focus on rational, logical thought processes to help them make decisions more effectively. Despite that formal training for his role, Arkan's always remained sunnier and more positive than the average monster.

"So," he continues, waving at the stadium around us, "this is the stadium. It was built last year by Ohken Stonesmith and the former Keeper, both of whom are casual players on the team. I was planning to give you a tour, but you've seen this much of it. Let's take a peek at the war room and locker rooms and what would be your office." He nudges me in the side. "It's extra tall. Your horns won't even hit the ceiling. That would be a nice change, eh?"

I snort in agreement, and he continues on, "I've got the team coming in half an hour. You mentioned wanting to see a short practice, and they're excited to meet you."

"Lead the way, kid."

He snorts and swishes his tail at me. "Not a kid anymore. Not hardly."

I shrug. "You'll always be a snarky, better-than-he-should-be-for-the-effort-he-puts-in player to me."

Arkan laughs. "I'll admit I was distracted on the best of days. I pulled through during the games, thank fuck."

We share a laugh at that, walking toward one end of the stadium. Arkan badges us into a private hallway that leads to the first locker room.

And it...is...amazing.

One entire wall is one-way glass, allowing the players to see the field without ticketholders seeing in. The view is incredible, the entire field visible from inside. The war room's even better, sitting at ground level with a wide screen showing the entire field from above. It's ideally suited for the type of planning I like to do.

Of course, Arkan already knows this. I suspect this part of the war room is an addition meant to entice me.

And it fucking does.

What doesn't thrill me is half an hour later when I meet the team. I know most of them—it's my job to know even those players who aren't full-time—but there's not a single monster on this team who's full-time or even *wants* to be. Not only that, but a vast majority of them seem almost skeptical about having me here for a trial period.

I plant both hands on my hips as I stare at the row of centaurs, gargoyles, and a big green troll who eyes me with his arms crossed.

The only one who looks excited to be here is Hana Canterbury, Arkan's beautiful centaur mate. She was a kickass player at the academy too. She didn't go pro, but she could have. My wheels start spinning, wondering if it's possible to get her to *consider* full-time now. I'm not sure how much extra responsibility she takes on as the Keeper's mate.

"I'd like to see what you're capable of." I count the players out. "Split into two teams, and let's play a quarter. Even though most of you aren't full-timers, you're what I'd have to work with in the beginning. Let's see what you're made of."

Arkan stands by my side as a few muttered grumblings reach us. I glance up at him. "This whole team needs to be rebuilt."

Arkan frowns, sucking at his teeth. "I did tell you we didn't have any pros, Manorin. I was serious."

I match his expression, lifting my whistle and biting it between my teeth.

Arkan holds a skyball under one arm. Cantering to the center of the field, he winks at his wife before tossing the skyball in the air. The flurry of activity happens fast, the bridge troll executing a perfect flip as he snatches the ball off the ground.

Damnit, he's good, and, of course, he doesn't want to be full-time.

As I watch the team play, it's clear there's a lot of talent despite the fact that, to my amazement, they haven't practiced since last year's skyball finals. I debate if I should bother with any other practices while I'm here. There's no point to piss off the locals, considering not one of them would remain on the team if I get this job and accept it.

One thing is clear—building a skyball program in Ever would be a ton of fucking work. This isn't a rebuild. We are literally starting from level zero.

Sigh.

CHAPTER THREE

CATHERINE

Vikand smiles down at me as we walk up Sycamore Street toward the stadium. Alo happened to mention there was a practice this afternoon, and I'm curious to see how that goes. Since Vikand and I were headed past the stadium for our picnic anyhow, I thought it would be nice to pop in for a few minutes.

I'm curious. That's all it is.

Pointing to the bend in the road, I look up at my date. "Once we round the corner, the skyball stadium will be there."

Vikand nods, quiet as ever with both thumbs looped in the pockets of his fitted vest.

He clears his throat. "Do you think we'll be there very long?"

I laugh, tossing my hair over my shoulder as I beam up at him. "Not a skyball fan? I thought Arkan played when he was at the academy…"

Vikand nods. "Yes, well, his dam went to all the games so I didn't have to. Sports aren't really my thing." He laughs lightly, removing a hand from his vest to wave at himself. "I suppose you've already guessed that, though."

I fight disappointment… It bothers me that he didn't want to see his son play, despite his own feelings about the sport. I'm already aware that he and Arkan's dam split when Arkan was very young, but still.

"Oh, I don't know. Arkan had to get his skyball skills from someone."

Vikand clears his throat again, something I'm learning is a nervous habit.

It's fine.

It's definitely not annoying me.

I expect him to say something else, but he falls into an uneasy silence, despite his pheromones telling me that he's very excited to be together. It's easy for me to read desire. What others *say* doesn't matter as much as what their scents reveal...and his reveals a lot. Unfortunately, he seems less inclined than some to act on a natural attraction.

We walk in silence across the parking field. By the time we enter the skyball stadium and hear faint shouts drift from the field, I'm a little surprised he hasn't attempted to carry the conversation any further.

Encouraging myself not to be frustrated with the shy scholar, I lead him through one of the entry hallways until the field comes into view. Anticipation brews in my stomach as shouts echo from the field.

I *love* skyball. I'm a huge fan. Which is how Manorin and I met one another all those centuries ago. Our time together was hot and heavy, but I eventually went on to mate a male who was absolutely not right for me. I don't think Manorin ever took a mate, if I recall correctly. I've seen him dozens of times during televised games, but it will be nice to see my old friend in person.

Well, perhaps "friend" isn't the right word. We didn't exactly keep in touch after we parted.

Vikand and I walk through the final archway, the clip-clop

of his hooves ringing off the beautifully etched stone. I reach out and touch the wall, looking up at him as I do.

"Ohken built this entire stadium, and Abemet designed it. They did an absolutely lovely job, don't you think?" I trail my fingertips along the rough-hewn wall, admiring the craftsmanship.

Vikand looks down at me, then over to where I stroke the stones, dark brows furrowed as he stares at my fingers. His scent deepens. Dark lashes flutter against his cheeks, highlighting elegant, high cheekbones.

"Oh...mmm, yes, I suppose so." He looks up and around, tucking his hands at his lower back. After a quiet moment, he returns his focus to me. "It's...quite lovely. Yes. Do I know Ohken or Abemet?"

I bite back a sigh as I nod. "Abemet is our former Keeper, the vampire your son replaced. Ohken was in the leadership meeting last week. The troll...perhaps you remember?" I beam up at him. "Or perhaps you were distracted?" It's the perfect opening for him to say something complimentary.

He nods and halts just beside the skyball field, the team coming into view.

"I'm afraid I have difficulty concentrating during those meetings, that one in particular. I've been offered a job at the protector academy teaching a course on dark magic. I've been mulling over their offer. They're expecting an answer by the end of the week."

I must have a horrified look on my face, because he sputters, "I'm not certain I'll take it, or if I'd stay in Ever or move if I do. It's all up in the air still. Don't worry!"

The statement irritates me for competing reasons. First, that he'd potentially begin dating me while considering a move, even if it's simply a first date. Second, that he'd assume I'm worried about what he just revealed. It's the age-old feminine need to be wanted and chased and pursued by a man, but only in precisely the way I want it to happen.

Frustration eats at the edges of my good mood, and I glance away to compose my thoughts. It's not as if I expect Vikand to make a life choice based on one date with me, but this is going very poorly so far.

Figures rush across my field of vision, players chasing the skyball as someone drops it. A gargoyle bullets out of the sky and snatches the ball, bouncing off Ohken's shoulders and leaping into the air as he swoops toward the opposite goalposts.

"Excellent, Alo. That was beautifully done!"

Time slows as I glance toward the voice—that voice—the voice I've only heard via televised games for the last few centuries.

A brutally handsome minotaur male walks toward the fray, even as his glittering red-and-black eyes follow Alo's path toward the goal. Long, thick horns stick out from his head and then curve forward and up. Light brown fur covers most of his body, his ears sloping low beneath tan-and-chocolate mottled horns. At his back, his tail hangs low, just the tip swishing from side to side. He's visibly irritated despite the compliment.

I shift from one foot to the other. Those horns used to make excellent handles, and they're longer and thicker than before.

Absolutely beautiful.

He's bigger everywhere else too. Manorin was always tall for a minotaur, but he must be approaching seven feet at this point, hundreds of pounds of bulky muscle. He's usually dressed in impeccably tailored suits for skyball games, but today he wears thigh-hugging jeans and a collared polo shirt that does nothing to hide chunky chest muscles and steel-cut abs.

He seems to have hardly aged. If anything, Manorin's even more handsome like this with a dash of white at his temples. The gold nose ring is new, but, gods, he looks good with it. He wore a much smaller one back when we dated. That made a good handle too.

I resist the urge to wave away the heat flushing my skin.

"Goodness," Vikand murmurs. "That must be the minotaur Arkan's been raving about. He told me some stat or another that I can't recall just now. Another skyball meathead, I suppose."

I can't recall any stats either, or respond to his insult, because Manorin's crimson eyes flick to the sidelines and drift down my figure as he halts on the field. The players rush past him toward the opposite end of the pitch, but he keeps staring, the edges of his mouth curling into a barely-there smile.

Vikand says something, but I'm too busy deciding what the appropriate greeting is for an old lover to pay attention.

Manorin grins, revealing sparkling white teeth and short fangs. A shout from downfield pulls his attention, and he spins on a dime to jog away.

Vikand clears his throat. "Catherine?"

Blinking, I look up. "Hmm? Sorry, Vikand. Did you say something?"

His dark brows bunch together. "I said, would you like to sit for a few minutes? Or shall we go on to our picnic?"

Oh, that's tempting. I probably shouldn't subject Vikand to any more skyball than absolutely necessary since he's already made it clear he doesn't like it. But on the other hand, I *love* it, and I wouldn't give up my skyball love for anyone, date or not.

I grab his hand, threading my fingers through it. "I'd love to sit for a few minutes, but I'm very excited to get to the picnic portion of our afternoon."

"Me too," he says with a soft smile, his fingers tightening around mine. "I'm pretty hungry."

Oh. Ermmm. Normally on a date with a male, I'd take that comment in a sensual way. But I'm fairly certain Vikand did not mean it the way I'd *like* to take it.

Shoving dismay down, I pull him toward the front row of

seats. There's a combination of regular seats and benches meant for the larger hooved monsters like Vikand. We find a spot in the middle of the field, and to my surprise, he asks a lot of questions as we observe.

I'm feeling better about things until the comm watch around his wrist beeps, a monster's name hologram hovering over the blue band. Vikand looks down. "Oh goodness, this is my potential boss. I've got to take it, alright?"

"Of course." I squeeze his forearm, even as he rises and trots back the way we came.

I let my hand fall back into my lap as I watch him go, admiring the shift of powerful muscles beneath his dark coat. A trail of pheromones follows him, plucking at the edges of my power.

"You out of practice, Cath?"

Whipping my head toward the field, I jolt at finding Manorin standing right in front of me, both huge arms resting on top of the wall as he grins. I can't help a quick once-over as he clasps enormous hands together, smirking at me. This close, he still smells of glycerin soap and pine musk.

I lift my chin. "He'll be back in a moment."

Manorin snorts, the round gold ring in his nose flopping against his upper muzzle. "Maybe, maybe not. I don't think he's the male for you."

Irritation swirls in my stomach as I rise to tower over him. "Oh?"

He takes a step back, gripping the railing as he looks up at me. He makes a show of perusing my figure, crimson eyes appreciative when they finally return to my face.

"Yeah. I'll be by later to check in. We're just about done here with," he waves dismissively at the players on the field, "whatever this is." He grins at me. "Let me take you to dinner so we can catch up. It's been a long time, and I'd love to hear what I've missed in the last few centuries."

"No thanks." The words are out of my mouth before I can stop them. "I've got plans."

The smile never leaves his handsome face. "If they involve that male, I suspect you'll be left wanting. Come to dinner with me; I insist."

"I don't like your immediate assessment of him." That's all I can manage as I recline into my seat, laying one arm over the back of the seat next to mine.

Manorin watches the movement, nostrils flaring. He's scenting me, I know he is, and minotaurs have excellent senses of smell. It's one of the things that made him a particularly skillful lover.

Back in the day.

When he returns his gaze to mine, his mouth curls into a knowing smile. "Suit yourself, Cath. You look good, by the way. Been a long time, but that gray hair's a nice change." He reaches over the wall and grabs a stray wave, twirling it around his finger. "Gorgeous." His smirk grows.

I hmph and look in the direction Vikand went. Manorin takes the cue and returns to the field. I'm woman enough to admit to staring at his long tail and broad back, admiring the view as he returns to the team.

The next quarter hour passes at the speed of molasses while I wait for Vikand to rejoin me. As the players wrap up, the sound of hooves echoes from the entry hall.

Smiling, I fluff my hair and stand to find Arkan trotting toward me with a baleful expression.

"Catherine, I'm so sorry, but I just saw Dad trot off toward downtown. He was muttering something about deadlines and contracts, and I thought you two were on a date. He's been so excited by it, but, if I'm honest, he's disjointed on the best of days."

I plant both hands on my hips. "Arkan, are you telling me he went home and left me here?"

Arkan runs both hands through his braided hair, shifting from one foot to the other. "Yeah, I think so. Why don't I call him and tell him to co—"

I put my hand up. "That won't be necessary, friend. I'll catch up with him some other time."

Arkan frowns. "He's always been like this, honestly. Part of why he and Mom never worked out, if I had to guess."

I sigh as I stare past him at the empty, quiet hallway.

Stood up? Me??

Maybe I *have* lost my touch.

CHAPTER FOUR
MANORIN

"Nice job this afternoon." I stare at the players as we wrap a short but effective game. I've seen what I need to see. "I don't think we need regular practices, but I'd like to schedule one or two sessions over the next couple of weeks to help you get a feel for my leadership style, if nothing else. If anybody's not down for that, let me know, alright?"

A few sideways glances between the players are my only answer. I suspect Arkan's going to get a couple phone calls afterward from players who have no intention of coming to those. That's fine. I've got a couple Hellions players in mind who aren't doing anything during the break and would probably love to come here and fuck around on a gorgeous field. It might even do the current team some good to see my academy folks.

When no one says anything, I resist the urge to bark that they hit the showers. But, of course, these aren't my protector kids, and they're probably all heading home. I dismiss the team gruffly, mulling over if it would even be possible to salvage next year's season with a team like this. Likely not. It'll take a few years of building before the program's in a good spot. Looking back to last year's skyball finals, it was pure luck how well the Ever Misfits did, in my opinion.

As the team leaves, Arkan jogs over to me with Hana, a worried expression on his face. She's all happy smiles, though, pumping her arms victoriously over her head when they halt in front of me.

"That was *amazing*, Coach. It was so nice to play with people my own age for once."

Oh my *gawds.*

I lift a brow at the beautiful centaur female. "Hana, you're the only one even worth keeping on this team because you're the only one with the right work ethic. Even then, do you have an intention of going pro? Because that's the mentality this team would need to be successful long-term."

She and Arkan share a glance. They've obviously discussed this.

I cross my arms. "Right. My job isn't to pressure you into something you're not dying to do. There are players who've worked their whole lives to get to the skyball pitch." I move my focus to Arkan. "But you weren't kidding when you said this is a rebuild. I don't think there's a single player here I'd keep."

He shakes his head, crossing his arms to match my stance. "I truly was not. This team needs building from the ground up, which is why I want you to do it. I can't attract pro talent the way you can, or any of the other things that need to happen to make the team successful."

I suck at my teeth as I stare around the bright green pitch, lights overhead cutting on as the sun begins to set. After a moment, I look back at Arkan. "You have time to take me to dinner? I've got questions."

Hana bumps her mate with an elbow. "Go. I'm headed to Shifter Hollow. Got a game with the kiddos down there."

He laughs and slides his arm around her waist, rubbing his

cheek against hers. When she turns, nuzzling at him for a kiss, I avert my eyes to give them a moment of privacy.

That easy-seeming, obvious love is something I've never had. Being famous makes it even harder, because it's nigh impossible to figure out who wants you for you and who simply wants your fame. I found myself returning home to Pine Gulch for nearly all of my vacations, because the one thing I can count on the Gulch to do is treat me like Manorin the Longhorn, not Manorin the Coach.

"Come on, Coach," Hana's voice breaks through my thoughts.

When I return my focus to them, Arkan's kissing her neck playfully even as she laughs and bats him away. She finally manages to stop him when he reaches for her hand and threads his fingers through hers. "I'll walk you to Main."

We leave the field, and I resist the urge to walk the stadium one more time. Realistically, I'm a poor sleeper, so when I wake up at two a.m., I'll come back here and poke around a bit. I glance up at Arkan. "Stadium open all the time?"

He snorts out a laugh, swishing his tail against his dark sides. "Yeah. If you want to come get a three a.m. and get a workout in, you can."

I crook a brow at him. "Oh, is there a weight room? I missed that on the tour."

Arkan's laugh grows louder. "Is there a weight room? Of *course* there's a weight room. You're right, we skipped that on the tour, but there's a kickass weight room in the basement."

"I brought weights in my bag," I muse offhandedly, glancing to where I left my luggage at the side of the pitch. "Just in case."

Arkan snorts. "Of course you did. Gods forbid you miss a workout." He punches my arm. "Might lose all of this hard-earned muscle in a day or two, old man."

We share a laugh at that. I couldn't lose the muscle if I tried.

Minotaurs are naturally strong. But I'm bigger and stronger than most due to my strict routine.

An hour later, we're seated at Herschel's Fine Dining, discussing the trial period, but my mind drifts back to Catherine. It's been almost two hundred years since I've seen her, but damn, she looked better than ever. I've always brought out her sassy side, and that doesn't seem to have changed.

I noticed she was on a date, but I never did see the centaur male return. Only an idiot would stand up a woman like her. I mull that over for a moment before returning my focus to Arkan, who chats animatedly about his vision for the skyball program.

The next half hour's a blur as I grill Arkan within an inch of his life about the realities of this job. Some of it excites me. Some of it doesn't.

My biggest worry is that he seems to be the only major champion of bringing bigtime skyball to Ever. Not surprising, but it doesn't bode well. If Arkan were to be called to another haven to serve as Keeper there, my program's major supporter would leave.

I don't love that.

This isn't just a team build; it's a community build too.

Do I have that level of effort in me?

I consider that as Arkan and I part ways. Striding up Main Street, I look around. Ever's really a gorgeous little place—all cozy small-town charm. Monsters wave to one another as they pass, calling each other by their first names. That reminds me of Pine Gulch. Hearth HQ, where I live now, is big and sprawling and cold. Everyone's usually too busy fighting the wind and snow to exchange pleasantries in passing.

A shifter couple passes me, and the male nods deferentially, a little smirk on his face. I smile back, but as they go past, I hear his whispered explanation of who I am.

My smile grows broader. Some vain part of me loves to be

recognized. I consider that as I make my way up the street, heading for the Annabelle Inn.

When I arrive, the lovely bed and breakfast waggles white shutters at me, pale pink siding rippling in a friendly way. Double glass-paned front doors swing open wide to reveal Catherine standing behind the check-in desk. She glances up with a thoughtful smile.

I miss admiring any more of the inn herself, because the innkeeper is so very, very delightful to look at.

Catherine's once-dark waves are salt-and-pepper gray now, curled elegantly and hanging over one shoulder. High cheekbones accentuate a heart-shaped face and a chin with a tiny divot in it. Intelligent gray eyes give me an abrupt once-over even as her nostrils flare slightly.

How many times have I nuzzled my way up that elegant neck and bitten that chin? How many times have I scented her, marveling at how she could tweak the way she smelled to entice me?

She's fuller-figured than when we were young, heavy breasts enough to fill even my large hands. The wrap dress she's wearing only accentuates those plump curves.

I've always had a healthy libido but a short list of partners I was willing to share a bed with—another downside of the fame. But desire roars to life as Catherine rounds the check-in desk with a smile, opening her arms wide. "Manorin! Glad you made it!"

Dipping low, I sling my arms under hers and pull her up against my chest, hugging her tight to me. I'm selfish, because part of me just wants to feel her against me, this gorgeous succubus who ruled my heart all those centuries ago. I breathe in, her familiar scent a near physical caress.

When I put her down, her cheeks are pink, and she smooths her wrap dress.

Thinking back to earlier, I wink at her. "Your date ever come back, Cath? I didn't happen to notice him."

Her smile falls, and she rolls her eyes as she returns behind the check-in area.

"You know he didn't, Manorin. Perhaps you should worry about your dating life, though, and not mine? Or just the skyball opportunity, since that's why you're here."

I wave away the comment. "Ah, I'm only here for a few weeks. If I decide to stay, I'll worry about it then." I grin wickedly at her. "Told you he wasn't for you. Looks like I was right."

She matches my smile, her crisp apple scent growing stronger. "Manorin, *friend*, much as I'd love to catch up, Vikand isn't a topic we need to discuss."

I laugh and bend over the desk, leaning onto both beefy forearms. I know Catherine, and whether she means to or not, she'll be reading my pheromones as we speak.

"Cath, what you need is someone big and strong with gorgeous horns to hold on to while he fucks you senseless. It's not that guy."

Her return smile is nearly feral, gray eyes flashing in the fading light. "And I suppose you think it might be you?"

I shrug. "At least you know we wouldn't lack for chemistry."

Around us, the inn creaks and groans. Catherine smiles sweetly up at me. "Credit card for incidentals, please."

I hand the plastic over, staring at her while she enters the card into her computer.

"Your inn's gorgeous, and I think she agrees with me."

She looks up at me. "Isn't she, though? This building has filled my heart fuller than anything in my entire life."

I notice she ignores my comment about the Annabelle agreeing with me. The full heart comment feels like a barb, but I probably shouldn't take it that way. Still, it brings me back to asking Catherine to get a minotaur mating tattoo, to be fully and irrevocably mine.

She said no.

My heart shattered.

We split up.

And here we are.

The Annabelle creaks again, sounding happy to me and thankfully breaking through my self-pitying train of thought.

Catherine slides my credit card toward me with a big smile. "I'll take you to your room now, Manorin, and if you'd like a tour of Ever at any point, please allow me to show you around."

I grin as I grab my bag, staring as she emerges from behind the desk and heads for the stairs. "Just keep walking in front of me," I say. "Best damn view in town."

She tosses me a sassy look, but her scent strengthens anyhow. She always loved my dirty mouth, and I'm not feeling too inclined to clean it up, despite the years between us.

Annabelle creaks happily again, the carpet on the stairs rippling to grab my attention.

"I'm happy for you, old friend," I manage, even as something deep inside me aches to be filled the way she described her love for Annabelle. What would it be like to have the same level of success in my personal life as I have in my career?

Is anyone ever that lucky?

CHAPTER FIVE

CATHERINE

Hours later, I'm in the kitchen baking quiche for the morning buffet when an insistent scratching at the back door announces my neighbor Iggy's arrival. Before I can even turn to let the young gargoyle in, he rips the door open and zips through, executing a wild spin before he lands on the countertop, narrowly missing the uncooked quiche.

Annabelle groans in warning.

Iggy throws both purple hands on top of his horns. "Catherine! Come quick! Minnie had her *puppies*, and they're so cute! You have to come see!!"

Without waiting for an answer, he grabs my hand and leaps into the air, dragging me toward the back door. Annabelle swings it open, and we rush out into the night. I can barely see where I'm going, but that doesn't stop Ignatius from dragging me down the small path leading to his cottage next door.

When we get there, Alo stands there with arms crossed and a wry smile on his handsome face. "Sorry, Cath, there was no stopping him."

Miriam, his pixie mate, pops out with a smile and a twinkle

in her fuchsia eyes. "But I've got a pitcher of margaritas, so there's that!"

I laugh as Iggy drags me into their kitchen, situated at the back of the cottage. He opens the pantry to reveal his hellhound, Minnie, lying in a cushy-looking dog bed as puppies squirm at her swollen teats. Lazy rivulets of fire run under her black fur, red eyes halfway closed.

Iggy pulls me to the ground, then sits next to Minnie's head. She fully closes her eyes as he strokes her fur softly. "Well done, Minnie girl." He looks up at me. "That's what Dirk the hunter used to call her before she decided she liked me best."

I reach out and rub one of Minnie's big ears softly as I smile at Iggy. "She's bonded to you for life, Ignatius. What an incredible gift."

His return smile is thoughtful. "But her puppies won't be, right?"

"They'll bond with you for a while, but not forever," I admit. "Once they're grown, they'll go off into the world and find their own monsters. Who knows when that'll happen though. If we're lucky, they'll all remain in Ever."

His eyes go glossy with unshed tears. "Or maybe Dirk will take them back to his hunter work at headquarters, and they'll have law enforcement jobs. That's what Minnie did."

"We can't know, son," Alo says cautiously as he hands me down a margarita. "But you'll always, always have Minnie."

Miriam drops down next to us, translucent pixie wings fluttering at her back as she rests a hand on one of three squirming puppies. "And don't forget, we still have a lot to do to help take care of them as they grow. Starting tomorrow! We're still making collars for them, right? Did you decide on names?"

He shrugs as he keeps petting Minnie. "Minnie's name isn't that cool, so I kind of want to name them something badass like Brimstone."

"Ignatius!" Alo and I shout his name at the same time.

Minnie jolts and looks up at us, lips curling into a warning snarl.

"I mean something *cool*, like Brimstone." He rolls his eyes at Alo and me. "Can't I just use cuss words at home? I promise not to say them at school. Kevin and I don't even use them on the playground!"

I resist the urge to laugh as he picks up one of the puppies and cradles it to his neck. It nuzzles against him, whimpering as its long black tail flops quickly from side to side.

Reaching out, I stroke the pup's black and red fur as Minnie watches intently, ready to spring into action if I become a threat.

"Hey." I ruffle Iggy's dark hair, careful not to jostle my margarita. "I've got a really cool new guest, an old friend named Manorin. I'm going to invite him to family dinner with the Hectors tomorrow. Would you like to come and tell him about the puppies? I think he'd be delighted to learn about them."

The idea just came to me, and I love it. Manorin would be a fabulous choice for our new skyball coach, and if I can do anything to welcome him to Ever, it's to help him make friends. He'll feel more invested, and maybe he'll stay, and that'll be good for the town.

And my deep, deep love of skyball.

"Yep," Iggy says with a pop. "I'll bring them over tomorrow. The triplets are gonna want to see them too. I bet they've never seen hellhound puppies before!"

"Shit, none of us have," Alo says dryly. "Minnie alone was enough to spark terror in most of the Evertons when she arrived."

I smile as I think back to Minnie's arrival with Dirk, the elemental sylph who used to work for Hearth monster headquarters. He came here hunting a warlock who threatened to ruin everything I hold dear.

My former mate, Wesley.

Good riddance.

Shoving unpleasant thoughts away, I catch up with Miriam and Alo while Iggy plays with the puppies and shouts exuberantly at Minnie.

"Iggy's birthday's coming up," Miriam says as he zooms in circles through the house. She looks at me. "He wants to have a party in the rose garden, if you're okay with it." She chuckles. "Apparently it's good for hide and seek because his friends don't want to go near the thorns."

I beam as I sip at the margarita. "Perfectly reasonable of him. That sounds delightful."

Alo leans against the island. "His invite list is about twenty kiddos long. You sure you're alright with all of them running through your roses?"

The mental image of it is so adorable.

"Yeah." I set the drink down. "Annabelle will love that, and, of course, the Hectors will be there. Wren can always fix the bushes up when the kids are done."

"It's gonna be awesome," Iggy shrieks as he zooms back into the kitchen with a puppy slung over his shoulder. He rubs its tiny bum as if it were a baby, eyeing his father and schooling his expression to neutral. "Maybe I can even have a soda, like, the one day a year I get to."

I resist a laugh. Iggy's obsessed with soda and never allowed to have it.

Alo scowls but eventually relents. "Just one. 'Cause that sugar high seems to go on for days."

Iggy whoops and takes off again. Minnie grumbles from the security of her dog bed, as if asking Iggy to return her pup but not fussed enough to chase him for it.

Eventually, I take a second margarita to go and head home. When I get there, I consider scrawling a quick note for Manorin about dinner but decide I'll ask him directly instead. I don't examine that desire too closely as I leave the margarita in the kitchen, ascend the stairs, and knock quietly on the door to the rose-themed room.

I smell him before I see him. That same glycerin and pine musk I used to love when we were young and lustful. When he's hot, it takes on a dark, needy edge that—

The door swings open, and Manorin stands there shirtless, with said shirt in one hand. He grins and leans against the doorway, the tee dangling from his fingers. His chest is covered in pale brown fur, yet it does nothing to hide a body still tight with muscle. Somehow, Manorin's even manlier than before.

Twin bars pierce his nipples, though—that's new—and his jeans hug thighs so thick, I don't know if I could wrap both arms around them.

He leans down. "Smells good when you stare at my body, Cath." He wrinkles his snout. "Actually, you smell like tequila. You come up here for a good time, pretty girl?"

Such a flirt. I forgot how *insanely* flirtatious he is. Is he like this back home? Does he flirt with the females there?

It's such a stark contrast to Vikand, who couldn't string a flirtatious sentence together if he tried. I told myself I wanted that because Wesley was also a charmer. Such a charmer that I didn't see the red flags until it was too late and monsters got hurt.

I choke grief back as I look up at Manorin.

His sexy smile falls, and he reaches out, capturing my chin between his fingers as crimson eyes scan my face. "Your scent changed. Is everything okay?"

I force a smile. "I got lost in thought for a moment. I'm fine, thank you."

He winks at me. "If I need to defend your honor against a wayward centaur, I'm there, Cath. In a heartbeat."

I nearly choke at the idea of Manorin taking Vikand on in some sort of fight for my honor. It's laughable. I think Vikand would likely crumple to the ground in a heap, begging not to be beaten.

Manorin's smile grows wicked. "Are we envisioning the same ridiculous scene right now? That male on the ground in front of me, cringing and promising never to insult you again?"

I swat his big chest, resisting the urge to curl my fingers through the soft, flat fur there. "Stop it. He's perfectly pleasant, and very much a gentleman."

Manorin scoffs as he rolls his eyes. "Just what every male wants to hear from his bed partners. Oh, Manorin, how perfectly pleasant he was." He winks playfully. "Never let it be said that I was anything but a ravenous beast in the bedroom. If you ever look back on our time as perfectly pleasant, I'll expire from disappointment."

That reference leads me back to all the good times we had. It's been centuries. But years of memories flood back all at once.

"Errr, no." I clear my throat. "Perfectly pleasant isn't really the right description for you."

He leans closer again, bringing his hands to either side of the doorframe. He fills the entire doorway as he leans into my space, the low light glinting off the ring in his nose. "Is that what you came here to discuss, Cath? A reigniting of all those *imperfectly filthy* times we had?"

I shake my head; I've got to get out of here. The mere suggestion of our past times has my power rising and roiling, desperate to be unleashed. "I came to invite you to dinner tomorrow. One night a week, I have the Hector triplets over. Long story about how we met, but I figured it might be helpful to introduce you to some Evertons, and they're lovely. All witches, and all mated to various haven leaders."

"Done," he says simply. No twenty questions about where we're going and why. No thoughts about how he's not really into the same sort of things I'm into.

He cocks his head to the side. "Did you not want me to agree?"

I laugh and pat his arm. "Just lost in thought for a second. I should warn you that my neighbors come as well. Ignatius, who's about to turn seven, is particularly excited to introduce you to his new hellhound puppies."

Manorin's dark brows rise. "Hellhounds? That *is* interesting. Well, I can't wait. Arkan's scheduled meetings most of tomorrow, but I'm free all night."

I clasp my hands together and force a big smile. "Excellent. Dinner's at six in the private dining room at the back of the house. Come find us when you're free."

"Will do," he says with a smile, nipping at his lower lip as he smiles at me.

His scent wraps me up again, tugging at desires I've kept mostly dormant since Wesley. I'd hoped to start dating again with someone safe, someone easy. Vikand is all of those things.

"Good night, Manorin." I smile up at him.

But as I turn to go, the scent of his obvious attraction follows me, stoking long-dead flames. Annabelle ripples the carpet runner, the kitty cat timer in the kitchen dinging incessantly.

"Oh shit, the quiche!" I shout as I scurry toward the kitchen.

~

"He's like...*really* hot," Thea Hector whisper-hisses as she hands her triplet, Wren, a martini over my island the following evening.

I roll my eyes and purse my lips, barely holding back a smile as Wren thoughtfully sips the martini, smacking her pink-painted lips together.

Thea takes a loud sip from her glass, tossing blond waves over her shoulder. "He was meeting with Shepherd and Alo earlier, and I might have snooped because, well, why not, and, good lord, he's one hundred percent beefcake." She bats her dark lashes at me. "Don't you think, Catherine?"

I shrug. "I hadn't noticed, girls."

The triplets' aunt Lou, who's about their age, gives me a carefully neutral look, even though the edges of her lips curl upward.

Morgan, the third triplet, snorts and swats my side as she layers cheese on top of a tray full of penne alla vodka. "You're telling me this hot, handsome minotaur is staying at the Annabelle. And, oh, he's single, by the way, which I know because Abe told me. But you haven't happened to notice?"

I sigh. "My focus is elsewhere, as you might remember." I give the girls a sassy look. They've been front and center to my Vikand pursuit for a while now. I swear it's at least half of what we discuss during "family dinner" every week.

Morgan grabs the pasta pan and turns, slipping it into the oven. Annabelle kindly closes the door, ensuring it doesn't slam as Morgan returns to the island and sits next to Lou.

She throws a rag over her shoulder, then crosses her arms, an uncharacteristically serious look on her face. "Listen, we're not trying to be all up in your dating business, but we *are* highly invested in seeing you happy. And obviously you're interested in dating because, Lord knows, you've given Vikand all the signals he can possibly get. He's just not..."—she waves a hand around —"picking them up."

I blow out a breath. "Actually, we went out yesterday, thank you very much."

I don't know why I said that, because, the moment I do, the triplets pepper me with a barrage of questions so fast and furious, I find myself scattered trying to remember the first of them.

"Funny," Lou says with a saucy look. "I could swear I saw Vikand in his office at about that time yesterday afternoon."

The triplets' heads swivel toward me as I try not to look surprised at Lou's comment.

I'm mercifully saved when Alo, Iggy and Miriam enter through the back door. Iggy holds a hellhound pup under each arm, their little bums dangling as he zips through the air and greets the triplets.

Thea and Wren ooh and ah over the puppies, but Morgan turns to me with a motherly look. "Don't think you're off the hook that easily, Catherine. I wanna know what happened. Was it fab? Was it not fab? What's he like in bed?"

I snort out a laugh at that. "Not all succubi sleep with a partner on the first date, you know."

"Oh, but some do." Manorin ducks down to enter the kitchen, his tall horns nearly scraping the roof. He shoots a wink at Morgan and Lou.

I jolt and freeze.

The room goes silent as Thea and Wren spin on the barstools. I can't see their faces, but Thea drops the chips she's holding in one hand. They clatter to the floor as Manorin watches their descent, a pleased-looking smirk on his face.

Perhaps it wasn't my best idea to introduce the Hectors to him. He's going to charm them to death and th—

Well, isn't that exactly why I invited him here? Although, I'm not sure how public he's planning to be about why he's in Ever for the next few weeks. I assume he wouldn't want news that he's hunting around to get back to Hearth HQ. Although, if it did, beloved as he is there, he could probably wrangle a pay increase.

Maybe that's his end game anyway.

"You must be Manorin," Wren says smoothly, standing and putting her hand out for him.

Manorin's never been to the human world that I know of, but he's interacted with enough humans in his role, so he takes her hand easily, shaking it with care.

"You've gotta be the Hector triplets." He glances to Alo. "You I've met, so this must be your kiddo and lovely mate?"

Miriam rounds the island as Iggy settles on her shoulder, nearly dropping one of the hellhounds. Minnie lumbers tenderly after Miriam, snuffling at Miriam's wings as if to say "give them back to me!"

Miriam takes the puppies and looks at me. "Is it okay if I set them down here, Catherine? They just peed outside, and somehow, they're already potty-trained."

Manorin drops to a knee and lifts his hand out toward the closest puppy. It yips and growls at him, then just as quickly steps forward and tentatively licks his enormous fur-covered finger. He remains quiet as Minnie joins him.

I think it surprises us all when she flops down at his feet, rolling over and kicking her back legs up in the air for a scratch.

Manorin laughs, a deep, hearty noise that pebbles my wayward nipples—nipples that should be misbehaving for Vikand when I see him next.

The enormous minotaur reaches down, careful not to poke anyone with his long horns. He rubs Minnie's belly with rough, thorough intensity. Her tongue lolls from her mouth, and Morgan looks over at me suggestively, nostrils flared as she attempts to hold back a smile.

Iggy hops off Miriam's shoulder and flaps toward Manorin, landing on one of his horns. Crimson eyes flick up to the young gargoyle and crinkle in the corners, even as Alo rounds Miriam and grabs his young son.

"Ig. You can't just land on monsters, kiddo. It's not super polite, right?"

"I don't mind," Manorin offers, patting his horn. "If you wanna come back, I'll tell you all about the pit hells in my home haven of Pine Gulch."

Iggy shoves out of Alo's hands and zips back to Manorin's

horn, alighting on it and grabbing the tip with one hand as he wraps his tail around it.

Manorin stands and moves to the side of the island where nobody stands, crossing both arms as he focuses upward on Iggy. "Pine Gulch is also here in America. Have you learned what human state it's in?"

Iggy nods and hops up and down excitedly. "Yeah! Montana! Big sky country."

Manorin snorts out a laugh that jiggles his nose ring. "That's right. It's so big and wide open, all you see is sky. Anyhow, our sheriff had a hellhound for a while, and some dumba—err, idiot—brought a pit bull with him when he moved to Pine Gulch from the human world. One thing led to another, and now Pine Gulch has a pack of pit hells. Half pit bull, half hellhound."

"That's genius!" Iggy shouts. "What are they like? Do they have fire rivulets? Do they bond to monsters like Minnie did to me?"

"They're a bunch of big sweeties, honestly," Manorin says with another deep laugh. "A little smaller than hellhounds and a bit louder. They talk a lot, and they're sillier, as a general rule. They do bond like hellhounds."

"Aww..." Iggy's tone is tender. He glances over the island to Alo and Miriam. "Can we get one?"

Miriam shakes her head. "Kiddo, our house is full of hell-hounds right now, and I can already tell they're going to get into everything. Four doggos is probably enough, don't you think?"

Iggy scowls and rolls his eyes, peppering Manorin with more questions about the pit hells.

Manorin answers each question carefully until the kitty cat timer dings to let me know the baked penne alla vodka is ready.

I shoo everyone out of the kitchen and toward my small personal dining room just off the kitchen hallway. They flood noisily out of the room as I release a sigh and turn to the oven, grabbing a kitchen mitt.

"How can I help, Cath?"

Manorin's deep voice wraps tight around my body. I'd swear it was just yesterday he and I dated, because those memories feel so recent, even though there's a lifetime of experiences and heartaches between then and now.

Opening the oven, I reach in and grab the pasta, setting it on the countertop.

Annabelle opens the fridge and slings a packet of parmesan cheese at Manorin, who easily catches it and unclips the chip clip holding it closed.

He jerks his head at the bubbling dish. "How much?"

"Just spread it all on there while I grab a couple bottles of wine." I turn and duck down to the wine cooler built into the island, selecting a few reds—a tempranillo and a sangiovese—I think would go nicely with the dish.

When I rise, Manorin's got the dish in one hand—no potholder to be seen—and he's smiling pleasantly at me. "I'll just take this to the table?"

"Yeah…" I trail off as I stare at my only potholder, still sitting on the countertop.

"What?"

I shrug. "I forgot you were so—"

He takes a step closer. "Strong? Manly? Horribly charming and impossibly attractive?"

Easy laughter tumbles from my throat. "I *was* going to say impervious to things like heat, yes, but I suppose you're most of those other characteristics as well."

He laughs and turns, heading for the back hallway the dining room's off of. "Let me give you a view of my back to make sure you've nailed down the attractive part."

He stalks toward the dining room, and, truly, I do stare at his huge figure. He's stacked with thick muscle, his shirt tight and pants tighter. In the hallway, he has to duck partially sideways to get his horns through the arched doorway into the dining room.

I glance up at the Annabelle. "We need to do something about that, darling girl. If he stays and comes for dinner on occasion, I don't want him to feel uncomfortable."

I imagine if Manorin chooses Ever, I'll see him with regularity. He'd want to hang out with the only friend he already knows.

I assume.

Following with the bottles of wine, I join my neighbors and the Hectors at a dinner table already overflowing with charcuterie and snacks.

Morgan groans happily. "You love to overfeed us, Catherine, and I am honestly here for it."

Thea snort-laughs. "You can work off the calories when you get home. What's Abe up to tonight? Wouldn't surprise me if you left him tied up somewhere."

The triplets laugh together as Manorin watches them, a twinkle in his eye. "You wouldn't be talking about Abemet Zeniphon, would you? Used to be a damn good skyball player?"

Morgan smiles. "That's him! He was the Keeper here for a very long time, and he played on the skyball team. Now he's my full-time stay-at-home mate. I forced him into retirement to serve me."

Manorin barks out a laugh as Morgan waggles both auburn brows at him. "Somehow I can't imagine Abemet retired."

Wren grabs a grape and pops it into her mouth, chewing slowly as Thea pinches Morgan's side playfully. "That's 'cause he's a full-time daddy."

Morgan blushes, and I can't resist the urge to see what Manorin thinks of the triplets' incredibly straightforward manner.

"Not a bad way to go," he muses, glancing at Iggy, who's

mercifully sitting on Miriam's shoulder, whispering something in her ear.

"He's been talking about jobs, actually," Morgan muses. Her typical smile grows wicked. "Actually, I'm trying to convince him to oust his mother so he can run the monster world. I think he's coming around to the idea."

There's silence for a moment before Lou looks at her niece and pops a bite of pasta in her mouth. "Why don't you do it, Mor? You'd be kickass, and you're already so drawn to serve with your black magic. You could heal, but at scale, maybe..."

Morgan's eyes roll up as she seems to consider it.

Manorin looks between the girls with a playful smirk. "Am I now party to a revolution? That's delicious."

Morgan snorts. "Well, errr, you might be. You don't happen to have a close personal *friendship* with Evenia, do you?"

He chuckles. "I suspect the concept of friendship is foreign to her, so, no, but she *is* my boss."

Morgan pales, if that's even possible. "Oh, well, perhaps don't say anything to her. We're all talk at family dinner anyhow, right?"

Lou shrugs as blue flames dance in her eyes, her battle magic rising at the idea of an altercation with Evenia. "Oh, I dunno. I'm the only blue witch in the haven system. I could always run her out of the office at HQ, and you could simply take over."

"Yessss, queen!" Thea shouts, depositing a ladleful of pasta onto her triplets' plates. "Revolution away, girl. We are here for it."

Manorin places a hand over his heart, which draws my eyes to his chest. "And I promise not to breathe a word of this to anyone. Cath knows me well; I can keep a secret." Crimson eyes flick to mine as he takes a sip of wine. "I'm good at secrets, right?"

I clear my throat as I nod. I can't trust myself to say anything else about what an excellent secret-keeper Manorin used to be back in the day.

Two hours and six bottles of wine later, the triplets cackle as he delivers the punchline to a joke. Iggy's asleep against Miriam's chest, and my heart is so full.

This is what I love about Ever. This friendship, having my dearest Annabelle filled to the brim with laughter. Family dinner with monsters who are in no way related to me, yet my family all the same.

But what about love? a little voice whispers in my head. *What about romantic partnership?*

My mind drifts to Vikand, but I can't honestly see him at this sort of thing. I've invited him to these weekly dinners a few times, and he's always declined, saying it wasn't really his thing.

I'm starting to think nothing is *his thing* outside of his books.

"Manorin, how'd you let Catherine get away?"

Morgan's question jolts me out of my errant thoughts, and I set my wine glass down. Oh gods oh gods, how did that topic come up? I dart a look at Alo, but he raises both hands quickly in a denial of guilt.

Manorin's expression goes serious as he looks at Morgan. "I didn't. She moved here to help develop Ever, and I remained at Hearth HQ, eventually taking over the skyball program." He sits back in his chair and rolls his shoulders, smiling softly at me. "We just sort of fell apart, if I'm honest." He glances at Morgan again. "It was a long time ago."

I look around the table, but it's Wren I land on. She sips her wine quietly, looking at me with a thoughtful expression. Of the Hector triplets, she's the most brutally observant. She won't pepper me with questions later like Thea or Morgan would, but she *sees everything.*

"Hundreds and hundreds of years," I confirm. "Lifetimes, seems like."

The table falls silent until Alo clears his throat, gesturing at

Iggy, whose head flops back against Miriam's upper arm. "We should get outta here and get Ig to bed." Dark eyes flash to me. "Thank you for a wonderful dinner, as always, Cath. This is the highlight of our week."

I look under the table where Minnie nurses all three hell-hound pups. "Shall I bring them to you when they wake?"

Miriam laughs. "Oh no. As soon as we take Ig out of here, Minnie will follow, and the puppies will too. They're at a compliant age, it seems, but I'm sure that'll come to an end inconveniently soon."

The moment Alo and Miriam stand, Minnie grumbles and shifts onto all four legs. When she falls back down with a yip, looking at her back end, we all drop to the floor to peer at her.

Morgan crawls under the table and places a careful hand on Minnie's belly, closing her eyes. After a brief moment, she looks at Manorin. "Any chance you can carry her next door and lay her in her bed? Her stomach's bothering her, but I think I can heal it. I'd just rather she be in her comfy spot first."

Manorin stands and grabs the table, pushing it to the side to expose Minnie and the pups.

The hellhound licks her lips, tail wagging softly as Manorin approaches her, speaking in low tones. When he scoops her up into his big arms, my heart nearly melts. He talks quietly to the big hellhound, who whines as he begins walking toward the hall.

"I'll grab the puppies." Morgan reaches down and picks them up, cradling them to her chest.

As they leave, Wren starts grabbing plates from the table, headed for the kitchen.

Thea and I do the same, but the moment Manorin and the rest are out the back door, she turns to me, grabbing my arm.

"Catherine! You let a dude like that get away? Tell me you're not gonna let him get away again."

I look between the Hectors, but even Wren nods. "He's

totally into you, Catherine. Strike while the iron's hot, ya know?" She sets the empty pasta crock down with a wink.

I sigh. "I'm…it's not the right time, girls. I just went out with Vikand yesterday!"

Wren smiles at me. "One date does not a relationship make. You could just…have fun. With two dudes." She points at Lou. "It worked out for her."

Lou giggles and pumps her hands in the air. "Double the dick is better, for sure!"

Oh, I know. I've done that plenty of times in my life.

Not with Nor though. No. One of him is plenty of dick to handle.

Oh fuck, now I'm thinking about his cock, and I really need to *not*.

"It wouldn't be right," I reiterate, more to myself than anything.

Annabelle clatters all the dishes on the countertop, slamming the oven door open and closed in rapid succession, causing the triplets to jump.

She doesn't agree with me.

CHAPTER SIX

MANORIN

Catherine's "family dinner" was so lovely. It's clear the Hectors and her other neighbors adore her. And a hellhound with puppies? I've never seen another hellhound outside of Pine Gulch. I thought about that a lot overnight, given that sleeping isn't one of my better qualities. Eventually, I gave up on the shut eye and relocated to the gorgeous gym at the stadium.

Now I'm seated at what would be my desk in my office at the stadium, staring at my computer and a stack of paperwork. Figured I could do a planning session and get a feel for what it'd be like if this role is formally offered.

And if I take it.

I've still got concerns after a handful of meetings yesterday.

It's clear that building up the skyball program is exciting to folks, but primarily driven by Arkan. The town leadership crew is aware of the need to expand, but they're mostly doing it in response to the new Grand Portal Station, not so much out of a deep desire to have pro skyball here.

Before the portal station was created, each haven was linked to only one other in a giant ring of sorts. Monsters only traveled when absolutely necessary. If I'm honest, it's the one thing that held skyball back from being adopted more widely across the haven system.

If you've got to go through fifteen individual portals to get to the haven hosting a skyball game, you're pretty devoted to the game itself. Casual viewers won't go to the effort. And for skyball to take off the way many human sports have, we need die-hard and casual fans alike.

I consider that as I begin sketching out what would have to happen to get the rest of the town on board with skyball expansion here. The pages in front of me contain lists of folks I'd need to win over, given my few conversations with Arkan so far.

My mind picks and turns over a handful of ideas before a knock at the office door pulls me from my thoughts.

Looking up, I find Catherine standing in the doorway wearing a dark blue wrap dress, a picnic basket over one arm. Gray waves are piled high in an elegant bun, highlighting her high cheekbones and those shocking gray eyes.

Gods, there's really nothing like a succubus in all her glory.

I set my pen down and lean back in my chair, taking her in as she approaches the desk.

"Hello, Catherine." I can't help the deep timbre of my voice. She's single. I'm single. We go well together. I don't know how long I'll be here for, but I don't see why we can't have a good time for the next few weeks. I'm gonna ask her out again, most definitely.

She dips her head. "Manorin." Sashaying into the office, she sets the picnic basket down on the edge of my desk. "It occurred to me that I was a little, well, perhaps sassy is the best word, when we saw each other again on the pitch. I wanted to bring you some treats as a reminder that we're excited you're here."

"Are you?" I shift back in the chair, clasping my hands behind my head.

Gray brows furrow. "Am I what?"

"*You* love skyball. I know that. And Arkan's obviously obsessed. But to be honest, not a single monster outside of you two seems devoted to building a program."

She sighs. "I've thought about this a lot. I don't think it's that they're not devoted to the idea of it. I think it's more that a lot's changing with the new portal station. Tourism's up. Ever's not as quiet and remote as it once was. And then, of course, they're worried about being pressed into full-time service."

I shrug. "I don't want players who don't want full-time."

Catherine perches on the edge of the desk. "You shouldn't. It would probably be good for you to tell them that. It would go a long way toward building a truly professional team, don't you think? I suspect they're wary of you because they don't want to be busy with skyball practices and games… They're not pros."

"I need more," I muse aloud. "I need community outreach to build support. Actually,"—I shift forward, leaning onto my elbows as I stare at her—"you can probably help with that. It's clear the Evertons adore you, and as long as nothing's changed, you adore skyball."

"Oh, I'm down," she says immediately. "You *know* I love skyball."

"I'll get some thoughts together, and then take you to dinner to discuss."

She quirks her head to the side. "I'm happy to come to your office, Manorin."

I shake my head. "Conversation'll be better on a date."

Her elegant nostrils flare, pink lips parting slightly. "You're asking me on a date to discuss business? How very romantic."

I rise and round the desk, placing a finger beneath her chin as I tip her gaze up to me. I love that she barely comes up to my chest.

"I'm telling you we're going on a date because we're single, attracted to one another, and have a lot in common. I'm going to take you on that date, talk about skyball for half an hour, talk about you the rest of the time. Then take you home and fuck you long and hard and deep, Cath. That's how this is going to go."

Her gray eyes flash with a range of emotions.

Need. Lust. Power. Indecision.

"Let it out," I croon. "All that power you've got stored up. I can smell it, Sunshine."

"It wouldn't be appropriate," she says smoothly, ignoring her old nickname. "Ever's courting you for a job."

I lift my chin. "Who gives a fuck what's appropriate at this point in our lives? The time for caring what others think has come and gone for me." I slide my hand down to grip her throat, noting how her nipples pebble under the soft-looking fabric of her dress.

With my free hand, I grip the tie holding it all together and pull. The fabric goes lax, falling open to reveal big, round breasts encased in navy lace.

"Stunning." I bring my focus to her beautiful eyes. "How long has it been since you've been filled?" I bend down and brush my muzzle over her chin. "And I don't just mean physically, Cath. Mentally. Emotionally. How long has it been since a male brought you pure joy? I could do that…"

She opens her mouth to answer, but I squeeze her neck tighter, just as her comm watch pings, a single name hovering over the flat surface.

Vikand Canterbury.

Catherine jolts, but I grip tighter, forcing her to ignore the watch and look into my eyes.

"Let me take a stab at this," I growl. "You're attempting to date that male because you need it, your power needs it, and you want something. But you know he will never, ever give you what you need. He's safe, and that's it. So it's all falling apart in front of you because he's not right, just like I said."

Her scent explodes as she drenches me in needy

pheromones. I don't even know if she knows she's doing it as she brings both hands to mine and claws at me. At the same time, she sinks closer, her body doing what her mind's still trying to catch up to.

The watch falls silent as her mouth drops open. "Manorin," she whispers, "I—"

The godsdamn watch blares to life again, the centaur's name flashing incessantly at Cath's wrist.

She shifts out of my grip, backing away from me as she re-ties her dress. Her fingers tremble as she glances up at me, then refocuses on the knotted belt.

"I've...I've got to take this, Manorin. Enjoy the picnic!" She dashes from the room, leaving the air saturated with her crisp apple scent.

Catherine used to love being cornered. But now, there's a harsh edge to her scent, a *tornness*, if that can be a word. That name I saw must be the centaur male who ghosted her on their date. I assumed, but I'd bet a thousand dollars I'm right.

What an idiot to leave a woman like her wondering and frustrated.

Flaring my nostrils wide, I suck in great big breaths, pulling her scent deep into my lungs as my cock pokes from my sheath, pressing painfully against the front of my jeans. Crisp fall apples. But when she's aroused, like now, even if she's also frustrated, it takes on an almost burnt, sugary gingerbread edge that makes my mouth water.

She needs what that other male will never give her.

I've just decided that, starting tomorrow, I'm going to see that she gets it.

CHAPTER SEVEN
CATHERINE

I rush from Manorin's temporary office as if my skirt's on fire. Pheromones drip from me, filling the air. That scent calls Manorin, I know it does, because now that he's in town, our chemistry is painfully obvious to me.

Vikand's name flashes again over the watch.

Rounding the corner, I back against the wall, half expecting Manorin to stalk toward me, rip the watch off my wrist and shove me up against the wall to take what he wants.

Gods, that sounds fun.

I half pray for that as I direct the watch to answer Vikand, my voice tremulous.

Vikand clears his throat. "Err, Catherine? Is that you?"

I resist the urge to remind him that he called *me*. Instead, I smooth back my hair.

"Yep, you've got me."

He pauses for a long, awkward moment. "Well, I'm not sure how to say this, but Arkan let me know my behavior at the field wasn't acceptable, so I'm calling to apologize for leaving you when I got a call."

I slap a hand over my face. Could he be any more obtuse?! In that moment I know one thing for sure—*nothing* about Vikand is right for me. If I'm honest with myself, Manorin's correct—I picked Vikand because he was safe and easy and available. But none of that is enough. I'm better off alone than dealing with a square peg, round hole situation.

A smile tips my lips upward at realizing I don't have to force a connection where there's not enough of one to mean anything.

"Listen, friend," I say gently. "I understand. I thought perhaps there could be something between us, but it's clear to me that you're on your own path, a very exciting path, I might add, and—"

"You don't want to reschedule? Catherine, I—"

I interrupt him the same way he just did me. "No, Vikand. I'm absolutely sure. There's no need to reschedule."

He pauses for another moment. Another clearing of his throat.

Gods, this is starting to annoy me.

"Well, if you're sure, I suppose that's fine, then."

What would Manorin do in this situation? That unhelpful voice in my head pops up again. This situation would *never* happen with Manorin, because he's always perfectly clear about what he wants and when he wants it. That doesn't seem to have changed in the two centuries since we parted.

It occurs to me I could hang up this call and return to his office to take exactly what he offered me.

But, no, I'm not going to do that. I'm going to let that play out later. I'm a little curious to see what Manorin will do next.

"Goodbye, Vikand," I say with confidence, relieved to be done attempting to court a male who doesn't have any common sense.

～

Hours later, I'm prepping three apple pies in the kitchen, considering how much relief I feel at, well, I can't even call it breaking up with Vikand. We never even dated, and I don't count the failed picnic attempt. Vikand was so much the opposite of my Wesley. Wesley was brash and brilliant and charming, and he used those assets to hurt monsters I cared about, attacking Ever and unleashing thralls within our wards. He betrayed me in the deepest possible way.

I should have known he was bad news... Annabelle never loved him.

But I don't have to worry about Wesley anymore. He's dead and gone, thank the gods.

My kitty cat timer hops from the windowsill to the island, flipflopping over to me as the sound of the front door opening echoes down the hall to us in the kitchen. The timer's tiny features curve up into an honest-to-gods smile.

Moments later, Manorin ducks into the kitchen with a smirk on his face. He slides onto one of the barstools, which creaks under his enormous weight. Leaning onto his forearms, he stares at me, crimson eyes scanning my face and dropping lower. His perusal is a heady thing, my power rising to the obvious call of his interest.

Without the distraction of Vikand, my sensuality is roaring back. I lick the spoon I used for the pie, running my tongue suggestively over the curved end.

Manorin's nostrils flare as he rises, planting both hands on the countertop.

"There you are, woman." His tone is low and suggestive, crimson eyes narrowed as he stares at me. "Let me guess, it didn't work out with what's-his-name?"

I grin. "It didn't."

His red eyes drop down my body then back up, and in that

moment, I feel more beautiful than I've felt in a very, very long time. Because the way Manorin looks at me is worshipful.

Just then, my pixie guest, Gilbert, pops his head into the kitchen with a smile, glancing at Manorin's enormous back. "Err, sorry to interrupt, Catherine. I'm out of towels, and I know you told me where I could grab more, but I've already forgotten."

I flash him a big smile. "No worries at all, Gilbert. I'll bring a stack to your room as soon as I get these pies in the oven."

The pixie male waggles his brows. "Tell me I don't have to wait until morning for the pies? They smell delicious!"

That pulls a laugh from my throat. "You don't have to wait until morning for them. As soon as they're done baking, I'll set them out in the formal dining room, and you can grab a piece. Come fast, though. They move quickly." I shoot him a friendly wink.

"Thanks, Catherine!" He waves as he turns and heads back up the hallway.

I set the spoon down, then round the island. When I'm close enough to Manorin, he grabs my hand and pulls me close, dipping low. He nuzzles his snout against my ear, sending white-hot rays of heat through my body.

"You're fucking dripping pheromones, Cath," he murmurs. "Needy little Sunshine. You've been a godsdamned faucet since I got here. After you help him, let's go to dinner and talk about doing something with this heat."

I turn to him with a smile, summoning my power to tweak my pheromones in the way I know will drive him wild. The slight change has an immediate effect.

Manorin lets out a quiet low. The sound is a combo of a moo and a growl and it's so deep, I nearly gasp from the reverberation of it.

Now that we're playing like this, I want to drive him utterly wild. A switch has flipped somewhere inside me, and it's all systems go.

"Not tonight, Manorin." I bat my lashes up at him. "I've got quite a lot to do around here."

He drops his grip on my hand, lifting his chin as his smirk grows. "Alright, Catherine. Tell me how I can help, and let's get it done together. Either way, I'm taking you to dinner. You turned me down yesterday, but tonight, I'm not taking no for an answer."

I wave away his offer. "That's alright. I've got my methods and—"

He silences my refusal by bending down and licking a hot path over my bottom lip. His tongue is rough and wet, and everything inside me clenches up tight. Pulling slightly back, he stares at my mouth.

"You could have this hot tongue on your pussy tonight, Cath. Because I've got a proposal for you that involves friends with benefits simply because it'll feel good." He plays with a strand of my hair. "No strings attached, woman. Use me up because we both know you want to."

He straightens, his expression a challenge.

Come to me. Give in.

But this is how it always was with us. Teasing and pushing until we fell ravenously into bed.

"I can agree to dinner," I manage.

He straightens with a satisfied smile. "Good, Sunshine. If you won't let me help you, I'll wait out front."

The kitty cat timer meows and flip-flops head over heels across the countertop. When it halts in front of Manorin, he leans onto both forearms on the counter, still looking at me. "Actually, looks like I'll be here having a little chat with Annabelle. Find me when you're done."

A chat with Annabelle? Surprise courses through me. She's a

wonderful hostess, but she doesn't typically do more than make her opinions known to our guests. For her to initiate a conversation of sorts with Manorin is a surprise indeed. I stare at the timer for a long moment, but she studiously ignores me as she purrs and scoots closer to Manorin's hands.

I mull that over as I grab Gilbert's towels and consider my old friend's proposal.

A succubus's deepest desire is to fill and be filled, but contrary to what many seem to believe, it's not solely from a sexual standpoint. It's true that I can tweak my pheromones and easily read others'. But it's also true that I have an innate need and ability to read monsters in *general* and to ascertain what they need emotionally and mentally. Making monsters happy is my thing.

It's why I'm the unofficial mother of Ever. I welcome guests and new citizens alike. I give the welcome tours. Now I'm the one handing out the stunning new welcome books, designed by my friend Betmal and his mate, Ama. And filling those roles brings me joy. I've focused almost entirely on that, casting aside the more physical aspects of my power.

But Manorin brings *all* of it to the forefront.

My belly flutters with anticipation as I return to the kitchen. He stands with his back to me, the cabinet doors in front of him flung wide. The kitty cat timer sits on top of his head, nestled in his short waves as he screws the cabinet hinge.

I clear my throat, but he moves slowly, I assume not to dislodge the timer. She spins too, her kitty face splitting into a grin as a tiny meow echoes from her.

"What are you two doing?" I round the island and join him just as he sets a multitool down on the stove.

He swings the cabinet door open and shut a few times, and the timer meows happily. She leaps off his head and onto the countertop, then hops up and down excitedly.

"All done, sweet Annabelle," he practically croons.

My mouth drops open as he reaches out and brushes a big knuckle along the timer's round head. "Are you flirting with my house?"

He crosses his arms and leans against the island, smirking at me as the timer rolls away to her resting spot near the back windows. "She indicated she wanted my help."

I scoff. "Is that so?"

He shrugs and grabs the belt of my wrap dress, pulling me between his big thighs. He's hot, even with all that fur and clothing between us. But his body's still hard as a rock, his gaze reverent as he stares down at me. Big fingers come to my curls and twist the ends.

"She did. Cabinet door was a little loose, and you know I always carry a multitool, Cath." He winks at the word "multitool," and I resist a groan. Manorin doesn't make many dad jokes, but I swear he can turn anything sexual.

He grins now. "Haven't lost my touch, I see. You smell as good as your pies, Sunshine."

"You shouldn't call me that."

His dark brows bunch together. "And why not?"

I wave my hands around, getting flustered at how easily he can get under my skin, all these hundreds of years later. "You called me that when we dated."

He laughs. "Ain't that kinda the point, Cath? Because now that Gilbert has his fucking towels, I'm taking you to Herschel's, and we're gonna discuss an arrangement for the duration of my stay. You've got needs, woman, and I can take care of those, even if it's only for a little while." He leans down and nuzzles his way along my neck, his nose ring slightly less warm than his skin. "Long as I'm here, Sunshine's your new name."

He straightens. "Unless you want me to be your big, filthy secret. In which case, I'll agree to call you by your given name in public."

"Please do." I step backward as my stomach rumbles. Am I

really doing this? Considering taking him up on this friends-with-sexy-benefits situation?

As he holds his elbow out for my hand, I decide, yes, I definitely am.

I deserve a little fun.

~

Herschel's is jam-packed by the time we get there, Herschel himself scrambling around to seat groups of monsters. Every table's full, but when we arrive, Herschel seems unsurprised to see Manorin.

"Ah, good, you are here. Follow, follow!" He grabs two menus and waves us toward the back of the restaurant.

I glance up at Manorin, but he only grins down at me as he pulls me in front of him, guiding me through the busy restaurant.

And this is one of the things I loved about him when we dated. Manorin's always been a planner—romance was his forte in a way Wesley never bothered with.

By the time Herschel leads us through the kitchen and up a tiny, twisty flight of stairs, I'm literally gobsmacked. On the restaurant's roof sits a tiny gazebo crawling with rose vines. The red and white awning on the front of the building is tall enough that no one could see the gazebo except from above.

"I had no idea this was here," I muse, shooting Herschel a look.

He blushes and waves his hands frantically around. "Ah, a secret, sweet Catherine. I reveal the gazebo only to those who take the time to plan something special." He looks at Manorin. "Which he did. So…enjoy yourselves!"

But the surprises don't stop there. A beautiful arrangement of pink roses sits in the center of the table, a card poking out the top. I recognize Ohken's work, not to mention he's the only florist in Ever.

I take the card, flipping it open as Manorin joins me. He presses one big hand between my shoulder blades, then slides up to grip the back of my neck. And just like that, my power flares to life again, loving how he touches so easily but in such a commanding way.

He brings his snout to my neck and nuzzles softly. "That's it, Sunshine. That scent. Gods, there's nothing like it."

I hold in a moan, canting my head to one side to give him better access. He lets out a soft, grumbly growl as he nibbles the edge of my ear.

Footsteps echo toward us from the stairs, breaking the moment. He moves away from me and pulls out a chair. We manage to seat ourselves by the time the waitress arrives to take our orders.

Half an hour later, we're on our second bottle of wine, and I'm laughing more easily than I have in years. We've already covered a dozen topics and caught up, and it's really, really nice.

"So." He leans onto the table with both forearms, a vicious glint in his crimson eyes. "I mentioned my proposition, Cath, but I was serious. Let's have fun while I'm here."

I take a sip of my wine, then set the glass down. "You can't tie me to a bed for the next three weeks, Manorin."

He chuckles. "Enticing as that sounds, three-week sexcapades are over on account of real life and all." He shakes his head. "No, I was thinking more like me creeping into your room every night and taking care of you. Maybe during the day sometimes too. You could come fuck me in the gym at the stadium. Gods know nobody else will be there, so we'd have the place to ourselves." His smile falls a little at the mention of the stadium.

I resist the urge to nip my lip, an old nervous habit. "We'd need rules," I hedge instead.

He sits back, laying one enormous arm on the back of the chair next to his. "I'm listening."

I clear my throat, pondering what sort of rules a dalliance like this might need. "Absolutely no strings attached," I say finally. "You're only here short term, for now, so no emotion, in as much as that's possible."

He grins. "There's a lotta history between us, Cath, but I'll do my level best not to fall in love again."

When his nostrils flare, I straighten in my chair, knowing he's scenting me. My scent is likely telling him what I haven't said aloud yet—that my body, at the very least, is fully on board with whatever Manorin wants to do.

"No need for checking in or scheduling or any of that, either," I say. "Let's just let things happen naturally."

He cocks his head to the side. "I'd like to spend time with you like this, too, Cath." His smile goes slightly feral. "Even if we're talking about work some of the time."

I wave my hands around, trying to gather my thoughts. "I just mean we don't need to make a huge production of it."

He spears a bit of apple and munches it slowly. "Seems to me like you're trying to find rules and struggling to come up with good ones, so I'll make this easy for you, Sunshine." He drops his fork and stares at me, and I feel that red stare straight to the middle of my bones. "I'm gonna make this fun for you, but if you stop having fun at any point, you tell me."

Heat spreads through me, my cheeks flashing hot when Manorin doesn't break the intense eye contact.

"Fine," I say before I can rationalize this away. "Let's just have fun, right?"

His smile grows wicked again. "No strings attached, Cath. Just lots and lots of delicious sex."

We're really doing this. Oh my gods.

I beam at him, tweaking my pheromones to the specific scent I know he loves.

His answering chuckle sends a needy flash of heat down my spine as pleasure swirls low in my belly.

I deserve fun at this point. If that's what Manorin is offering, I should absolutely take it. This is nothing serious. Just two friends with a fun agreement.

Two friends who want to have really, really, really damn good sex.

CHAPTER EIGHT

MANORIN

L ast night was a prelude to what's coming. Dinner with Cath was lovely, and she agreed to my sexy proposition. But when we returned to the Annabelle, I didn't so much as touch her. I could tell she expected me to, but I know her. She loves to be chased and teased. And I love doing both of those things. I'm sure a psychologist could talk about how, in ancient times, minotaurs were thrown into mazes to hunt down hapless women. The idea of that makes me hot.

So, tease it is.

But teasing her meant I went to bed horny as hells, thinking about the beautiful woman upstairs I'd left wanting. I didn't sleep well, not that I've ever been a good sleeper. Not even after fucking out my frustration on my favorite toy helped. Toy succubus pussy is nothing like real succubus pussy. There's no replacement for Catherine.

That's why I'm in the stadium gym now, pumping iron and tossing weights around to work off the excess energy. The stadium's all dark stone with flashy new equipment. The weights have no dings in them. It's clear nobody's used them at all. All that'll have to change.

I consider that as I go through my leg day routine, but Cath is never far from my mind.

A two-hour workout doesn't even take the edge off, though, because my dick is hard and dripping still by the end of it. It's been a dozen years or more since I've taken a lover and longer since my last relationship. I've been so focused on the Hellions and tired of dealing with the push and pull that doomed relationships mean. I'd set that aside for a while, content to focus on work.

But Catherine reminds me of what I haven't had in a long time—a true partner who fits me in all the important ways.

I take a cold shower and dress in the locker room. I'm starving, though, so I decide to head back to the Annabelle for Catherine's famous buffet. By the time I get there, I'm nearly desperate with need, thinking about bending her over the dining room table and eating something that ain't food.

When I walk up the Annabelle's front stairs, I notice an old can of paint in the corner. Sweet girl waggles her shutters at me until I cross the porch and take a peek. The white paint is peeling off the shutters in sad little strips, exposing the wood beneath. I stroke my way along one of the slats, and tiny shreds of paint fall off it.

"You need some help, sweet girl?" I glance around at the front of the inn.

She ripples her pale pink siding in a sad little pattern, then dangles the shutter from one hinge, letting it swing as if the whole inn is about to fall down.

I laugh at her dramatics. "Point taken, Annabelle. If you want me to help, I'm happy to. But we gotta sand these shutters before we paint. If I paint over this, it'll just peel right back off."

She lets out an ominous groan from deep inside, but I pat the siding. "Promise I'll fix it, okay?"

She doesn't respond, but I make a mental note to grab sandpaper later today. Cath has her hands full with this place. Makes sense she doesn't have time for upkeep. I'll handle that so she doesn't have to.

All reasonable thoughts fly outta my head when I find Catherine flitting around the kitchen in a fitted pink tee, tight-ass jeans and a ruffly apron with hearts all over it.

Gods*damn.*

Just like that, I'm aching again.

This woman might be the death of me.

A bowl of juicy-looking red apples sits on the kitchen island. I don't recall that being there before, and it makes me smile. She knows I love red apples, even though minotaurs are primarily meat eaters.

When I enter the kitchen and grab one, she halts and turns, smiling up at me.

Gray eyes sparkle with mirth as she plants a hand on her round hip. "Sleep well, Manorin? I'm not sure if everything's quite your size in that room, but let me know if you're at all *uncomfortable.*"

I resist the urge to discuss my *comfort* at length right here in the dining room, but the male pixie flits in and starts picking over a stack of scones, so I hold back.

Instead, I level Catherine with a heavy stare. "I need you this morning. I neglected to mention it last night, given our other topic of discussion, but I'm meeting Arkan at the Galloping Green Bean to discuss recruitment and what that might look like. I'd like to have you there to give your opinion, if you're free?"

A pretty pink blush spreads over her cheeks, and she smiles, a tiny dimple appearing. "I'd love that. Let me just wrap up the breakfast buffet and set out a sign letting the guests know how to contact me. I can be ready in about five minutes, if that works?"

"No rush." I wave toward the front door. "I'll be waiting outside."

She smiles bigger and turns, heading for the dining room. I watch her go—who wouldn't?—but then realize, just in front of me, Gilbert the Fucking Pixie is watching her go as well.

I don't mean to glare; I really don't. I don't even realize I am until he looks over at me, pales, and drops his scone. When he rushes toward the stairs and up them, it occurs to me that I'm acting like a younger bull, and that just won't do. What if Gilbert's here for the same reason I am, considering a move to Ever and reevaluating his priorities?

I can't sow that sort of ill will, so I grimace on my way to the door, considering if I should find Gilbert and apologize, maybe offer to bring him another stack of towels or a piece of Catherine's pie.

Fuck that. I don't want anybody tasting that pie but me.

Once outside, I lean against Annabelle's pale pink siding and munch on my apple, watching the world go by as I wait for Catherine to appear.

As I'm staring at the lovely Community Garden across from the inn, my communication watch pings. When I look down, I'm surprised to see Bishop Rygold's name flashing above the blue band. It's bad news if Pine Gulch's sheriff is callin' me.

"Rygold, what's u—"

"When you coming home next?" Bishop's deep voice cracks a little when he speaks, the result of a wartime injury that permanently damaged his vocal cords.

I cross my legs at the hooves. "I don't have a plan, Bishop. I'm on b—"

"Break, I know," he interrupts. "Listen, I've got a situation here with some cattle rustling and your godsdamned nephew."

I sigh, rubbing a hand over my face at the Pine Gulch sheriff's comment. This shit seems to come up when I don't get home frequently enough.

"I've got plans the next couple of weeks, but I can get home for a quick visit."

"Gotta be a week or two," he snipes. "You know how it is. You don't come take care of it, and I'll be forced to. I don't think either of us want me to hafta do that."

It's not a threat, per se. But we both know if he has to deal with my knucklehead nephew, it'll go poorly for said nephew. Bishop is a broken, bruised soul who doesn't give a fuck about Alarion's comfort.

"Gimme a couple of days. I'll make time early next week, okay?"

"See that you do, Longhorn." That's all I get before he signs off.

Resting my head against the Annabelle's siding, I don't notice Catherine standing there with a wry look on her elegant features.

"Everything okay, Nor?"

I turn toward her, leaning my shoulder against the siding. "Better now if you're gonna start using that old nickname with me." I resist the urge to reach out and tuck her gray waves over one shoulder, just to see if they're still impossibly soft. "You're the only one who's ever called me that."

She laughs, the sound joyous and tinkling. "Well, it doesn't hurt that you always demanded everyone else call you by your full name."

I join her in laughter. "If I could force everyone to address me by the full Manorin Longhorn, I'd do it."

Wrinkles form at the edges of her eyes. "I know there's a lot of pride in your name; it's one of the things I really admire about minotaurs. That shared pride in *everyone* with the Longhorn name is really unique."

A memory of her declining to accept my mating tattoo flits through my mind. That tattoo would've magically added her name to the historical list of Longhorn family members.

"Well," I run a hand along my horn, "I wish I could say I was feeling pride at the moment, but you walked in on a conversation about my nephew."

She waves toward the street. "Shall we walk and talk?"

I nod and hold my arm out for her to take.

She slips her much smaller hand through the crook of my elbow, fingers curling around the muscles of my forearm. "What's going on with Alarion? Or do you have other nephews at this point? I'm embarrassed to admit I haven't kept up with your family since..." she trails off.

I wink at her. "Well, you did shatter my heart into a few hundred pieces. Don't know that they'd have wanted to keep up with you, Sunshine. I can't say my mother ever forgave you, if I'm being honest."

She blanches, her earlier blush returning. "That was a long time ago."

And I'd moved past it, I really had. But it's hard not to remember how badly I wanted her to be mine...once upon a time.

"Mhm." I sigh as I consider Alarion. "My nephew's always been wired a little differently than my brother. He's brash and confident when he shouldn't be. There's a kind soul *somewhere* inside of him, but he's easily led astray." I glance down at her. "You've never been to Pine Gulch, right? Still?"

She shakes her head.

"Well," I glance up Sycamore where the diner comes into view, "there's a den of ophiotaurii that settled in the northwestern corner of the haven, and they're mostly bad news. They cause a disturbance in town; they steal cattle. They're a general nuisance, and Alarion's gotten involved with them." I sigh. "I've heard they've even ventured outside the haven into the human world a time or two. To what end, I'm not really sure, but they're dragging Alarion into it with them." I rub her fingers gently. "That call was from Bishop Rygold, our sheriff, reminding me that if I don't come home and deal with Alarion, he will. We still don't have a keeper, so it's Rygold or nothin' keeping the peace."

Catherine frowns up at me. "What about your brother?"

I shake my head. "He can't handle Alarion, not since his mate passed. He's lost to the pain and grief of her death, and most times I call, he's drunk or doesn't answer."

Catherine clutches my forearm a little tighter. "Sounds like you need to take a trip home?"

I nod, then smile down at her. "Well, it doesn't have to be all bullshit. Why don't you come with me this upcoming weekend? Pine Gulch is beautiful, Alarion's nonsense aside." I waggle my brows at her. "Let me show you a good time in a place that's a little more country than this." I dip low. "It'll be easier to keep me a dirty little secret if we're away from prying eyes."

Catherine laughs. "What am I going to do about Annabelle?"

I glance skyward as I consider that. After a moment, I look down. "What do you usually do when you want a vacation?"

She grumbles, "I don't take vacations. I've never left her."

My mouth drops open. "Never?"

"Never." She looks up. "I'm not opposed to it; I've just…well, I think I've been hiding out here. This is where I took my first mate and where he tried to rip everything I loved from me. I'm tied to Ever in a way I could never be to another haven. So, I haven't left." She looks off into the difference. "For better or worse."

I'm not sure how much to reveal here, but I work at Hearth Headquarters. News of the warlock Wesley's attack on Ever and eventual death reached us there.

"I'm sorry he did that to you," I offer quietly.

Catherine squeezes my forearm a little tighter. "Me too, Nor. But we don't have to talk about that just now."

I check to make sure there aren't any cars coming before I guide her across. When we stop in front of the diner, I smile down at her. "I won't pry about Wesley, although I've seen the news, of course. But if you ever want to talk about him or what happened, I'm here, alright?"

She smiles, but it seems forced. "I know, Manorin. Thank you."

She doesn't want to discuss him right now; that much is clear. And it's probably for the best because, if I learn more about the male who hurt her, I'll want to dig him up just to murder him.

I pinch her side playfully. "So, we going to Pine Gulch this weekend then?"

Her smile grows broader. "I bet I could ask the Hector girls to watch over Annabelle for me. I'll comm them after breakfast to check."

Good, I think to myself, because there is a single bed situation in our future, and I'm gonna put her in the middle of it while I give her everything she needs.

~

"Walk me through this again," Arkan says, staring at the stack of papers we've been looking at for the last half hour.

"You're looking at a substantial budget for pulling in talent." It's not the best news for me to give him, but I don't know what he expects going from a volunteer part-time team to a team of pros.

Arkan frowns. Next to me, Catherine's quiet, smiling up at a big pegasus waiter as he clip-clops past us.

The Keeper slumps down into his curved centaur bench, crossing his arms as he jerks his head toward the stack. "Obviously I knew this was going to be a need, but I didn't realize just how much of a budget jump it would be."

Catherine clears her throat. "Keeper, if we're going to go in on skyball, we absolutely must go all in. Big budget, flashy new players. We should probably consider rebranding the Misfits a little. Abemet did the logo way back in the day. If we can attract even one or two skyball games here per season, we'll more than make up for that cost over a few years."

Arkan nods. "Okay, here's the thing I don't want to say, but I feel I have to say because I aim to be transparent." He looks at me. "You've sensed this, but I'm the primary driving force behind this change, and obviously Catherine's on board, but the rest of the haven leadership needs more convincing. Any additional budget would need their approval."

Catherine reaches across the table and pats the stack of papers. "That's where I come in. We need a grassroots initiative to get the excitement up about skyball. I think we should plan an exhibition game, get the Evertons excited about it. The playoffs game was a huge hit last year...we can bring that excitement back!" She glances at me. "I wouldn't plan to broadcast this outside of Ever but we can really do it up with painted signs and glamouring or decorating downtown. It'll be fun."

Surprise courses through me as I look at her. "First I'm hearing of *this*, Cath."

She looks between Arkan and me. "It came to me overnight, but isn't it the best idea?" Clasping her hands together, she rushes on, "We can get specialty shirts made and have folks get together to paint signs, decorate Main Street. Really do it up and make it a big deal for town. That should get even our grouchiest of leaders on board, if the whole town is excited."

Arkan wears a pleased, if amused, expression. "I love it. Let's do it. Assuming..." He looks over at me, a dark brow curving wickedly upward. "You're into this, right?"

I laugh as I look between them. "Oh yeah," I stare right into Catherine's gray eyes, "I'm into this."

Her scent explodes, although I don't know if anyone but me can tell. A muscle under her eyelid twitches. I suspect she's holding back from snarking something sassy at me. Instead, she tosses her long hair over one shoulder and looks at Arkan. "Manorin would have the entirety of my support in accomplishing this, of course."

Arkan snorts out a laugh. "Shit, Catherine, I don't think there's a single thing you *couldn't* do if you set your mind to it." His smile partially falls. "You really think you can get the others on board with an exhibition game? I think they're tired of hearing from me."

She sits back against the turquoise, red, and white bench seat and glances up at me with a big smile. "Leave it to me, boys."

I cross my arms, matching Arkan's stance. "Well, there you have it, kid." I grin at the young, ambitious Keeper. "There would be the matter of my compensation, too, and I don't come cheap. We can talk numbers, but as you might imagine, you're gonna have to pay me a shitload to come here and take this on."

Arkan's characteristic smile falls a bit, but he nods. "Of course. How would you feel about us announcing the exhibition game at a town hall meeting tonight? I'm calling one later to discuss expanding downtown's footprint. I think it'd be good timing even if we don't have all the details hashed out."

"Yeah," I say as I consider if there's any reason not to. I can't find one, and it'll be nice to get the whole town in on skyball. "Let's do it."

~

Hours later, I'm standing at the corner of Main Street and Sycamore as a bell tolls, ringing throughout downtown. Hordes of monsters exit every building and the homes back behind downtown. Catherine mentioned earlier that town hall meetings typically happen either in town hall or at the gazebo, so I'd guess that's where everyone's headed.

"You lost, big guy?"

Turning toward the voice, I smile at finding Morgan Hector standing behind me with her arms folded at her back.

I jerk my head down the street. "Town Hall's that way, as I recall?"

She smiles. "Walk with me?"

I hold my elbow out for her, and she slips a hand through it, curling her fingers around my forearm.

She squeezes my forearm. "How are things going?"

Oh, she's nosy. I kinda like that.

I glance down with a smirk as I guide us along Main. "In what way?"

She shrugs as if it could be any old thing. "Your time here. Thoughts on our expansion." She clears her throat and looks up at me. "Catherine."

The shortest version of the truth is probably best. Morgan knows Cath and I dated—we covered that much at family dinner.

"Ever's lovely. I've got concerns about how widely the skyball expansion will be supported, but there's a plan for that. Catherine's an excellent hostess, as I expected. She's literally made for that, you know."

Morgan's smile grows. "You know that's not what I meant. You dated. There's obvious chemistry. What's up there?"

"Why?"

"'Cause I wanna know."

"Why?"

"I'm nosy."

"We're just friends," I confirm as we pass by Ohken's store, Fleur. "If you're worried our past will at all affect who's chosen for—"

Morgan snorts out a laugh. "That's not it, and you know it. If you don't wanna spill the beans, that's fine... I'll just bug Catherine instead. I will find out though." She looks ahead with a soft sigh. "On another note, what do you make of our expansion? Is it in line with how you've seen other havens do it over the years?"

I look at her with curiosity. As far as I know, she doesn't sit on the town's leadership committee even though her mate does.

"Nosy," she says like she's reading my thoughts.

I glance down the street, checking for cars as we cross over toward the big white gazebo in front of Town Hall. "Well, there's usually an order of things. Infrastructure planning is typically first, but it's harder in havens like this one that are fairly small. Ever's actually one of the smallest havens in the network, if you can believe it."

Someone shouts Morgan's name, and we turn. Her sisters and aunt jog up the street toward us. By the time they arrive, it seems like Morgan's moved on from her line of questioning.

Interesting. I wonder if she's just asking out of curiosity or what.

Ahead, the gazebo creaks, groans and begins to grow to accommodate all the Evertons. Even so, some monsters opt to stand just outside the tall white structure. Arkan and Hana stand at the front with the rest of haven leadership, including Catherine.

Gray eyes flick to me and wrinkle in the corners as I walk into the space with the Hectors. The girls find seats toward the front, but I lean against a railing. Normal-sized chairs were never meant for males my size. Catherine glances at me again and smirks as I cross my arms over my chest.

It takes a few minutes for everyone to file in and quiet down. I find this process fascinating. Hearth HQ doesn't do anything like a town hall meeting. Evenia emails updates to residents, and that's pretty much it. Hearth HQ is gorgeous and cultured and fascinating, but it's tiny and tucked away and stiff, too. It's wildly different from Ever in every possible way.

Once the gathered group falls quiet-ish, Arkan opens his arms wide. "Welcome, Evertons! Thanks for joining our biggest town hall meeting to date! I've got a couple topics to cover with you this evening. The first is the proposed expansion of downtown. I'll be emailed detailed plans this week, but I wanted to make you all aware of the discussions happening with myself and town leadership."

He points to his right, where a wide swath of grass covers the space between the gazebo and the nearest building. "I think it's safe to say you've all felt the pinch as Ever grows. Our restaurants are full, there's never any parking on Main, and the Shifter Hollow folks are running out of space."

A few grumbles sound like they agree with him.

"That spot over there," he waves toward the grassy area, "was originally meant to be a cross street to Main, just like Sycamore is. To the west would be more neighborhoods, and the east was always meant to be an extension of the shopping area. What we're talking about now is doing the infrastructure expansion to begin bringing more businesses to Ever."

Lots more rumbling and a cacophony of questions ring out at his announcement.

He indicated for everyone to quiet down. "I'm gonna answer questions in a minute, but let me just say that we'll have a question period for a couple of weeks before the plans are voted on and finalized by the leaders you see here at the front. That being said, what questions can I answer now?"

The next half hour is full of question after question, some of which are pretty good and give me more to think about.

How will the infrastructure changes be prioritized?

What changes will be enacted to improve the situation for monster species who've indicated past challenges with Ever's infrastructure? That one from a harpy who honestly shocks me when she stands and shares the question. I've never even known a harpy to live within the haven system. Between her and Lou Hector, the blue witch, it seems like Ever's full of unusual beings.

The questions go on and on, but Arkan finally announces he won't take any more and to save them for the question period. His dark lips curl, the smile wicked as he glances at me.

"On an even more exciting note, part of our expansion includes Ever having a formal skyball program. And, if we're lucky, a kickass coach." He grins at me. "Manorin, wanna come up here for a sec?"

Every head in the gazebo swivels toward me, murmurs rising again as I stalk to the front to join him. When I stare out over the crowd, it's easy to see that most seem to recognize me. They look excited, at a quick glance.

Arkan continues, "Manorin's here with us as we talk through what pro skyball would look like in Ever. You'll see him in town for the next little bit, culminating in an exhibition game for the whole town."

Cheers break out, and a lot of monsters stand and whoop. I hear shouts of the Ever team name, Misfits, ring out. As the cheering dies down, a lone monster toward the back screeches, "Go Punishers!" and I have to hold back a smile, hometown team and all.

Arkan looks at me. "Coach, you wanna say anything?"

I wait for the crowd to fully quiet, looking around at the gathered monsters.

"I couldn't be more excited for the exhibition game, but I need your help making this a big deal with our neighbors. So, let's paint signs, decorate Main Street, wear the green and gold. Let's get excited, right?" When I lift my hands, the shouting erupts again, and most everyone stands, stomps, cheers. I risk a glance at Catherine, who's beaming at the other Evertons.

"Skyball deserves a bigger place in Ever," Arkan shouts above the crowd. "Whaddya say?!" The crowd erupts even louder, the excitement tangible.

It raises the hair on my nape, that same thrill as walking out of a locker room onto the skyball pitch. I love that the Evertons seem super jazzed about bringing skyball more to the forefront.

It takes a while for folks to calm down. When they do, Arkan reminds them about the question period then closes the meeting. As the crowd dissipates, I turn to Arkan and Hana. Cath comes to my side.

"I've gotta head home for the weekend to take care of some family business, but I'll be back Monday." I glance between the Keeper and his mate. "Didn't want you to think it meant I was in any way less excited about this opportunity. I've just got a nephew being an asshole, and I gotta deal with him."

Hana punches me on the shoulder. "Go get 'im, Coach. We're not worried." She looks over at her mate. "We'll use the weekend to get started on decorating Main."

Catherine clasps her hands together. "Perhaps you can do a little subversive recruiting while you're there, too. The Punishers do have quite the lineup this year, as you know."

I match her feral smile. "Oh yeah."

We share a laugh, and I picture Catherine in the corner of a bar, whispering sweet nothings to a skyball player to bring them to Ever. I'm more and more excited that she's going home with me. I oughta turn her loose on every Punishers player we run across just to see what'll happen.

Arkan was right about one thing he said this morning—there's nothing Cath can't do.

CHAPTER NINE

CATHERINE

"We'd love to redesign the logo!" Amatheia claps her hands excitedly as she and Betmal smile at me across the booth at the Green Bean later that evening.

Betmal stares at his beautiful young mate, love obvious in the way his dark eyes eat her up. I've known him for centuries, been friends that entire time, and I've never seen him like this.

I want a stare like that for myself, a perusal that makes me feel beautiful.

She glances at him, nips her lip, then looks back at me. "Catherine, do you suppose the Evertons would consider a name change while they're at it?"

I cock my head to the side. "For the team, you mean?"

She shrugs, aqua darkening her cheeks. "Well, Betmal has taken me to games in six or seven havens at this point, and all the names are pretty strong, but ours is, well…it sounds more childlike to me?" She lifts both hands quickly, as if to apologize. "I don't know who came up with it, and I don't mean to offend. But most of the other names are alliterative, as well. Hearth HQ

Hellions, Pine Gulch Punishers. But we're the Ever Misfits. Sounds like a ragtag band of preteens."

I don't mean to gawk, but I'm sure I must. She's absolutely right.

I tug at one of my waves before flipping it over my shoulder as I stare at my half-eaten burger. Eventually, I nod as I return my focus to the stunning young mermaid. "Alright, why don't you two take a stab at a new logo and new name? Surprise us. You're our resident creatives. Arkan and town leadership would have to approve it, but see what you can do."

Betmal strokes a thick lock of Amatheia's dark hair back behind her frilled ear. "What about the Enforcers, ma sirène? Epics? Eternals? Hmm." He glances up in thought, then over to me. "Amatheia's right, of course. We'll come up with something for you, sweet friend. When do you need it?"

"Welll…" I draw the word out long. "It would be great to share it ASAP if we want to include it in the exhibition game. But maybe, now that I'm thinking about it, it would be better to keep the Misfits for now and unveil a new name later?"

By the end of lunch, Betmal and Ama agree to design not only a new logo and merch, but signs for the competing teams. Now I just need to talk to Manorin about this, because I sprang it on him at the meeting as well. It just came to me, and I couldn't wait to share it.

"How are things going with Manorin in town?" Betmal eyes me carefully as he takes an elegant sip of his drink.

Rascal. He knows I dated Manorin for many years. Betmal was front and center to the way that turned out…he's been my friend for a very, very long time.

"Just fine," I hedge. "He's absolutely lovely and it's been nice to catch up."

Betmal grins at me, revealing twin white fangs. "Oh I just bet it has, darling. How much catching up are you doing?"

Ama nudges him in the side with a little laugh. "Stop needling her, mate."

Betmal slings an arm around Ama but continues grinning at me. "And yet I sense a moment of rekindling, and I'm nosy, so tell me, Catherine, how much catching up is happening?"

I roll my eyes as I take another sip of my cocktail. "None of your business," I manage finally.

We share a laugh, but it does occur to me that keeping this arrangement with Nor under wraps might be harder than it initially seemed.

Especially if Betmal is going to insert himself up into my business.

Nosy vampire.

"You're absolutely sure?" I stare at my comm watch where Wren's name hovers.

"Absolutely," she says with confidence. "Annabelle loves us. We'll come hang out so she's not lonely, and, honestly, I'm an excellent cook. I can keep the buffet going while you're gone, do the sheets, all the things. Oh," her voice goes thoughtful, "I can spend some time in the rose garden too. I'd love that."

"So would the rose garden, so long as you work your magic on her."

Wren laughs. "Well, I don't know. How enormous do you want the roses to be when you return?"

I join her in laughter, considering how her green magic could be used to do incredible things to my flowers.

After we hang up, I clean the kitchen and prep breakfast, but my thoughts don't stray far from Manorin. He was with Arkan most of the morning after our meeting, then he came back and went to his room to make calls.

The Annabelle's quiet. It's late. I should probably let him

know the Hectors agreed to watch Annabelle for our trip to Pine Gulch.

Am I really leaving Ever for the first time in centuries? I didn't realize how hermit-y I'd gotten over the years, but the prospect of seeing another haven excites me after all this time.

Smiling, I ascend the stairs. When I get to the rose room, I rap lightly on the door.

"Come on in, Sunshine."

Manorin's greeting makes me smile, and I swing the door open to find him huddled over a stack of papers, his comm disk on the table in front of him. When I enter and close the door, he sits back in the chair, focus drifting lazily down my body and back up.

"Beautiful," he murmurs, almost to himself.

His praise lights something inside me, something that was dead for a long time, then kindled slowly back to life. It turns into a roaring bonfire in Manorin's presence, though.

I sashay into the room and sit in the chair across from him, looking down at the papers. "What are you working on?"

He grumbles, "Did you really come here to ask me about work?"

I laugh when he grins. "You've got me. I came to tell you the Hectors agreed to watch Annabelle next weekend, so I can go home with you. It might not be the best timing, though, if we want to get a grassroots support system going for the exhibition game."

The corners of his mouth turn up into a wicked smirk. "Nah, we'll only be gone two nights. It's the running of the steers, and there's a huge barn dance, and I promise you don't want to miss that." His eyes drift down my body and back up. "I definitely need to take you to that. It'll be fun."

Without even meaning to, I tweak my pheromones, sending him signals about what I need. He's right, I didn't come up here to talk about work, but I don't think I *fully* realized that until right this second. But looking at that gold ring in his nose and the appreciative look on his face, what I came for has changed.

Across from me, he stiffens, then grabs the entire table and shoves it aside. The yawning space between us seems too big, so I cross to him.

"Your need is obvious, Catherine," he growls. "Let's do something about that."

Reaching down, he pulls me into his arms and turns, depositing me on top of the table. He grabs the belt of my dress and yanks, the fabric falling down on either side of me. With an expectant smile, he grabs the halves of the dress and fully opens them, revealing a scarlet matching number that's my favorite.

Crimson eyes flick to mine. "Your taste in lace has gotten decidedly more expensive, woman."

I grin and shift onto my elbows. "Belleza makes the absolute best lingerie."

He nods as he brings both hands to my belly and strokes the dips and creases admiringly. When he brings both hands down over my pussy, rubbing at my clit with the pads of his thumbs, I let one thigh fall open.

He leans down, burying his snout between my thighs to suck in great, greedy-sounding breaths. He's slow in his perusal, dragging his muzzle down my inner thigh to my knee, the tiny whiskers on his snout tickling me. Working his way back up, he nuzzles at my pussy before moving higher, nipping at the soft rolls of my belly. His attention feels like worship, the way his nostrils flare and his eyes never leave my body.

"I'm going to enjoy this." Sliding two fingers between the silk and my pussy, he pulls the fabric to the side.

I'm still not ready for the first swipe of his enormous, hot tongue. Scrambling, I grip onto one of his horns to hold him where I need him as I gasp and watch. His tongue is even softer than I remember, and I arch as he licks a broad, flat path up my slit. Crimson eyes narrow on his work as he shifts the tip of his muzzle over my clit, then licks again.

I clap my hand over my mouth as a groan tumbles from me. Falling onto my back, I lose myself to sensations I haven't felt in so long.

So long.

Manorin's fingers dig into my hips as he holds me in place, despite my squirming. I need more. I need that tongue deeper. I'm equally desperate to come and to start this whole thing all over again.

Crying out, I pull at his horn, trying to get more of him, harder, hotter.

Manorin chuckles, a low, satisfied sound that has me clenching on nothing. But that nothing shatters as he slides two thick fingers into my pussy and curls them, rubbing at my G-spot. Blissful heat overtakes me, back arching as my nipples pebble. Everything blurs except for my focus on that tongue, those fingers and the masterful way he remembers what I like.

The steady thrust and curl of his fingers has me rocking my hips to meet him. But I need more of that tongue too. Mewling, I try to shift lower, to get closer, to open my legs wide enough to take everything he's giving me. Instead, he throws one of my legs over his left horn, opening me wide.

His scent strengthens, wrapping me up in a wash of pheromones so masculine and strong, I clench around his fingers. He grunts and laves harder along my slit, the long path teasing because it's not enough to get me off, not without focusing fully on my clit.

"Nor," I gasp. "I'm begging, please..." But words fail me as he surges forward and pulls my clit between those big, flat lips. The sudden roughness sends a jolt of pleasure that snaps up my core and radiates outward.

It seems just moments later, orgasm overtakes me, and I snatch at both his horns as I grind against his face, riding out mind-bending waves of bliss. I can't scream in this room and risk everyone hearing, but my mouth is open all the same as I force myself not to make a sound. My eyes roll and lips curl back as Manorin keeps up that damned licking, his fingers never stopping their movement.

He licks until I'm over-sensitized, and then he flips me over on the table. After parting my ass cheeks and lifting my hips, he licks my pussy from behind, cleaning me of all that sweet honey he brought forth.

"So fucking good," he groans.

Another lick.

A nuzzle at my pucker.

I claw at the table, desperate to get more of him, to get him deeper, to be filled the way only someone of Manorin's immense size can fill me. I'm a succubus; I can partner with anyone and be physically capable of enjoying it. But there is absolutely no replacement for minotaur cock.

Manorin uses his grip on my hips to rock me along his tongue as heat swirls again.

But I need more. I *want* more.

Growling, I shove backward and spin. I reach up and pull at the buttons along his shoulders, ripping his shirt from his torso. The sight of all those thick, fur-covered muscles makes my mouth water.

"The way you look at me makes me hot." He grips my throat. "Take everything else off, woman."

He shoulders his way out of the half-undone shirt and tosses it aside. For a moment, I can't do anything but stare at giant pecs, so familiar and yet not at the same time. Thick bars pierce them. That's new. His nipples were always sensitive before, but I'll bet they're more so now. He's huge everywhere.

"You're bigger than before."

He chuckles and lifts my chin. "Wait until you see the rest of me, Cath. Lotta male for you to enjoy." He sighs with pleasure as I reach down and unbutton his jeans.

"I'm ready to enjoy it." I slide the jeans over his ass, careful with his tail. Once it's free of the fabric, he swings it and curls it around my waist, holding me tightly to him. Stepping backward, he sinks into the chair and pulls me on top of him, nestled into his lap with my thighs wide around his torso.

Between us, his cock extrudes from its sheath, sticking up obscenely thick and tall. I take a moment to admire how damn perfect it is with thick rings of flesh a third and two thirds of the way down.

Manorin strokes his knuckles along my shoulder. "Still think we'll fit, Sunshine?"

I force myself to look up from a cock so gorgeous, my mouth's watering.

"Yes," is all I can manage before I grip it and stroke the tip.

Crimson eyes flash with need as his lips curl back into a snarl. He reaches behind his head, clasping his hands together as he watches me explore him.

Tucking my legs so I can move up and down on top of him, I nestle his cock between my thighs and ride a stripe along it. His sigh matches mine, but he doesn't move as I take pleasure from him. His shaft is thick and hot, dripping creamy white strings from the flat tip. Each pass over the thick rings that separate it into sections caresses my clit, nudging it to one side and the other.

"Take what you need, pretty girl," he murmurs, bringing one of my hands up to his long, curved horn. He grabs his cock with the other hand and thwaps it against my clit, sending a shudder zipping down my spine.

I stiffen and moan as my other hand moves to the golden ring in his nose. I love that I don't have to be careful with it because minotaurs are so incredibly strong and impervious to pain. Slipping two fingers through the ring, I hold tight as I ride up and down him again. Gods, it feels good to do this after so long. My pussy clenches, honey dripping from me with every pass along his shaft.

"Soak me in that sweet cream, Cath," he growls, bringing both hands to my hips. Big fingers dig in and help lift me on and off him, but I need more. I need to be filled.

When I reach down and grab his cock, guiding it to my entrance, he swats my hand away. "Not tonight, Catherine."

Shocked at his words, I angrily flash my eyes gold at him, a sign of my power to entrance. Power I've used to control him in the past, with his consent, of course, but it was natural, so natural to use that power with him.

He snarls, "You gonna *make* me let you, Sunshine?" Grabbing my hips, he bucks upward, bouncing me into the air so I slide back down his length, coating us both in his sticky precum. "Don't think so, woman." Bounce. Slide. Soak him. "Use me like this," he commands, "and if you're good, I'll let you have more tomorrow."

"The nerve of—"

He cuts my words off with a hand around my throat, his grip tight as he uses his hold there and my hip to fuck harder. His nostrils flare as I yank on the gold ring and twist. Manorin gasps and lows, a rumbly, deep noise that has heat splashing through me in waves. The buck of his hips thrusts his cock through my folds, teasing every inch of me while not giving me nearly enough of what I want.

Gasping, I ride him as the heat builds and swirls into a hurricane. My thighs tremble as he bucks and thrusts with methodical, incredible force. The chair creaks beneath his heavy weight, rocking as the sounds of fucking that's not actually fucking fill the room.

Stars burst behind my eyelids as bliss overtakes me, muscles tightening as my pussy floods his hard, hot length. I clap a hand over my mouth to avoid screaming as every sensation I can catalog pinpoints to Manorin and the satisfied sounds he makes as he drags orgasm from the depths of my soul.

It seems like hours that I come, clenching on nothing as he holds me steadily, his cock rubbing up, down, and through my pussy lips until I'm begging, honestly begging, for more.

"Just soak me with your cum, Cath," he commands in that low, sultry way of his. I'd forgotten about it, just how dirty this minotaur's mouth is.

"Tomorrow, maybe, when we can steal away for a minute, I'll let you suck me off. Nobody ever could take all of me the way you can." He guides my trembling hand to his cock head.

I moan at finding him coated in sticky precum, slick and perfect for—

The moment I drop down to take him into my mouth, he chuckles and pulls me tighter to him. "Naughty woman thinking she can have what I just told her she can't."

"Give it to me," I command, sliding my hand down his length and pulling the way he used to love.

He cocks his head to the side, crimson eyes flashing. "No, Catherine."

When I flash my eyes gold at him, he chuckles. "I'm stronger than I was as a young male, pretty girl. You think you can still control me so easily?"

My nostrils flare at his challenge. He was *always* like this, under my skin and pushing, pushing, pushing until we became a wild frenzy of heat.

"Do you want to find out, Manorin?"

He shifts me off his lap and stands, pulling jeans back up over his huge thighs, although his enormous cock pokes out and presses against his stomach.

"Not tonight, Sunshine," he says with a blistering smile. Gripping my throat, he backs me across the room until I hit the door. "But tomorrow when we can steal away for five minutes,

I'll press you to another wall somewhere and fuck you good. What do you think?"

"You're playing with me." I cross my arms and pout, yet he does nothing but chuckle.

I'd swear there's a twinkle in those familiar crimson eyes. "You know I am, and you know I should. Because the best, hottest sex comes when you're so desperate for it, you're ready to tackle your partner in the sheets just to get what you want." He drags his gaze down my body and back up. "You're not there yet, pretty girl. Maybe tomorrow. Maybe the next day."

Stepping back, he releases his grip on my throat and turns, grabbing my dress. He hands it to me as he reaches for the door handle. When he pulls it open, moving me bodily out of the way and nudging me toward the hall, I scoff and tie the dress quickly around my body.

"Well, I never..."

"Good night, Catherine," he says with a smirk.

I wave at the obvious erection still pressed to his belly. "But you're not even, I mean—"

His smirk grows feral. "Oh, I'm gonna take care of it, Catherine, here in my room by myself." He pulls close, nuzzling his way up my neck until the gold ring in his nose presses below my ear. "Maybe I'll even think of you when I do it."

Before I can respond, he steps back inside and closes the door.

CHAPTER TEN
MANORIN

Teasing Catherine is half the fun of pursuing Catherine. I gave her just enough last night to stoke the flames, and not nearly enough to sate her. I half expected her to barge back into my room in the middle of the night and demand what she wants. Her scent was fully burnt pie by the time I kicked her out of my room.

I'd have given in to her if she'd come to me later that night.

I'm a simple male, after all.

Instead, I slept like shit, woke up at three and hit the stadium gym again. Then I showered and worked on a plan for the exhibition game. I even called a couple of monsters from the academy team back home and asked them to come to town for the game, folks I know won't run to Evenia to tell her what I'm doin' in Ever.

Not that it won't come out eventually. I just don't need little birdies whispering in my boss's ear.

This morning, Arkan's busy, so Catherine's promised to give me a tour of the infrastructure expansion plans. I won't relocate without knowing if what they're building will accommodate increased traffic. I'm going to be distracted by her, but if I know her, she'll get me back for last night.

I'm standing in front of Fleur when she saunters up the street wearing thigh-hugging jeans and a dark gray wrap shirt that accentuates her stunning figure. That's part one of her teasing. She knows I fucking love jeans and a simple top. Stick a cowboy hat on her, and I'd be fucking done, getting indecent in the middle of Main Street.

"I wouldn't have taken you for much of a flower lover," she says, tossing her hair over her shoulder, gray eyes flashing. Her lips are painted the palest of pinks, accentuating how plump the bottom one is. It's slightly swollen from last night's play.

I push off the brick wall and slip both hands into my pockets, looking my fill of her before I answer. When our eyes meet, hers are full of a powerful challenge. She's so much smaller than me, and so terrifyingly mighty at the same time. If she wanted to unleash that power to beguile on me, she could wrap me up right here and turn me into a mindless, need-filled male, content only to obey her command.

I love that.

"I liked your suggestion of being more direct with the part-time players that I have no desire to press them into full-time service. I met Ohken here this morning and had that chat with him. He's a great skyball player, but as he's mentioned several times, he wants *more* time with Wren, not less."

Catherine nods slowly. "Did he say anything else?"

I smile and offer her my arm. "Just that you're right—this would be an ideal conversation to have with everyone else. It definitely seemed to unblock something with him. He was much more excited about changes to the program after I made it clear that I don't want him as a player." I smile at her as we head toward the end of the street where the new construction is slated to start next month. "He loved your exhibition game idea too. You've got a real knack with monsters, Cath."

She winks up at me. "It's sort of in the nature, you know?"

"Don't discredit yourself," I say quietly. "While *some* of that's in your nature, I've met dozens of succubi in my lifetime, and there's never been one who read others as well as you."

Her lips curl into a smile, but she says nothing, walking quietly next to me.

When we reach the movie theater, she halts, pointing at the empty grassy area across the street. "That entire area between the last building and Town Hall was always meant to be our next expansion area. It was originally designed to connect to the road leading to Hel Motel, so there'd be a nice little feather-shaped area where we could expand with another road and more businesses. Doing so would put Town Hall smack in the middle of Ever, and, honestly, that was always the plan for growth."

I stare at the empty space for a while, considering what else will have to change with Ever growing busier. Sucking at my teeth, I glance around the downtown area. The reality is that Downtown Ever is pretty small, all things considered, and it's not immediately clear that Shifter Hollow has another sort of downtown closer to the portal station. Even then, it's a solid quarter-hour walk along Sycamore Street, and there aren't even any signs letting folks know where to go.

All of that will have to change.

"What about public transportation since the Ever portal station's quite a ways from downtown?"

She sighs. "That one's harder. I was always in favor of something cute and homey-feeling like a streetcar. That feels very *Ever* to me, but nobody else has ever agreed with that plan. Richard, the shifter pack alpha, always wanted to put a monorail system in that went back and forth between Shifter Hollow and downtown, but we weren't growing enough to ask HQ for that sort of investment."

She glances up at me, irritation evident in the scrunch of her brows. "We could potentially fully fund it as a town, but it would be better if we could use some of HQ's funding programs for infrastructure growth."

"And parking?" I wave at the street. "Every time I've walked down here, there've only been a handful of open spaces."

Her smile is wry. "It didn't used to be like that prior to the Grand Portal Station. But, yes, parking is an issue. There's always been a plan to add parking behind the shops on either side, but I honestly don't know if that's enough." She jerks her head toward the other end of the street. "The stadium has that giant field, and that's sufficient for game traffic. But as for general tourism, that's harder."

I look around. "Are these conversations moving fast, Cath? Because I've seen other havens struggle with this. Even Hearth Headquarters has faced its share of growing pains. Parking's a bitch there and getting worse all the time. Of course, being nestled against the mountain range is limiting…"

She nods, stepping closer to me. "They're happening, but they need to be happening more quickly. Thankfully, Arkan's on top of it. Morgan and Abemet have started to get more involved too. Mor's very interested in the growth plan, Abemet used to be an architect, and I think they've been talking with Valentina, who lives here. Since she's Evenia's Chief Haven Planner, she's an excellent resource." Cath winks. "Speaking of your boss, are you sure it's not Evenia who's the limiting factor at HQ?"

I bark out a laugh. "She's unfriendly but effective. I'll give her that. Arkan's pushing hard for this expansion, but what's an actual timeline look like?"

Her tinkling laugh fills me with joy. "He first brought this up about two weeks ago, and he's already got plans for us to review at the leadership meeting next week. Between you and me, I know he's already seeking quotes from construction companies in other havens for the new streets. Ohken and the other trolls can help us with the buildings, but the streets are best done by someone more familiar with infrastructure needs."

I pull her toward the far side of the movie theater. "Let's walk. I want to see how much space there is for parking. I've got some ideas, but I need a better visual."

An hour later, we've walked all over downtown and along the space where the new street will go, once it's officially approved. Downtown's got a couple cutesy stores, the things a town doesn't have to have but make it feel nice—the flower shop, a candy shop, an ice cream store. There's Ohken's General Store and a couple restaurants, but not much else on Main.

I feel pretty okay overall, but parking's still likely to be an issue. It's my opinion that the entire footprint of the haven will need to expand. There's a lot of pretty forest spread throughout, and we don't necessarily want to lose that, either. Nobody wants to live in the middle of a parking lot.

Eventually, Catherine's stomach grumbles, so I insist we stop at Herschel's Fine Dining—noting that it's one of only two restaurants in downtown Ever, the Galloping Green Bean being the other. That'll have to change. Pine Gulch has more restaurants than that and half as many citizens. Of course, Gulchers are foodies.

Herschel himself leads us to a gorgeous little table set in the back away from the main dining area. "My second-best spot." He winks as he sets the menus down.

Half an hour later, Cath looks sated and full, dragging a piece of crusty French bread through the last dregs of marinara.

"I like seeing you this way," I muse as I swirl whiskey in an etched crystal glass. "Full. Happy. Smiling."

That pretty blush I'm such a fan of appears, pinkening her high cheekbones.

"It's hard not to be happy with such excellent company."

I lean over the table onto my forearms, holding my glass between my hands. "Talk to me about *your* plans, Cath. You love

Ever and the Annabelle. You're not going anywhere. Do I have that right?"

She sits back in her chair, clasping her hands in her lap. "Truly, I love it here; I've told you that. You'd have to blast me out of this haven with dynamite. Even then, I'd only go kicking and screaming." She laughs at that last visual. "What about you? What'll you do if this job doesn't work out?"

I've been thinking about this a lot in the last day or so. I consider how much to share with her, since technically she's on the committee deciding whether to offer me the job or not.

Eventually, I sit back in my chair and level her with a serious look. "I'll go back to my current role for a bit, but it's always been my heart's desire to get home to Pine Gulch at some point."

Some unnamed emotion flits through her gorgeous gray eyes. I'd bank on disappointment, but I'm not really sure, so I shrug. "I don't know if or when it'll ever happen. I'd love to coach the Punishers, but I'd have to murder Rip Shorthorn to get him outta that job, so I don't see it happening. Well, ever. It's long been my dream job, but the chances of it happening are basically zero, so I've never made a plan assuming a place for me back home. I'll stick around at HQ until something else pops up, if this doesn't work out."

Catherine nods, but it's slow and thoughtful.

Suddenly, I'm regretting sharing that much with her.

I cock my head to the side. "I'm sorry, Cath, maybe I shouldn't have said that much. I don't want it to seem like I'm not thrilled for this opportunity, because I am, absolutely."

"I get it." She smiles, although it looks forced to me. "The way Ever feels to me is probably the way Pine Gulch feels to you. Like you're where you belong."

I'm too wary to nod in agreement, so I take a sip of my whiskey instead.

Herschel shows up with the bill then, so I slap down my credit card and change the subject.

When we leave, I nod toward Ohken's General Store. "Can we pop over there for sandpaper? Annabelle's shutters need a little love."

Catherine looks up at me in surprise, her gaze softening. "I've had a can of paint out there for a while but she never lets me mess with the shutters. I'm not sure why because as you can see, they need to be painted."

I chuckle. "She waggled them at me this morning, so I'll tackle that for you."

Cath falls silent as we enter the General Store. I make quick work of grabbing a packet of sandpaper and a fresh gallon of stark white paint.

When Catherine's said nothing by the time we get back to the inn, I glance at her. "You okay?"

She sighs as she looks up at the Annabelle, who waves her front doors open and shut at us. I think Catherine will say something, but she falls silent and shakes her head.

I jerk my head toward the front door. "Got something for you inside, Cath."

When we enter the check-in area to find a gigantic floral arrangement at the front desk, Catherine rushes over to it and I set the sandpaper and paint down just inside the door.

Smirking, I lean against the wall left of the desk while she takes the card and reads it. Her smile's huge when she looks up at me, stroking the beautiful pink and red arrangement. "You sneak, you did this while you were at Fleur, didn't you? Ohken knows all of my favorites."

I reach out and tuck a stray gray wave behind her ear, staring deeply into her eyes. "I had multiple reasons for visiting Fleur today, one of those being the flowers. Enjoy them, Sunshine." I glance up. "And sweet Annabelle. I had him match your siding, darlin'."

Annabelle lets out a series of delighted squeaks.

Catherine leans into my touch, although her lashes flutter against her cheeks. Placing one of her hands over mine, she nuzzles into my palm. But just as quickly, she steps back and straightens, snapping up walls around herself as a guest emerges from the dining room and passes us to go upstairs.

I should have kept my damn mouth shut at lunch. If I was a betting man, I'd guess Catherine's thinking about how I said I'd love to have the chance to move home. Why the fuck did I admit that? It's never happening, and I tried to make that clear, but it seems like she's thinking about it.

A name flashes over my comm watch, interrupting the explanation I'm about to dive into.

Bishop Rygold.

"Fuck," I manage, eyes flicking to Catherine's. "I've got to take this."

She nods. "Of course. See you later, Manorin."

Back to my full name. That won't do. I far prefer a moaned "Nor" falling from her lips.

I head for the stairs, and the minute I answer Bishop, he starts barking about my nephew again.

By the time I get him settled with an update on my plan to come home, Catherine's nowhere to be seen.

CHAPTER ELEVEN

CATHERINE

I don't sleep well that night, not after Manorin shared his desire to go home. Even if the chances of him going back to Pine Gulch are small, they're not zero. And more than that, it's what he *wants*.

And if it's what he wants, it's what he should get.

I'm old and experienced enough to know that life is too short to settle for anything less than.

My power roils and simmers all night, ready to be unleashed. As much as I'd like to do that, our lunchtime conversation holds me back despite our arrangement. On some level, I recognize that Manorin's going far beyond what a friends-with-benefits situation calls for. So far, he's feeding me and buying me flowers, and it feels far more like dating than sexcapades. Sexcapades, I agreed to. We agreed no rules, just fun. Dating has the potential to lead to feelings, and that seems like a bad idea considering what he shared over lunch.

I'm still mulling that over the following morning when I descend the stairs at the crack of dawn. For the first time in a while, I'm not looking forward to prepping the breakfast buffet for my guests.

I enter the kitchen to find Manorin there, leaning against the window as he grins at the kitty cat timer. Annabelle swings a cabinet open and tosses a bag of white table sugar at Manorin. He doesn't seem to notice me enter, focused as he is on the tiny cat.

He easily catches it and sets it next to the timer, who meows angrily at him.

"No, Annabelle. This is Azuro coffee, which means no sugar needed." He snorts out a laugh, the ring in his nose brushing against the flat surface. "Thank you, but no."

I clear my throat, and he smiles up at me as if he knew I was there the entire time.

"Good morning, Sunshine."

I love that nickname.

I saunter past him, unable to resist brushing my ass against his thigh as I lean into the cabinet, hunting for my favorite coffee mug. When I don't find it there, I emerge from the cabinet with a confused look.

He sips his coffee. "You still thinking about what I said at lunch yesterday?"

"No," I lie.

"You're a terrible liar." He takes another sip of his coffee, lifting the cup quickly out of the way when Annabelle tosses several sugar cubes from the container on the island. The cubes fall to the ground, and she shuffles them toward his feet. "Also, your inn is incorrigible."

I laugh. "Much like me, I'm afraid. Set in my ways and persnickety."

He gestures at the microwave. "Your coffee is in there. I came down a little early. Didn't realize you were planning to sleep in."

I scoff as I plant a hand on my hip. "It's five forty-five, Manorin."

"Nor," he corrects. "And you used to get up at five."

I frown. "You've been down here since then, waiting? Surely you've got better things to do?"

He sets his coffee cup down on the island, covering it with one enormous hand as he stares at me. "I'm meeting the leadership folks at the stadium, but I want to take you out tonight on a date. A real date. No skyball chatter. Just romance. A continuation of the night before last."

My mouth drops open. "Oh, are we finally going to get to the benefits portion of this friends-with-benefits situation?"

He rounds the island and looks down at me, crimson eyes flashing. His attraction would be obvious to me even if I didn't have the ability to read him with my power.

"We're doing too much dating," I manage. "This is supposed to be no strings attached, right? Just fun and no emotions?"

He slides his free hand around my waist and pulls me close against his huge, hard body. "And yet I still feel compelled to take you out. That's because what's between us is easy and natural. I promise I'll make it fun. If you don't have a wonderful time, I won't ask you out again. You've got my word. We can just dirty fuck at night in your room. You can milk me dry, Sunshine."

I...I can't find a reason to say no to that because I *want* to go out with him, even though the logical side of my brain is looking for all the reasons this is a bad idea.

Before I can answer, Iggy shoves his way through the back door, flying with a hellhound puppy clutched in his arms. "Catherine! Catherine! Dad said we get to keep the puppies!"

Minnie lumbers in the open back door after him, red eyes focused on the pup in Iggy's arms. I feel quite certain Alo and Miriam didn't agree to keep all three hellhound puppies, but...

"It might not be up to you, kiddo," Manorin says gently, dropping to a knee to scratch under Minnie's chin. "You know how Minnie's bonded to you? That same thing could happen with these puppies and any monster they meet. It makes sense for you to keep them for now. You can help Minnie take care of them. But, one day, they'll probably find their monster the same way Minnie found you."

Iggy's smile falls, and he clutches the puppy to his face. It turns and licks at his mouth, mewling against him.

"I know, I just… Dad agreed we could keep them for a while, at least." He looks at Manorin. "Do you want to hold one?"

Manorin chuckles but takes the puppy when Iggy holds it out to him. "What if this thing gets attached to me, and I have to keep it?"

I stare at him as he and Iggy go back and forth as to the advantages of being bonded with a hellhound.

There's a softer side of Manorin that wasn't there when we were younger. He was aggressive, brash, and I thought I wanted someone more elegant and powerful. When he asked me to get the traditional mating tattoo I said no—I wasn't ready for it and it didn't feel exactly right at the time. When I glance up at him now, he's holding the puppy with a wry look. Iggy's hanging on to one of Nor's horns like it's a gymnastics bar, swinging around it as he lashes his tail from side to side.

I shouldn't make the same mistakes twice. Even if Nor and I only have fun for a short time, we'll make good memories I can look back on.

"I'll take you up on that dinner offer," I say quietly.

"What offer?" Iggy shouts. "Is it something good? Can I have it too?"

Manorin laughs and hands the wriggling hellhound puppy back to Iggy. "No, you may not." He pauses and stares at me, wrinkles appearing at the corners of his eyes as he smiles. "But you, Sunshine? Yeah, you can have it for sure."

CHAPTER TWELVE

MANORIN

Thank fuck Catherine agreed to go out with me tonight, because this day is a shit show otherwise.

I pinch the base of my snout between my eyes as I stare at the monsters seated in the stadium war room. "We've already ascertained that none of you want full-time roles on the team. That being the case, the only way to grow it is to recruit heavily and spend money on a solid first string and solid second string."

Dropping my hand, I look around at the gargoyle brothers, Arkan and Hana, the former Keeper, Abemet, and a handful of others. I throw my arms wide. "If you want to be successful at growing skyball, this is what you have to do at a minimum. Plus all the infrastructure expansion I've outlined. Plus paying me."

Silence. Furtive glances.

I resist the urge to knock heads together.

Finally, I sigh and lean back in my chair. "Why'd you call me here?"

Alo, the older of the Rygold brothers, crosses his arms and sits back in his chair. "To be honest, we might have been a little hasty in that, in my opinion. We're growing whether we want to or not—that part is clear from how busy everyone is. But the more you talk about infrastructure, the more I wonder if we should focus there first."

This is an important crux in their decision-making path. I can't force this, and I shouldn't. So I remain silent, waiting to see who'll tack on another opinion.

Arkan walks a slow circle around the room, a habit I see he's never managed to kick. "We should do both at the same time. We *can* do both at the same time. Looking back on the plans from when Ever was first designed and built, it was always the intention for this haven to be larger and accommodate more Evertons."

"Was skyball mentioned?" That from Shepherd Rygold, Alo's younger brother.

Arkan's pale eyes flick to me, softening, and then he shakes his head. "Not specifically, although it looks like Abemet did a fair amount of work when Ever first began ensuring we'd be set up for a skyball team." He looks at the tall vampire. "Any chance you can provide context here?"

Abe leans forward over the long oval table in my—their—war room, glittering red eyes rounding the room before he halts on me. "As a group, we've gone back and forth on this, but it's my opinion we need to go all in on skyball. Havens that do so experience not only better financial growth, but they get better scores on the headquarter's satisfaction surveys. There's a better sense of community in havens with teams. Not only that, but residents tend to remain longer in havens with skyball. It's a quality-of-life improvement. For a moment, set aside your personal feelings about playing and just assume you could all be spectators with no other skyball responsibilities."

I nod at the reports I'd put together for the team prior to this meeting. "If you flip to the backmost section of that report, you'll see specific stats from the best- and worst-performing skyball teams in the league. What Abemet's saying is backed by the data."

I look around the gathered monsters, wishing Catherine were here. She had an unfortunately timed meeting with Morgan this morning, but I'd dearly love her perspective here.

"There's already a lot of chatter about the exhibition game even though we just announced it," Hana says after a short silence. "We asked Manorin here for a trial period. We can't keep wiffle-waffling about whether or not this is a priority. Ever's going through growing pains now; I know you all feel that. It's my opinion that we start on the infrastructure immediately, and I think we're already aligned on that. We have to do that to keep pace with the natural population growth. That part's a given. But as Ever grows, let's give them that symbol of community to rally around."

She smiles over at me. "The reality is that we basically don't have a team now. If Manorin can pull one together for next year's season, that would be a miracle. The likelihood is that we'd need a building year, and the following year we'd launch more fully."

"That's right," I offer. "I'm headed to Pine Gulch this weekend, and I plan to do a little subversive recruiting. But I don't wanna dive deep into that without your full backing."

"We should vote," Abe says quietly. "Those in favor, raise your hand."

"We're missing Catherine," Alo notes.

"She's a yes." I stare at him. "You know she is."

Alo sighs when everyone's hands go up but his. After a long pause, he runs both hands through his dark waves. "Honestly, I think I'm just missing the days when Ever felt like it was hidden from the world, even the monster world. We're not remote anymore with monsters visiting so easily, and I just think I'm going to miss how it used to be."

"It's still Ever," his brother says softly. "And change isn't always bad."

I stare at him until he lifts his gaze to mine.

"We can build thoughtfully. There's absolutely no need to lose Ever's charming vibe. That's why monsters come here to visit. It's one of the reasons Ever's been such a successful haven. If we're conscientious of that as we plan, we'll keep that small town feeling even as we grow. Pocket neighborhoods over sprawl, things like that. There are already two downtowns that feel like two separate entities. There's space for more of that."

He nods, but it seems clear he's still not fully on board.

"That settles it then," Abe says in a confident tone, smiling over at me. "We're in your corner, Coach."

He's saying the right words, but I can't shake the feeling that they're not entirely true, which puts this entire job on some-what tenuous footing.

~

As evening rolls around, I double-check my preparations for my date with Cath. I've stuck an extra set of clothing, snacks, and a bottle of wine in a small sling bag.

I'm ready. She mentioned earlier that we were doing too much dating, but I can't find it in me to stop. I thought I could be her dirty little secret for a few weeks—shit, the idea of that is appealing—but I find myself wanting to spend a lot more time with her than that.

Excitement moves me out of my room, heading downstairs to find Catherine. I comm'd her earlier and asked her to meet me in the front room.

Still, nothing prepared me for seeing her in a short leather miniskirt and white tee. The shirt highlights her heavy, large breasts and the roundness of her waist and hips. I halt at the bottom of the stairs, my mouth dry as I drop my eyes to the black stilettos on her impossibly adorable feet. Her nails are painted red, my favorite color.

She did that for me. Her favorite color is pale pink.

"Love the red," I murmur, bringing my focus back to her face.

Her smile lights up the entire room, and I'd swear I can almost see glittery stars dancing around us.

Dating someone you've dated before is a wholly different experience from what I'm used to.

No, not dating. Hooking up. Because I promised her there were no strings attached, and I'd do well to remember that.

But I *know* her already. There'll be none of those awkward first-date silences. None of the having a good time, only to discover the person's life priorities don't match yours. None of the worry that she's only with me for the paparazzi photos and glamorous evenings out.

"I'm excited for our date, Nor," she says in a bubbly tone, smiling up at me. She crosses the small space between us and slides a hand to the middle of my chest, rubbing soft circles. "I had a couple ideas if you're looking for something spec—"

"Stop that," I say with a laugh, pulling her closer. With one hand, I sling the bag over my shoulder and tip her chin up. "I made a plan for this date. This is all about having fun with you. You don't need to plan a thing, Cath."

The familiar pink blush crawls along her cheeks and down her neck. "Is that so?"

I lift my chin and stare at her. "It's so. You ready?"

She nods, so I grab her hand in mine and guide us toward the door. When Annabelle swings the double doors wide, I thank her. The little inn's so friendly and hospitable. I'm *thoroughly* enjoying my time staying with her. I rub a spot outside the front door as we leave.

"Bye, sweet girl. We'll be back in a few hours, alright?"

Annabelle wiggles her shutters at me, reminding me I promised to get those sanded and painted.

"Tomorrow," I promise her, pointing at the sandpaper and fresh gallon of white trim paint. "I'm all yours tomorrow, Sweetheart."

Annabelle rolls the sandpaper toward me but I shake my head with a laugh.

Grabbing it, I set it on top of the nearest shutter and pat it lovingly. "Tomorrow, I swear."

Cath is quiet as we descend the stairs and head up Sycamore toward the skyball stadium.

She laughs. "Are we going to your office?"

My nostrils flare, and I chuckle. "Not my plan, but the idea of doing things to you in my office is very appealing." I wink down at her. "Some other night." Glancing farther down at her pretty red toes reminds me I should let her in on a little bit of tonight's plan.

"We're going for a ride," I say. "I just don't wanna get naked in front of Annabelle for all of Ever to see."

Catherine grips my hand tighter. "That sounds absolutely fabulous, Manorin."

I can't resist a dig, though, and I tug her hand to pull her focus up to me. "Did that centaur ever take you for a ride, Cath?"

Her throaty laughter tells me everything I need to know.

Halting, I pull her to my chest and bend down enough to bring my muzzle to her ear. "Tell me, Cath. Did he ever put you up on that big, broad back so he could feel your pussy on his fur?"

She growls softly.

"That's what I thought." I nip at the skin just beneath her ear. "You're gonna ride me, woman, and I want to feel every naked inch of you."

She curls her fingers into my chest fur and strokes, her scent exploding between us.

Tonight's the night. I know it. She knows it. It's just a matter of time before I get inside her and please her.

We walk about five minutes, just far enough to get well past downtown. Monsters aren't overly fussed about nudity per se, but disrobing in the middle of town might get an eyebrow raise or two.

I halt and hand Catherine the bag. "Take this, Sunshine. It's got everything we'll need."

She lifts the bag over her head, careful not to muss perfectly arranged gray waves.

I can't resist touching her. Reaching out, I twirl a long section around my fingers. "Still so soft," I murmur. "Just like it used to be."

She beams up at me. "I guess some things haven't changed, hmm?"

It feels like she's talking about more than just the texture of her hair. I hope we'll cover that and more on our date tonight. A level set about my intentions seems in order here. Have fun. Make her laugh. Make her come. Not in any particular order. I want dates to be part of our "arrangement," if she'll allow me. They're not technically against the rules as they're still fun.

Smirking at her, I reach for my shirt and unbutton the shoulder and down one side, pulling it off my big figure. She watches me, her blush deepening as her scent grows stronger, nostrils flaring.

Gold swirls in the depths of her eyes when I reach for my jeans. Pulling them down, I step out and shove them in the pack she holds.

I'm nude in front of her again, and I love how she stares.

Gray eyes drop down my chest to my stomach, my sheath, my thighs. She trails her gaze lazily back upward, a smirk on her face. "It's been a long time since I've seen you shift."

"Been a long time since I did it, if I'm being honest." I drop forward onto my hands and close my eyes, calling my power to shift into my other form.

My muscles pop and pull, joints cracking and reforming until everything's configured four-legged style. It's the closest I'll ever look to a bull with hooves.

When the shift's complete, I open my eyes and look at Catherine. In this form, my senses are sharper. I twitch one ear to listen to her heartbeat.

It's fast but steady.

Dropping to both forelegs, I wait for her to carefully climb onto my back.

She laughs as her thighs stretch around my midsection. "If I'd known we were doing this, I wouldn't have chosen a miniskirt."

I join her in laughter. "I'm glad I didn't mention it. Feels good that there's nothing between us."

"Well, besides my underthings," she says with a laugh.

"Not for long," I manage, tossing a wink over my shoulder. "Hang on, Sunshine."

"I've never fallen off you a single time in my life," she reminds me.

Turning, I walk up Sycamore, feeling for her to get settled on my back. It's been a long time since I did this with anyone. Allowing oneself to be ridden is significant to most minotaur males. It's not done lightly.

When she seems comfortable, a hand on either side of my neck, I break into a slow lope, heading toward the skyball stadium.

Catherine lets out a delighted-sounding whoop as I pass the stadium and head up along the twisty road toward the depths of the forest. I canter along for a solid fifteen minutes before veering into the trees. I ran the path earlier today to make sure I knew what I was in for. Worst case scenario would be tripping and throwing my Sunshine because I didn't check the path.

Rookie mistake, and I'm no fuckin' rookie.

Five minutes later, we come to the gorgeous clearing I staked out earlier. I paid Herschel to come out here half an hour ago and leave a charcuterie setup. Looks like he did it, because there's a pretty little picnic on a thick striped blanket.

Catherine tickles my side. "You weren't kidding about a plan. This looks lovely."

I reach for her, helping her slide off me as I shift back into my usual form. I'm still naked, but I plan to stay that way. "We might just be scratching the itch, Sunshine, but romance is what makes that good, in my opinion."

She studiously ignores my comment as she looks around at the setup. I bend down and swoop her up into my arms, loving the little squeal that falls from her lips.

"You feel good in my arms." I smirk at her as I carry her to the blanket and drop to both knees, setting her down. As I do, I fall over top of her, pushing her carefully onto her back. Hovering above her, I reach up and drag my knuckles along the slim column of her throat.

She closes her eyes and lets out a little sigh, arching into my touch. I run my fingers down to the vee of her shirt, tugging it down to stroke her bare skin.

"Still so soft."

She smiles, even though her eyes remain closed. "You seem to have an obsession with my softness. That's your second or third comment on it this evening."

"Who wouldn't?" I bend down and drag my snout up between her breasts, nuzzling against her neck to breathe her in more fully. "Your lack of fur entices me; it makes you seem extra naked."

Gingerbread, crisp apples. She's a godsdamned pie.

"Let's get you fed, Sunshine," I manage, even though all I

want to do is lie here with her and talk about the last few hundred years and all the things we haven't had a chance to cover yet.

She shifts onto her elbows, a glint in her eyes. "Are we eating lying down?"

I manage a laugh. "Lovely as that sounds, I don't need a choking hazard situation. That being said," I sit upright and pull her into my lap, a thick thigh on either side of mine, "I don't plan to let you go far."

Reaching to my side, I grab the picnic basket and open it, pulling out a variety of cheese and crackers and some of the fancy grapes Herschel told me she loves. A small tray of chocolates comes next. I ordered those from a tiny shop in Arcadia the day I arrived in Ever and realized I was gonna ask her out.

Catherine's eyes flash at seeing the chocolates. She looks up at me, eyes wide. "How did you manage this?"

I take a chocolate and lift it to her plump lips, dragging it along her skin. "There aren't any lengths I won't go to to make you smile, Cath. And I remember *everything*."

She sucks in a deep breath and presses my hand away from her lips. Before I can ask what's wrong, she leans forward and peppers the tip of my snout with soft kisses.

I can't kiss, not like other monsters, not with a snout this shape—too flat. It's possibly my only regret about being a minotaur. Everything else is fucking fantastic, but kissing looks like a lot of fun.

That being said, there's a lot I can do with this mouth.

Catherine settles back, eyes glistening. "Thank you, Nor."

I slide a hand up her back, pressing her closer to me. She sinks down, legs spreading wider so she's nestled perfectly against me.

"Eat," I encourage. "Because, once you're nice and full, I'm going to fill you in other ways."

Gold swirls in her irises again, her power rising to my dominance.

"There she is," I murmur. "You gonna use that power on me, Sunshine? Maybe beguile me until I'm wild with need?"

"Would you like to be controlled, Manorin?" Her irises have gone full gold, and I can already feel my agency leaving my body. All there is is Catherine, and what Catherine wants. Whatever she wants. Whatev...

She chuckles, slapping my stomach playfully. "Too easy, Nor. You gave in too easily."

I shrug and lean back on both hands. "It's been a long time since you used your power on me like that. Maybe I'm desperate to be at your command." I sink onto my knees and tuck my hands at my back like I'm chained. "Keep me on my knees, Catherine. Take what you want."

When we were younger, we played a lot with her power to beguile. I've always loved it, that total loss of control, and she's the only succubus I've ever met who could fully bewitch me. Catherine's might is a nearly unstoppable force. She could topple cities with it. She chooses not to. She earns trust.

And that's why it's so hot when she binds me up in that power and makes me do whatever she wants. Because when she controls me, there is nothing but the desires of my mistress.

I level her with a teasing look. "I've dated other succubi, you know, and I've never done that with them."

She feigns surprise. "No? Missed me too much?"

I smile. "Something like that. I've never let another woman ride me either. Not since you—the last time."

Her teasing smile falls, her expression serious once more. "That's been two hundred years!"

"Mhm."

Silence stretches long between us as I rest on my hands, staring at her. Finally, I break it.

"You're smart, powerful, beautiful, kind. There's never been anyone who could live up to you. I've often regretted our breakup over the years. If I'd been smarter as a young male, maybe I could have kept you."

It's a truth I think about a lot.

She shakes her head. "There were lessons I needed to learn." She stares off into the distance, squinting as if the memory's almost too painful to conjure. "They were so costly, but I guess someone up above thought I needed them."

I dip down and nuzzle her shoulder. "What could you have possibly needed to learn, Cath? Perhaps some things are just shit that happens to us."

She sighs. "I stopped trusting so easily."

I bring my gaze to hers. "That's not necessarily a good thing, Sunshine."

She lifts her eyes to mine. "No? I won't get hurt like that again."

"Not if I have anything to do with it," I confirm.

Her gaze goes shuttered and unsure, but then she plasters a big smile on those pretty pink lips. Her eyes flash with need. "I'm not hungry for food, Manorin. You've been teasing me for days." Gold swirls through her irises again. "It's time to *stop* teasing."

I rise with her in my arms. Turning, I stalk to the glowing green ward that forms a bubble over the entire haven, protecting it from the outside world. I press her against a tree that sits right at the edge and lift her arms over her head. Green misty magic—her magic—streams and swirls on the ward's surface, straining toward her.

Very few monsters in our world know that Catherine's the mother of the haven system in more ways than one. She created it and the magic that protects us.

This beautiful, powerful woman.

Dropping to my knees, I sit back on my haunches with her legs draped over my shoulders. I spread her thighs wide and stare. She's soaked the panties through with need, her scent strongest here.

I bend forward and nuzzle at them, licking a rough path over the lace shielding her pussy from me.

She jolts and moans, the soft, needy sound tightening my cock in my sheath. It slips partially out, seeking her heat.

Another lick. Another moan.

Holding her with one hand, I use the other to pull her panties to the side, giving me space to bury my tongue inside her. I lick a hot path along the seam of her pussy, reveling in tasting her.

I didn't realize just how much I'd missed this, missed her, until I had her in my arms again. Groaning, I lick over and over again, using the flat part of my tongue and swirling it over her clit as her cries rise, echoing through the small glade.

Something hits the ward behind us, and Catherine jolts.

Pausing, I glance to the side to see a thrall—a soul-sucking monster who'd love nothing more than to get in here and turn us—snapping and lunging at the ward. This one looks like it might once have been a shifter. It's wolf-shaped, with that same twisted, nearly decayed look all thralls have.

It's her magic that protects us, and it's her magic that draws thralls to havens all over the world.

Not that many monsters even know that. No. Catherine's power is a well-guarded secret.

"We've drawn a crowd," I murmur, smiling up at her.

Her nostrils flare as she turns and stares at the thrall. But gold swirls in her irises again when she looks back at me. Seeing the danger amps her power, pushing her to protect, to serve. It's one of the most beautiful things about what she can do.

And it turns me on. It's *always* turned me on.

Rising, I slide her down until I can put her thighs around me.

She's still focused on the glowing ward and the pacing thrall outside it. Gripping her chin, I redirect her to look at me, loving the flash of gold in her irises as she stares hard.

I reach down and unsheathe my cock, guiding it to her pussy. In one swift thrust, I fill her, sinking deep into that impossible heat. Moaning at how good she feels, I marvel at being able to fully fill a woman with no reservations. I haven't been able to do that with a woman since her.

She feels. So. Good.

Catherine's head falls back, and she cries out, clenching around me, brows scrunched together in pleasure.

I bring my mouth to her ear as I pull out, then fill her again. "Nobody's ever taken me like you do. I don't have to be careful with you, do I, Sunshine? This pretty pussy's gonna swallow me whole, isn't it?"

A desperate, lusty moan is my only answer.

Catherine plants both hands on my chest, using the leverage to rock her hips as a flush travels down her neck and chest. She's still fully clothed, and something about that makes this even hotter to me.

"I like this," I rumble as I thrust in and out slowly, cock dripping precum that mixes with the scent of her need. "Feels like I came upon a hapless little woman in the forest and took exactly what I wanted from her. I can see it now. You'd be bent over a log looking at something, and I'd come up behind you and fuckin' fill you..."

She levels me with a devastating smile, even as I rock my hips, entering her again.

Heat swirls in my balls, tightening them as I widen my stance and fuck her harder.

"Maybe it's me who came upon a hapless male," she says sweetly. "Maybe it's you who are about to be taken advantage of, Manorin."

"Good," I bark as I snap my hips again, my sack slapping against her ass as pleasure drives higher and higher.

"Stop," she commands, eyes fully golden.

My vision goes hazy, the snapping thrall outside the ward amping my need to protect her, to serve her. But even that fades away as I stare at her. There is only her and what she wants.

And anything Catherine wants...

CHAPTER THIRTEEN

CATHERINE

T he snapping thrall outside the ward draws another, and another, and another, until a herd of them lunge and bite at the green surface.

It'll hold because I *will* it to be so.

Still, the proximity of danger calls my magic, my need to protect, along with it. The danger is right *there*, but I don't feel unsafe. Instead, it lends a heady, intoxicating edge to the sex.

Manorin's eyes are glassy as he stares at me, breathing heavily with that perfect, huge cock buried to the hilt inside me. When I smile, it flexes, arching against my G-spot and sending a swirl of need through me.

He lows, the mooing sound deep and full of longing.

My power to beguile fills me, producing a nearly depthless sensation of confidence, like I could do anything in this entire world. I could leap off a building and fly. I could level armies.

I could rule this giant male buried inside me.

"Put me on my hands and knees," I command.

He backs us away from the tree and sets me down, facing the ward and the thralls. After spinning me away from him, he drops me carefully to the ground, pushing me forward onto my hands and knees. My power swirls like a hurricane beneath my skin, loving being used like this for the first time in so very long.

I toss a smile over my shoulder. "Eat, Manorin."

He grunts and presses me forward, fully tangled in my magic. I'm controlling him, and he allows it because he trusts me. That he still does, after all this time, warms something inside me that's been dead and cold for ages.

Thought scrambles as he licks a path up my pussy, over my back pucker, sucking at it with his big, flat lips. It's always bothered him that we couldn't kiss, per se, but it never bothered me when we dated.

That *tongue*. It's incredible. Soft and hot and huge. When he licks, he covers all of me, heat tingling through me as my nipples pebble. I've never been able to last long when he eats me.

"Harder," I manage, eyes rolling into my head as I lose myself to the sensation of that enormous tongue and talented mouth, licking and nipping at my sensitive skin.

The moment orgasm threatens to crash through me, I command him to stop.

He does in a moment, a quiet, steady presence at my back, waiting for my next directive.

Instead, I shift backward and impale myself on his perfect, thick cock, filling myself deeply. I clench around him, spurred on by his low, needy groan. But he won't move, won't fuck, not until I tell him to. And I want to play.

I move forward and back, taking him slowly inside me and clenching before I release him and slide off. His soft groan rises, becoming a series of deep, needy groans mixed with the occasional rumbly snarl. He brings both hands to my hips and digs his big fingers into my skin.

He's hot, ready to come, ready to go wild.

"Not yet," I whisper, marveling at how it feels to be so impossibly full of a cock that would split other women in two.

He's long and thick, and that magical tip arcs and flexes inside me, dragging pleasure from the depths to build and swirl around him.

He roars, fighting the magic that binds his agency. Thralls smash into the ward, sending shimmering green rings radiating outward from where they hit. My power rises and sparks inside me in response to the danger and Manorin's barely restrained power.

Focusing, I snap the mental threads of my power, unleashing him.

He falls forward over my back, bringing his left arm around me to cup my breast, pinching the nipple. His muzzle comes to the back of my shoulder, where he nips and bites at my skin.

"Damnit, Sunshine. You nearly had me undone. I was seconds away from filling this perfect little pussy with gallons of cum. You ready for it?"

There's nothing in this world like Manorin's ability to talk me into an orgasm.

"Take what you want," I offer, curving against his far larger frame as I grind against him.

A rumbling growl is my only answer as he draws my hands behind my back, holding them captured in one of his. With his free hand, he lifts my torso, his cock nestled between us. It throbs against the cleft of my ass, dripping sticky precum onto my back as I wiggle my hips, desperate to feel him inside of me again.

"You can hold a horn for leverage," he says. "Just one. I want your other hand back here, my little forest maiden."

Reaching up, I grip a horn. Manorin brings one hand beneath my right arm, and the other guides his cock to my channel, pressing the spongy tip to me. I moan at how delicious it feels that he's so sticky, so wet, so ready for me.

I clench on nothing as I tighten my grip on the crook of his horn. Once I've got a hold of it, he brings a hand to my hair and wraps it around his fist, holding me taut. The knowledge that I'm about to be absolutely ravished has me preening in anticipation.

Behind me, though, he waits, teasing me with the hint of that perfect, huge cock.

"Nor," I growl, eyes flashing golden even though he can't see them.

"Quiet, woman," he commands, "I'm in control now."

A moan is my only answer to that, but it cuts off, becoming a strangled scream when he snaps his hips and fills me with a single, hard thrust. His shaft is blissfully hard and hot, the thick rings of flesh at each juncture rubbing on all those extra-sensitive places. Inside me, it kicks and flexes, sending washes of heat through me as goose flesh peppers my skin.

He's still for just a moment, allowing me to adjust as I tighten and loosen around him, my power basking in what only he can give me. He's familiar and new all at the same time, this hot, hard male at my back.

But conscious thought slips away as he fists my hair tighter and bucks his hips again, driving me off his cock and yanking me back down. I grip his horn harder as pleas fall from my lips: "Oh god, Nor, harder, please."

He drags my head to the side and bites my neck, sharp fangs poking into my skin and bringing a fresh wave of honey to soak his cock. "I said quiet, little forest maiden. I want you ravaged, unable to stop the onslaught of this enormous, feral male who came upon you. Do you understand?" When I don't answer, he bites harder, and I squirm, fighting off an orgasm that's going to destroy me. I know it will.

When he twists my hair, pain joining the pleasure, I cry out, "Yes, Manorin! Gods, please!"

"Not a god," he growls into my skin. "A monster." He thrusts again, dragging me off him and right back on, until I'm lost to the sensation of being filled and then left empty.

Mere moments later, bliss hits me, and I erupt, shockwaves of energy and pleasure radiating as I scream into the quiet of the forest. Nor claps a hand over my mouth as he fucks me, a devious chuckle his answer to my bliss. But I want him coming with me. When I clench around him, stroking his cock with my pussy, his chuckle abruptly cuts off.

Moments later, his thrusting goes harder, ragged, as he grunts against my neck. I clench harder, even as waves of ecstasy reduce me to a mindless being of pure sensation.

Nor gasps, tenses, then he roars so hard, the ground beneath us shakes. His hips snap against me furiously, almost bruising, sparking a second orgasm as I cling to his horn and beg for dear life.

When the fire fades, he sinks onto his haunches and holds me back to his heaving chest. Nuzzling my neck, he groans as he holds me steady, limp. I'm blissed out and sated, and I don't think we ever had sex that good even when we were younger.

"That was—"

"Extraordinary," he finishes. "Mind-blowing. The way you take me, little maiden." He chuckles as he snuffles against my neck and licks at the bites from earlier. "Let's do it again."

Manorin strokes my cheek, our legs tangled together as my chest heaves. Aftershocks from yet another of the strongest orgasms I've had in centuries roll through my system, my back arching as I press my breasts skyward. More, more, more. Now that he's opened those floodgates, I won't be sated.

Manorin chuckles, bending over to take a breast into his mouth. He sucks and pulls at my nipple, a needy whine falling from me as I squirm. The tiny hairs on his muzzle tickle me, even as I seek more of his touch.

"Been a long time, Cath? I figured you'd give me five minutes before you needed me a fifth time."

I guide my breast back to his mouth. "Less talking, more of this."

He laughs but sucks at it again. When he pops off my nipple, he shoots me a wry grin. "I still haven't fed you yet, woman."

I return the saucy expression. "You know, for a succubus, cum is a legitimate food group."

His dark brows shoot up. "Have I unleashed you, my sassy little forest maiden? Romance leading to no-strings-attached sex, and now you can't get enough of me? You're in serious danger of agreeing to yet another date."

I pause, because he's right. I agreed to this one, but emotionally I've held back for obvious reasons. What we just did is all this is meant to be. But as he strokes giant fingers down the front of my neck, between my breasts, down to the curves of my belly... I feel *cherished*.

I feel desired. And more than that, I feel supported, like I'm not alone, like whatever needs to happen, Manorin will take care of it. In this moment, the rules we created don't matter. They're as forgotten as my demand that we focus on just fun.

When I don't answer, crimson eyes flash to mine as he continues stroking my body. "You know, losing you nearly broke me. But being with you now feels right, Cath; it feels good in a way I haven't felt since you."

His words flay something open inside me, my mouth slightly parted as I try to suck air in without looking like his commentary's giving me heart palpitations. He rolls over, pulling me on top of his huge body. He nestles my legs on either side of him, then pulls my arms up around his neck so my face brushes against his snout.

"I didn't date for a long time after you declined my tattoo. Eventually, I dated a bit, nothing ever serious until more recently." He sighs. "There was a lovely pixie woman I dated seriously for a decade or two. We had a lot of good times, but something was missing, always missing."

His fingers trace a trail along my jawline.

"She and I didn't fit together in all the right ways. She was deeply submissive, and while there's nothing wrong with that, I could never really push and pull her the way you and I did. I wasn't right for her, either. She eventually left for a troll Dom in Arcadia who could give her what she needed better than I could."

He waves between us. "I share that all to say, chase the good feelings with me, Cath. Let me spoil the fuck outta you, if only for a little while. Otherwise, our Pine Gulch weekend might be awkward—I only booked one room, and it's only got one bed."

Laughing, I press forward and rub my cheek along his, loving the way his soft fur feels against me. He brings both arms around my body and strokes, his touch reverent.

"Thank you for sharing that with me." I rub the underside of one of his fuzzy ears. "I'm sorry she wasn't right, but I'm glad I have time with you again now."

As we lie there talking about everything and nothing, I can't help but feel a mix of elation and dread. This date has been everything I could have wanted.

But I'm already afraid to lose it.

CHAPTER FOURTEEN

MANORIN

S aturday morning, Catherine's eyes are saucers as we step out of the portal to Pine Gulch and into the vintage western-style train station.

I laugh at the look on her face as I squeeze her fingers. "I take it you've never visited, despite your...role?" I can't speak of how she architected the magic that holds the haven system together. I'm not even supposed to know that, although she confided in me when we dated. It would've been hard to hide that secret, serious as we were at the time.

She shakes her head as she spins a slow circle, taking in the wood-paneled floor, giant plate-glass windows and the wood plank ticket counter on the far end.

"I painted so many places into existence," she whispers, staring around before bringing her gray gaze to mine. "I've only ever seen most of them on canvas, though, and even those are in safekeeping at HQ. And I never know how they actually get developed."

"Well," I stroke gray waves away from her cheeks. "I can't wait to introduce you to Pine Gulch, pretty girl."

The Pine Gulch portal station's bustling with monsters

coming to visit for this weekend's moving of the herd and the associated festivities. It's busier than usual, though, I'm guessing because it's easier for folks to travel here with the new portal station. I'll admit, it was really fucking nice to take just two portals to get home. That'll make it easier for me to visit more often without planning two days of portal travel.

Not to mention dealing with my nephew Alarion, yet again.

I'm not gonna let him sour my mood today, though. I'll have to handle that soon enough. I sling Catherine's bag high over my shoulder and guide her toward the magic-powered train that'll take us into downtown.

I get my fair share of looks from the locals, but other than a few friendly nods, they don't crowd me the way monsters usually do when I travel. It's one of the things I love about coming home to the Gulch.

Here, I'm just Manorin Longhorn, Yet Another Minotaur.

We exit the portal station onto the train platform. Waving at the giant black and red locomotive, fashioned after human steam engines of old, I look at Catherine.

"The train runs on a useful bit of touristy magic we might want to consider for Ever, if the monorail idea becomes a reality. This same train travels all over the Gulch, to literally every corner and every town. The ride takes about six hours altogether, but it sits in its own time warp. So, if you're not actually on the train, it appears to show up at the station every quarter hour. It's perfect for when you're not in a hurry and just want to enjoy the ride"

Catherine's mouth drops open. "So you never wait longer than fifteen minutes?"

I nod. "That's right. Off the train. On the train it takes much longer, but it's a lovely journey." I point to a small parking lot beside the train station. "You can always rent a truck as needed if you don't want to wait around for Mabel."

The train's also an impeccable hostess, but I think I'll let Cath experience that for herself.

A door swings open in front of us, the train welcoming us into one of the passenger cabins. Catherine goes in first but stops dead in her tracks once inside.

"Another bit of magic," I whisper in her ear, pressing my body to hers.

The interior of the train's a bit larger than the exterior appears. A half dozen seating areas with big plush sofas and coffee tables sit on either side of the long train car. The aisle down the middle's wide enough for any species of monster, the roof tall enough to accommodate horns like mine, or wings, or whatever.

A train attendant pops round the corner with a welcoming smile. "Welcome to Pine Gulch, where the land kisses the sky! May I offer you a map of the train? Each car is a little different. It's almost like visiting a haven inside a haven when you ride us."

I hold back a chuckle at the innuendo in the pixie's welcome speech. It's another part of what I love about the Gulch. Everyone here has a sense of humor.

Well, everyone but our sheriff, Bishop Rygold.

Catherine takes the proffered map and thanks the pixie, who pops into small form and zips away. In front of us, the floor beams begin to flip and turn red like a carpet.

I laugh, pointing. "Mabel, the train, will give you the red-carpet treatment all the way until you reach your seat. I picked a spot for us ahead of time, thinking to give you the best view, so follow the red carpet, Sunshine."

She smiles up at me, eyes full of wonder. Mabel flipflops a couple more pieces of wooden flooring, catching her attention. With a laugh, Catherine follows the red flooring down to the far end of the train and a neat little walled booth at the back. It's got space for eight or so monsters, but when she takes a seat on the plush velvet bench, I slide in next to her.

When she looks up with a grin, I wink back. "We've got an hour to kill before we get to downtown, Sunshine. I've got a few ideas how we might do that."

Pink flushes her cheeks, and she looks around.

I chuckle and bend down, nuzzling at the side of her neck. "I can be very discreet, Catherine. Just don't scream. That would draw attention."

She opens her mouth to respond, but the wooden table in front of us begins to morph. The side closest to us flips over, revealing a hand-painted menu.

I pat the table lovingly. "Thank you, Mabel darling. Give us a moment for Catherine's order; she's a train newbie. I'd like my usual."

A tiny purple flag flips up, sticking a little way into the aisle, indicating we've submitted a partial order. If it takes Cath more than a couple minutes to figure out her order, the flag'll turn black and call an attendant to offer suggestions.

Catherine marvels at it all. "This is absolutely marvelous, Manorin!"

I point to the menu. "I've never had anything bad on the train. You can't go wrong, no matter what you pick."

It takes Catherine another five minutes to decide on a summer sangria. As always, the drinks arrive quickly, delivered by the pixie attendant.

While the train chugs through beautiful Montana countryside, I point out some of the bigger ranches we drive through to get to downtown. We won't pass through any other towns until we get to downtown Pine Gulch.

Catherine sips her sangria as I debate whether or not to turn and slide my hand up her skirt. Just as I'm about to do it, the table jostles the train overview packet toward Catherine. When it lands in her lap, she picks it up in one hand and pats the table lovingly with the other. "Thank you, darling Mabel."

The table vibrates with excitement.

"Do that vibration on the bench seat, though," I encourage.

Catherine playfully swats me with the brochure, then snuggles against me and opens it. The very first flap has a stunning picture of the library car, toward the back of the train. "Oh gods, that looks incredible."

I bend down and nuzzle the top of her head. "It's stunning, glass walls and glass roof and nearly sixty thousand books on the shelves, something for everyone no matter what you're interested in. It's also spelled so it looks like you're at the front of the train. You can grab a book and drink, sit at the front of the library car, and simply stare out at the Gulch as you go by. Heaven... I used to do thinking loops around the whole haven whenever I needed to sort out a problem."

Catherine rests her head against my chest and looks up at me. "It's been so long since I've traveled, and this trip is already magnificent. Thank you. I can see why you'd have no desire to ever leave this place."

I wrap an arm around her middle, holding her tightly to me. "Well, you haven't seen the best parts of the Gulch yet. I haven't even taken you dancing. You may remember I'm a better-than-average dancer."

She laughs lightly, rubbing my thigh with one red-nailed hand. "I do seem to remember something like that. The barn dance is tonight...is that right?"

"Mhm." I tighten my fingers over her soft belly, wanting to dig in and do inappropriate things. There's something about having her with me in my home haven that dredges up memories of all the plans I made when she and I first dated. Plans I didn't tell her about because I wanted to surprise her. Things that didn't work out when we parted ways.

"How long is the ride again?"

"An hour to town." I stroke her gray waves, breathing her in as I envision her swinging around the wood-plank dance floor I grew up dancing on.

"For today, I think I'd like to just relax here with you. But perhaps on our way back to Ever, we can check out the library car? I've got to tell the Hector girls. I think Wren, in particular, would be enthralled by such a thing."

"Done." I slide my hand lower, playing at the edge of her skirt. I slip it to the inside of her thigh and move up, up, up. Surprise rushes through me. "No underthings, Cath? My naughty girl."

She smiles up over her shoulder. "Thought you might appreciate that."

"Oh yeah." I snuffle against her shoulder as gentle tan and green hills roll by. "I'm going to *thoroughly* appreciate it until you're soaking this bench, Sunshine. Stay quiet, though. I'd hate for the attendant to come over to see what you need."

She wriggles against me as I cover her with my larger body, sliding the tips of two fingers along her outer pussy lips. She's as sensitive as ever, soft little moans tumbling from her mouth.

"Quiet, woman," I remind her, dropping my tone lower. She loves it when I get bossy. Reaching around, I clap one hand lightly over her mouth, the other stroking her softly as she lets one leg fall to the side.

She brings both hands to my forearm and pushes me, trying to get me where she wants me. Footsteps and a throat clearing indicate the arriving attendant, who carefully places our drinks on the table. Thankfully, she can't see what I'm doing to Catherine around my broad back.

"Will there be anything else, Mister Longhorn?"

I smile over my shoulder at the pixie as I slip a finger into Catherine's pussy. "That's all for now, thank you."

The pixie smiles and flits off to the next purple-flagged table.

"Oh gods," Catherine manages around my fingers. "More, Manorin. Now."

"Or what?" I add a second finger and stroke, curling the digits inside her to rub at her G-spot. I want her on the edge before I let her fall over. If I'm lucky, she'll squirt all over my hand, and I'll have a mess to clean up before we arrive at our destination.

Maybe I'll make her come until we get there. Once she's over the edge, it's possible to turn her into a blubbering mess of nonstop orgasms. I want it, I decide.

Chuckling at the idea of her soaking my fingers, I bend down and lick a path softly along her exposed neck, nuzzling her skin as I thrust slowly in and out of her. I use the pad of my thumb to rub her clit gently from side to side, pressing enough to activate that most sensitive of nerve bundles.

She rocks against me, legs falling open wider as she claws at my forearm. "Nor, oh gods, anybody could see us!" She's practically hissing, even as the sound falls off into a moan.

"No one can see you through the booth and my big, hard body, Cath," I whisper into her ear. "Enjoy yourself, my pretty little succubus. Enjoy watching the Gulch fly by outside as I finger you."

She groans, the sound cutting off when she remembers where we are.

Her hips rock faster, more desperately as she mewls against me.

I chuckle, delighted by the way she responds to me.

"Fucking you is my favorite thing," I growl under my breath. "Come for me, pretty girl."

On cue, she detonates, back arching as she claws at the seat and my arm and anything she can reach. Her nails leave great raised welts under my fur, and all it does is turn me on. I can't wait to get her into a bed and do more of this.

Stroking her through the orgasm, I wait until she's a heaving, soaked mess of honey. Murmuring softly, I praise her, telling her what a good, sweet girl she is, how pretty she looked coming on a public train, how much I want to see another orgasm from her.

And then I start it all over, because I'm an asshole who wants more. I need all of her. I want it. It's mine, and I'm taking it again, and again, and again. I shouldn't let this obsession continue. I shouldn't let it build and blossom the way it is. But if I'm honest with myself, it's too fucking late.

Far too fucking late.

I am. Obsessed. With. Her.

CHAPTER FIFTEEN
CATHERINE

I'm a sopping mess by the time the train stops in downtown Pine Gulch. Manorin's a hard, tense presence at my back. I've been quietly teasing him with pheromones for the entire ride, and as excited as he is to show me Pine Gulch, I think he's most excited to get to a bed.

As he should be.

Friends with benefits is turning out to be a lot of fun. While Annabelle has my heart, there are needs she isn't meant to fulfill. Manorin does that and more. I'm already dreading this trip being over because I'm having such a good time.

Before we disembark, he finds the pixie attendant to give her a tip and a quick thanks for being such an excellent hostess. Or maybe for looking the other way while he gave me a half-dozen soul-shattering orgasms.

Gods. It might have either been my best or worst idea to come here with him. He was always up for anything as a younger male, and that doesn't seem to have changed with age.

But all that worry evaporates when we step off the train onto a cobblestone street, a long row of two-story buildings in front of us. The train takes off with a steamy hiss.

"That's downtown's only BnB." Manorin points at a sign that reads *The Welcome Inn*. "We'll be there for the weekend, my brother got the family place when our folks died and I don't wanna subject you to him. Welcome's got a cute little saloon-style bar inside."

He jerks his head to the building next to that. "The Whiskey Business is your best spot for a really good drink, and the food's not half bad. There are a half dozen other good restaurants in downtown, and then, of course, the wraith hotel situated on the opposite side of the haven is its own property with a series of restaurants and shops. Great place to go for a little upscale shopping." He tucks a stray lock of hair away from my eyes. "I'd love to take you lingerie shopping there sometime, maybe on this trip if we've got time. Would you like that?"

It's hard not to shout yes and leap into his arms. Everything about Manorin is so...romantic. Thoughtful, well-planned, considerate. I didn't even have that with Wesley. Maybe a little when we first dated. But we were never partners the way I thought we were. I always gave more than I received, in every possible way.

But Manorin's not like that, and if I'm honest with myself, I'm enjoying it.

"I'd love to," I manage, reaching up to stroke his forearm.

He bends down, bringing his snout to me. "Good, I wanna find out how many businesses I can fuck you in before I get a slap on the wrist from Sheriff Rygold for public indecency."

"That'll be kinda difficult to do, on account of him currently stone sleeping away his troubles, so he'll be a statue for a few days at least."

I snap my eyes up to see who just *heard that.*

A handsome, tall dark elf with white hair in a high bun stands there wearing a tan uniform with a name badge reading *F. Zayle, Fish & Wildlife*. He stands with lazy ease, thumbs tucked into a black leather belt secured by a giant silver belt buckle.

Silver tattoos in the shape of various animals curve around both muscular forearms.

"Err, hello." I'm certain I'm blushing, but thankfully Manorin comes to my rescue, stepping forward to reach for the elf's hand, which he shakes vigorously.

"Furyon, good to see you, friend. What's this about Rygold?"

Furyon smiles lazily, black lips splitting to reveal sharp, white teeth. His pale blue eyes move from Manorin to me and back again. "Sicka dealing with you-know-who. Told me to pass along a message though." He winks at me, blue eyes crinkling at the corners. "Clean up your nephew's bullshit, or he'll do it when he wakes, and you ain't gonna like what happens." He shrugs and glances off into the distance. "I'm guessing he might feel ready to drop Alarion into the deepest part of the Gulch on account of the nonstop tomfoolery. Lotta places around here to hide a body."

Manorin laughs, honest to gods, as I stand horrified by the exchange.

The sheriff here would *kill* Manorin's nephew?

"Noted," Manorin finally says when laughter subsides to a chuckle. "Honestly, it might do that dumbass some good to get dangled over the Gulch for a bit. I might just ignore him this weekend and let Rygold take it from there."

Furyon shakes his head, rolling a toothpick between his teeth. "I mightn't do that if I was you, old friend. Bishop's in a right foul mood these days. Sidewinders got his tail all in a knot."

Manorin's smile falls. "I thought that mostly went away when Rezeth died?"

"Not hardly." Furyon's easy smile falls. "They got a new ophiotaurii in charge, and he's really somethin'. Most monsters don't even venture to the far west now. They've attempted to raid Mabel a time or two, if you can believe it."

Manorin chuffs. "And what's Bishop doing about this if he's stone sleeping for days at a time?"

"Honestly, Manorin, I think he's gearing up to bring a heap o' trouble to their doorstep. That old injury bothers him from time to time, but it's better if he gets in a couple solid days' rest. I suspect we're about to see shit go down next week. After the barn dance, of course, because what self-respecting monsters would fuck with that?" He scoffs, as if it's unimaginable for someone to interfere.

Furyon smiles at me. "And you must be Catherine. Manorin mentioned you'd be joining him. I've heard tell of the Annabelle Inn's beautiful owner a time or two over the years." He winks at Manorin. "This big lug finally got you back here, huh?"

I'm missing something, but I just smile and nod. "That's right."

Furyon sighs. "Well, have fun. I'll see y'all at the dance later?"

"See you there, friend." Manorin slides a hand up my back, resting it at the base of my neck. "Gotta get my woman settled in first."

Furyon grins, black brows sliding into two wicked curves. "Bet you do, you rascal." He dips his head at me. "Ma'am." With an easy spin on his heel, he heads toward the Whiskey Business and disappears inside.

"Well, shit," Manorin grumbles, starting us toward The Welcome Inn. "I wasn't planning to deal with Alarion until tomorrow, but I guess I oughta have a little chat with him today."

"Whatever you need," I confirm. "Family first, okay?"

He halts me in place, spinning and crushing me to his body. A finger beneath my chin tilts my focus up to glittering crimson eyes. "You first. Extended family second. Everything else third, including my job, Catherine. We clear on that?"

Something inside me unfurls and warms at his words.

"I've never been anyone's first," I admit, staring at twin pools of intensity.

"You were first for me, all those years ago," he says gruffly. "You're first now as well, and if that ain't obvious in the way I've treated you, then I'm doin' a shitty job." He gives me a wry look. "Even with our *arrangement*."

"I love how you've developed a country accent here," I say with a wink, trying to defuse a situation that's getting dangerously close to Real Feelings, trademark pending.

"Don't deflect." He slides his fingers down the front of my throat. "Wesley hurt you, and if he wasn't already dead, I'd put him under for that, Sunshine."

I place both hands on his big chest, grounding myself on the way it rises steadily with huge, deep breaths. Curling my fingers against him, I force myself to confront what I'm feeling and thinking, not to run from it.

Calling Manorin a hookup doesn't feel right. Nothing about the way he treats me is a no-strings-attached vibe. I can't seem to find my footing with that, because I crave *more*.

"He crushed my soul," I admit, looking up into crimson, sparkling eyes. "I didn't see what was wrong with him, but Annabelle did. She hated him from day one."

Nor says nothing but pulls me closer. "I'm sorry, Cath. I'm—"

I press my fingertips to his muzzle to quiet him. "It was a while ago, although his death was more recent, of course. I've put him behind me, but my point in sharing that was he never put me first, either. Not like you do. Even though this is just a short-term arrangement."

The words feel simultaneously important and hollow. The word "arrangement" barely encompasses what's happening between us. Does he feel that too?

"Need to feed you," Manorin says quietly. "Get you settled in our room. Maybe give you a nice little massage. And if you wanna keep talkin' about this, we can. Shit, maybe we'll head over to the tattoo studio, and I'll get my first one. A nice little typography tat over my heart that says 'Always *her* first.' Whaddya think?"

I smile up at his handsome face. "I think I'll need a box of tissues if you do that, because it might be the sweetest thing anyone's ever done for me."

He grins, the edges of his mouth curling up. It makes him all that much more handsome to me. "Consider it a date." He waves between us. "We talk about this arrangement a lot, Cath, but let me make this clear—even if this job doesn't work out, and we part as friends, I will always be there if you need me. One call, and I'm running to you. Are we clear?"

I push hard to keep tears from filling my eyes. The idea of having Nor in my corner warms me in a way nothing has since I first met and fell in love with Wesley. I thought he was in my corner, but, looking back, there were signs he wasn't.

Nor hauls my bag higher over his shoulder and takes my hand, walking us toward the front door. "C'mon, Sunshine."

The Welcome Inn soars up four stories of rustic dark wood, chunky red support beams punctuating the building's front. It's by turns rustic and elegant as the inn's emerald-green front doors swing wide for us.

"Thank you, beautiful girl," I whisper as we step through. The inside of the inn's as gorgeous as the outside. Everything has a lodge feel, all rustic wood and exposed beams. The two-story foyer is somehow cozy despite that. Huge antler chandeliers punctuate the ceiling and cast light down on us.

"Welcome in to the Welcome Inn!" a chirpy voice greets us from the right.

Turning toward the voice, I find a lanky black-haired woman standing behind a long check-in desk, wearing a big smile. She appears human, although with some monsters, it's hard to tell.

She beams at me. "Catherine, I take it? I've got you on a reservation with our resident celebrity." She winks up at Manorin.

I laugh at how people recognize him everywhere. That's new for me. That didn't happen quite so much when we were younger.

"That's me."

The woman pushes a small basket across the check-in table. "He pre-checked in, but please take this welcome basket as a thank you from us for picking The Welcome Inn. If you need anything at all during your stay, there's an attendant on call twenty-four hours a day. To my right, there's a great little bar." She points behind us. "Back there, we've got a coffee shop that's perfect for grabbing something quick." She leans in as if to tell a secret. "Although, if you want a really stellar latte, I recommend Brewhaha Beans across the street."

The inn creaks around us, expressing her dislike of the woman's suggestion.

She rolls her eyes with a little chuckle. "I'm going to be in trouble if I say any more, but please enjoy yourselves. I'm Kerri-ann, and I'm here, shit...well, I'm here a lot."

"Thank you, Kerriann," Manorin says easily. "See you at the barn dance?"

She grimaces. "I'm working, so no. But, honestly, a crowd of people being loud ain't really my rodeo, ya know?"

He laughs, and I grab the basket off the countertop, loving the idea of it. I don't do anything like that at the Annabelle, other than provide a haven welcome packet to those who are fully new to town.

"Do you have a welcome packet by chance?"

She sighs. "I'm fresh out, and I was told not to order more because they're being redone. So, we should wait for the new ones, I guess, but honestly, what a pain. So, I'm sorry to say I don't have any just now." She waves at Manorin. "Good thing he's an excellent tour guide, though. And definitely call down here with any questions!" She hands me a sheet of paper. "Here's a temporary map although I'm told the new welcome books will be much cooler. Sorry I can't offer more at the moment."

The inn creaks loudly around us and she laughs.

"I know, Welcome! You're just gonna have to share the name with the book…I can't do nothin' about it and if you have an issue you can take it up with Rygold."

The inn produces an unhappy sounding series of squeaks and squeals and I have to hold back a laugh. Her personality is as tangible as my Annabelle's, and it feels like home even though this building isn't *mine*.

I thank the attendant again, tucking my arm through the basket's handle. We ascend a set of wide, overlarge stairs meant for the bigger-bodied monster breeds. When I seem to note it, Manorin chuckles.

"Lotsa big boys out this way. We need a little more space sometimes." He points at his hooves.

I frown up at him. "Is it difficult for you at the Annabelle?"

He shakes his head. "Not difficult, per se, but I do pay a bit more attention."

When the Annabelle appeared for me in Ever, I didn't question her design. She felt perfect for me. But when I think about Manorin having to be extra careful to make it up my stairs, I don't feel comfortable with that, and Annabelle probably doesn't either.

"If we expand the Annabelle, we're changing that." I stare up at him, resolved to make Manorin and any other guests more comfortable where possible.

By the time we make it to our room, I'm in awe of the Welcome Inn. It's charming yet beautiful, with elegant little touches that speak to the brilliance of her design.

Manorin opens the door and strides in, setting my bag down on an entryway table. I stare in awe at the beautiful room, all powder blue and dark red. A large bed is covered in buffalo-check pillows, sheets and blankets piled sumptuously high. The back wall is all windows with a beautiful view of empty rolling fields behind the inn.

"These details are exquisite, Manorin," I whisper, spinning slowly to take it all in.

Which is when I focus on the singular bed.

Of course that's what it is. I knew that. And part of me relishes that fact, even as the part of me in charge of feelings worries over it. But he was right... I should lean into his desire to romance me during our arrangement. I should have a little faith that things will be fine.

Except, I thought that before, and all it ever brought me was a heap of trouble.

CHAPTER SIXTEEN

MANORIN

My intention was to get Cath settled in the room, fed downstairs, then maybe some alone time in the room before the barn dance.

But my sassy, beautiful woman demands the reverse schedule.

Sexy room time. Everything else later.

By the time I manage to sate her—albeit temporarily—it's time to head to the barn dance.

Catherine emerges from the bathroom in a pair of thigh-hugging jeans, a black lace spaghetti-strapped shirt and high-heeled cowboy boots.

I'm across the room without thinking, taking her hand in mine. I lift her arm and spin her around, revealing the low-cut back of the shirt that exposes the sexy dimples above her belt.

"Gods, woman," I manage, choking around a sudden surge in feelings. "You're stunning, Sunshine. I'm gonna be beating other males off with a stick. Good thing I'm big."

She spins in place, slipping both hands up my shirt and over my chest. "Pretty damn big, yeah."

Chuckling, I dip down and nuzzle her jawline. "I'm equal

parts desperate to show you off and desperate to chain you to this bed. Maybe do what my ancestors are famous for and throw you into a maze so I can hunt you down and have you."

She shrugs. "Why not both, Manorin? Let's go to the dance—you've been so excited for it. We don't have to stay all night. I didn't pack chains, but I'm sure you'll figure something out." Her wink has my cock rising again. "I can't sort out the maze part though, sorry."

She pops onto her tiptoes and kisses the tip of my snout, inside my nose ring. It tickles the tiny hairs on the surface of my skin, and I shake my head with a laugh, rubbing at my nose.

"Ticklish," I admit as one of her dark brows rises.

We manage to make it out of the room with minimal fuck-ery, which is saying something because that godsdamned outfit is going to be the end of me. Catherine exits the inn just ahead of me, her big ass fully highlighted in the tight jeans. It's perfectly peachy and round, and those dimples are begging for my tongue.

Again.

"I can feel you staring." She cuts me a saucy look over her shoulder.

"Who wouldn't?" I manage, pulling her to me, back to my front as we wait for the train to come through.

Catherine settles against me, pulling my arm around her soft belly. I slip my fingers into the waistband of her jeans.

I'm falling in love. Shit, I don't know that I was ever *out* of love, but she was far away and eventually took a mate, and I was focused on my career. I dated, but nobody was ever her. And now Catherine's here in my arms, and I don't know what the fuck I'm gonna do if I don't get the Ever job.

We said no strings attached, but I should have known it wouldn't be possible for me to do that. Being with her is as easy as breathing. I want to tell her, but she's already concerned about how much romance I'm putting into this arrangement. Part of me suspects it's because she's got feelings going on too.

We need to talk about that.

"Cath," I murmur in her ear, my arms tightening around her.

She rests her head on my chest, looking up at me. "Yes, Manorin?"

Just then, the train whooshes into view, whistle screaming as she rounds the corner.

"I'm excited for tonight," I offer. Now's not the right time to tell her what I'm feeling. Not as we're stepping onto a busy train full of partygoers. But soon—maybe later tonight.

Mabel chugs to a stop, every car's doors opening wide.

We enter to find the train packed to the brim, nearly every seat taken.

"The barn dance is kind of a big deal," I admit as I guide us toward the seats I pre-purchased. When we get there, a pixie mother holds a small child in her lap, marveling at the scene outside the window. Only one of our two seats is free. I offer the first to Catherine, and the pixie looks up at me with a bashful smile.

"Oh, this seat must be yours! We were just hoping to get a quick peek of downtown, but we'll scoo—"

"Stay." I widen my stance. "Enjoy the view, both of you. It'll only take about twenty minutes and I'm fine."

Catherine grins up at me, then stands, pressing her back to my front. "If you're standing, I'm standing as well."

Smiling, I bury my face in her hair as the train pulls forward, steaming into the night.

It's a quick quarter hour to the Shorthorn Double L Ranch, Rip Shorthorn's family home. When Mabel chugs to a stop and the train car doors open, gasps rise up as the revelers see the barn for the first time.

I recognize a lot of folks on the train, but there are plenty of new faces too. Seems like the Gulch is experiencing its own tourism boost thanks to the headquarters' new portal station.

When we exit the train and the famous Shorthorn barn comes into view, Catherine's surprised gasp joins the other monsters'. Shorthorn's barn is fucking gorgeous...I'll give him that. It makes a hell of a first impression. Not to mention the rippling siding highlights a fresh coat of red paint. Lights guide our way to the enormous structure—two stories with a paneled roof.

"It's even more beautiful inside," I say. Upbeat music echoes faintly from the open barn doors.

I slip an arm around Catherine's waist as we walk with the crowd toward the giant barn. Lights under the trim illuminate the left side, where a huge mural of dancing monsters hints at what's in store tonight. I point Cath toward it.

"Rip Shorthorn's grandfather painted that about a century or so ago, when they first started doing a barn dance to accompany the moving of the cattle."

Catherine glances up at me. "That part happens tomorrow, right? You mentioned something about staying out of the street between noon and four."

"Oh yeah." I chuckle. "Don't wanna get trampled. It's more symbolic than anything at this point, but the local ranchers drive their cattle through downtown to the pastures south of town for winter. It gets cold up in the mountains, and most of them own southern land too."

Catherine gasps anew when we arrive at the barn doors and find monsters already swirling around a jam-packed dance floor. Another dozen or so monsters hang on giant rings dangling from the ceiling. They spin, gyrate and swirl, putting on a show for those of us below.

I point toward the left-hand wall. "Bar's over there. Let's grab a drink. The opposite wall's all food for when you're hungry."

Keeping her protected with one arm around her, I guide us through the milling throng to the bar, where four monster bartenders work quickly to provide drinks.

The moment I catch a stout shorthorn's eye, he comes over, slinging a rag over his shoulder. "Dad'll be happy to see you here, Manorin. Been talkin' lots of shit about your team this year."

"Which one?" I snark back. "Seeing as how I've got responsibility for two."

The shorthorn snorts and smiles down at Catherine. "Don't know how such a beauty got mixed up with this rabble-rouser, but what can I getcha to drink?"

Catherine strokes my forearm. "Surprise me."

The minotaur bartender jerks his head toward me. "You?"

"I'm afraid to say 'surprise me,' so how about an autumn mead if you've got any?"

He disappears behind the bar as I press Cath to it, wrapping both arms tightly around her. "You hungry, Sunshine?"

"No. Dying to dance, though."

"Admit it," I say as I nuzzle my way along her shoulder. "You just want these big hands all over you, moving you around where I see fit."

She spins in my arms, irises flashing gold. "Perhaps, Manorin."

That look tightens my balls, my cock hardening in its sheath.

"Catherine," I warn. We can't play like that here, or I'll lose my mind and fucking stampede the place to get her home.

Red-painted lips curl into a wicked smile. "Yes?"

I bend down and collar her throat, my touch light but commanding. "Don't unleash me here, woman. I just managed to get us out of the bedroom, and I'm bound and determined to get at least a few dances in."

She snorts. "You started it." But she can't resist swaying along with the raucous music.

And I can't resist staring as she moves those hips and sidles along next to me.

The bartender returns, saving me from myself as he slides two drinks across the bar. I drop a few bills into his tip jar and thank him, but he's already moved on to the next partygoer.

"Manorin Longhorn, the nerve of you to show up here."

My laughter rumbles as I spin in place to see Rip Shorthorn standing there, a lazy grin on his face. His scarlet eyes drop to Catherine and wrinkle at the edges as he holds out a big hand.

"Hello, darlin'. I know you by reputation, of course, on account of you breakin' Manorin's bitty heart, but how'd you get wrangled into comin' to my party with this ruffian?"

Catherine laughs and tucks herself close to my side, lifting her chin. "You're the second monster to ask me that in the span of sixty seconds. He convinced me with those gorgeous *long* horns."

I hold back raucous laughter as Rip's smirk becomes a playful scowl.

"Length ain't always a good indicator of value, if you know what I mean," he offers, tapping the short, pointed tips of his own horns. He waves around at the party. "Party's never been quite this big, but I'm lovin' it. Enjoy yourselves. There's food on the opposite side, and apparently, I'm supposed to give a quick speech here in a minute."

He steps closer to me, clapping his hand on my shoulder. "Call me sometime tomorrow, if you would."

Oh fuck. If he's asking for a call; I'm gonna guess Alarion's in even more trouble than I thought. Rip Shorthorn doesn't get involved in others' business, not if he can help it. I don't want to open that can of worms here at the party, though, so I nod. "Will do, Rip."

His mouth flattens, and he nods before disappearing into the crowd.

A band positioned along the back wall picks up a rowdy tune

that elicits a huge cheer from the crowd. They play a few notes, and I recognize a fan favorite song I've been dancing to since I was a calf.

Finding an empty table, I set my mead down and look at Catherine. "Dance with me, Sunshine?" I'm gonna have plenty of time to worry about Alarion tomorrow, but for now, I wanna get lost in those gray eyes of hers and forget.

She sets her drink next to mine and takes my hand with a playful little bow. "Lead on, Mister Longhorn."

CHAPTER SEVENTEEN
CATHERINE

This place is incredible. String lights hung across the cavernous arched ceiling illuminate caged dancers hanging above the crowd. The dance floor itself is packed with young and old, dancing, laughing, drinking. It's merriment at its finest. About half of the monsters are short- or long-horned minotaurs, but the rest seem to be a healthy mix, like in Ever.

Manorin guides me to a free spot on the dance floor and slides his hand flat between my shoulder blades. With his free hand, he brings one of my arms up around his neck and the other to rest over his heart.

The first bit of light pressure at my back serves as a guide, even as he steps toward me. And then, in a rush of movement, we're spinning and swirling across the dance floor. Manorin's crimson eyes barely leave mine. He looks up just enough to keep us from hitting other dancers.

And I am *lost*.

Lost to the ease with which he moves me around the dance floor.

Lost to the sultry way he stares at me, like nobody exists but me.

Lost to the fun and joy he brings to my life simply by being himself.

I stare up at him in wonder and awe as he leads me through one song and into the next and the next and the next.

I'm falling for him, again. Hard and fast, and I don't think I could stop it if I tried. But instead of worrying about it, I embrace it as we dance around the floor, our bodies moving easily together. Comfortable. Secure.

I'm safe with him. And I didn't think I'd be willing to give in to that feeling after Wesley. Allowing someone else in. But Manorin weaseled his way right back into my heart as if he'd never left.

One song becomes two and ten and fifteen, until something catches his eye, and he grins over my shoulder. Halting us, he takes my hand and guides me off the dance floor. Standing at the edge are Betmal and Amatheia. The mermaid female hops up and down, clapping as she beams at us.

"My gods, Catherine, you two are fabulous dancers! I'm so jealous that I don't know a single dance move."

Betmal's crimson eyes wrinkle at the corners as he smiles down at his mate. "And yet your rhythm is perfect, ma sirène." She blushes up at him.

I pull them both into a big hug, delighted to see friends here. When we part, Betmal smiles at me.

"I'm sorry it didn't occur to me to ask if either of you planned to attend this weekend's festivities. I wanted Ama to experience it for herself as we're working on Pine Gulch's new welcome book."

Manorin reaches out to shake the vampire's hand. "Can't wait to see what you come up with. I was thrilled to learn that someone was finally redoing them. Evenia didn't seem too happy about the announcement when it came out, but then, she's not happy about much."

I keep my mouth shut on that one, but Betmal laughs. He and I have talked about this topic before. Nobody would like to see a replacement for Evenia more than the two of us. I've got ideas about it and I fully intend to pass those by him at my earliest convenience.

"No, she's not. Good thing I don't have to pretend to care anymore." He winks as he slides a hand around Amatheia's waist, curling his fingers into the scale-patterned skin of her hip.

He smiles at me. "Listen, Ama and I are going to lunch-time karaoke tomorrow just before the running of the steers. Why don't you two meet us? It'll be a good time."

I look uncertainly up at Manorin. "I'm not sure what our plans are for tomorrow…"

He grins down at me. "I wouldn't mind seeing you belt out a few songs, Cath."

I fluff my hair, grinning at Amatheia. "Once upon a time, I was a pretty good singer."

"Coach, that you?" a deep voice breaks through the din of the crowd.

I glance toward it to find Hadrian Alkazar—the Protector Academy's star player—walking toward us with a hand reaching toward Manorin.

Nor grabs the skyball prodigy's hand and shakes it vigorously. "Alk, how's it goin', kid?"

The tall, muscular gargoyle blushes a dark purple as he dips his head respectfully at Ama and me. "All good, Coach. Doing a little sightseeing in one of my favorite havens."

I risk a glance at Manorin, but I know neither of us believe that story. Hadrian's likely here being wined and dined by the Punishers' coach.

Manorin gestures at the other Evertons. "Hadrian, this is

Betmal of House Zeniphon, and, I'm sorry, I didn't catch your name..."

Ama blushes deeply but holds out a hand for Hadrian's. "Amatheia, also of House Zeniphon."

Betmal shoots me a wicked, pleased grin before turning the smile on Hadrian. "My mate, of course."

Hadrian flashes a toothy grin at our group. "Looks like I interrupted y'all in the middle of dancing, and I'm not one to stop monsters from having fun. I'm gonna do a little tour around. I was supposed to be meeting a friend here, but I don't see him yet."

"Have a good time, kid," Manorin says. "I'm gonna give you a call tomorrow, alright?"

Hadrian blushes even deeper, running a hand through pitch-black hair that nearly touches his shoulders. "'Kay, Coach. See ya later." He tucks his wings at his back and disappears into the crowd, shouldering his way past monsters who point and whisper as he goes.

When Manorin glances down at me, I raise a brow meaningfully as I plant a hand on my hip, my competitive spirit kicking into overdrive. "We've got to get him if we can."

"Good luck," Betmal says with a snort. "Every haven in the system is trying to snatch up Hadrian Alkazar, and word has it he's a country boy."

When I roll my eyes, he grabs Amatheia's hand. "Come, ma sirène, I promised to feel you up on the dance floor."

Ama waves goodbye as she allows Betmal to guide her to an empty spot.

When I look up at Manorin, he's staring at me with an intense look in those beautiful dark eyes.

"Ready to get outta here, Sunshine?"

I take his hand. "Lead the way, Nor."

CHAPTER EIGHTEEN
MANORIN

Catherine clings to my neck as I gallop over moonlit fields toward our destination. She's quiet, her thighs gripping me tightly as she rocks along with the rhythm of my easy lope. It's a solid half-hour ride, but it's fun.

More than fun. I want her to ride me everywhere, because there's nothing better than running across the rolling hills—my hills—with this woman on my back.

When dark forest comes into view, I slow down and slip her carefully off me. Her hair's wind-whipped and wild, her cheeks ruddy as she beams up at me.

"That was exhilarating!" She plays at the bird's nest of her waves. "There's truly nothing like being on your back."

I sweep her into my arms as I carry her toward the dark of the forest. "What about my front, Sunshine?"

She rolls her eyes and lets out a groan. "Gods, I walked you right into that one. That was terrible, Manorin. Are you a young bull again?"

I chuckle as I stalk between the trees, moonlight reduced to faded shards as the forest envelops us.

She smiles up from my arms. "We headed to the ward? That was very hot."

I shake my head. "Nope. This is my land, land I bought when we were together before. It's the land I thought I'd eventually build a house on and bring you home to."

She goes utterly silent, her playful smile falling. "What?"

I jerk my head toward a spot in front of us. "I started building, and then we parted ways, and I never finished it. I knew my brother would get our family plot and that was fine. I wanted something new for us. But when I need to think about anything important, I come back here. The only thing I did finish was statues to the minotaur gods. Want to see?"

She slips out of my arms as I halt in a clearing, the four statues standing in a circle facing each other.

Cath looks up at me. "I never knew, Nor. I—"

I press the pad of my thumb to her plump lips. "It wouldn't have changed anything if you did, Cath. It wasn't our time then, but I prepared for it anyhow."

I walk her to the first statue, noting the minotaur's long horns and the water droplets dripping from her fingers. "Viya, Goddess of Rain. Her mate, Ratek, God of Wind, stands across from her." I point to the next statue over from Viya. "Vejoom, Goddess of Earth, with Firbell, her God of Fire, across from her."

Catherine's gray eyes fill with tears. "I can't believe you bought this for us."

Brushing my knuckles along her high cheekbones, I smile. "I assumed a lot in those days, brash and young, as you've noted. I *assumed* you'd be okay coming here. I *assumed* you'd remain mine. And I didn't put in the work I needed to put in to keep you. I'm not making that mistake twice, and I'm not trying to convince you to come here. I know you don't want to leave Ever. But this place is special to me, and I wanted to share it with you."

She rubs her cheek against my palm, closing her eyes as a tear slides down her face. Pulling her closer, I press my snout to the top of her head, breathing her quietly in.

"It's beautiful," she says in a shaky voice. "So beautiful, Manorin." She steps back and looks up. "If I remember correctly, you'd traditionally put the house about a hundred yards that way, right?" She points to the west.

Nodding, I take her hand. "Yeah. We'd have had a killer view, Sunshine. Gorgeous sunsets." We walk quietly through the forest until it opens again onto the edge of a cliff. Every star in the sky's visible from this vantage point. I take her close to the edge and point at a wide river snaking through the valley below. "I planned to build the main quarters underground so we'd have a view from the front of the cliff below. We'd stare right down at the river all the time."

Catherine tucks herself against me. "You've really thought this through."

I wrap her up in my arms. "Like I said, I daydreamed a lot, and I made a lot of assumptions."

A faint noise echoes up from below.

Catherine tenses. "What's that?"

I kiss the top of her head. "Don't worry, Sunshine; we're remote and safe here. There's a band of wild mustangs that live in this valley. They were here long before this was ever a haven. It's a minotaur's belief that we should honor the land, so I come back once a year to help Furyon take care of them. Dewormer, hoof trimming, stuff like that. They nicker up at me when they know I'm home. Usually, they crowd me for carrots."

Catherine looks up at me, brows bunched and eyes wide. "Seriously?"

I laugh. "Yeah. Now that it's easier to get here, I'll come back to care for them more frequently. Once a year's not really enough to keep them in optimal health. I try not to disturb them more than I need to, but there's a great little spot down there to take a dip in the river, if you're inclined."

She laughs. "Wouldn't it be cold?"

I slide my hands down her body, groaning softly. "Yeah, which means you'd have to be all over me to keep warm."

"I'm feeling a little cold now," she says with a playful wink. "Will you warm me up, Manorin?"

"C'mere, Sunshine." I reach down and haul her into my arms. "Every time, sweet thing."

The walk to the river takes us another quarter hour, and Catherine peppers me with questions about the land and the horses and my vision for the house. But it's clear in the wild beating of her heart that she's anxious about it too. I might've told her too much about what I planned for in the past, but I lost her once when I pushed for too much, too soon.

The wild horses join us on the riverbank, shoving and jostling. The herd stallion comes toward Catherine, nuzzling her carefully.

"No carrots today," I tell him, keeping my tone low and soft. "Come back later, though."

The black stallion snorts and bumps me with his nose, snorkeling around my pockets as he hunts for the carrots I'm usually good about remembering. When he doesn't find his prize, he lets out an angry squeal and tosses his head. He's elegant and wild and when he squeals again, the mares trot off into the darkness.

Cath watches them go, gray eyes wide as her heart pounds behind her breastbone. She turns to look up at me. "That was so thrilling, Nor. Gods, they were beautiful."

"You're beautiful," I murmur as I slide her clothes off her. Then I remove mine and pull her into my arms. She gasps as I stalk into the cold river, chilly water splashing up to coat her feet and lower legs. The gasp turns into a yippy screech when I duck down and submerge us in the water.

"Godsssssss," she cries out, clinging to my neck. "This is so fucking cold, Nor!"

Wrapping my arms around her, I hover my mouth over hers. "Let me warm you, woman."

Gray eyes flash golden momentarily before returning to their usual storm-cloud shade. With a smile, Cath tilts her head to the side, giving me access to that slim, elegant neck. I grin as I dip forward to nuzzle and lick my way along her neck and shoulder, then back up.

She squirms in my arms, rocking her body against my core. My cock extends from my sheath, eagerly seeking her heat as my bites grow harder, more insistent. Catherine keeps one arm around my neck and reaches down with the other, guiding me to her channel. The warmth of her pussy lips is a delicious shock against the freezing water.

But when she grabs my nose ring and hangs on, using it for leverage to impale herself on my cock, the only thing I can do is let out a desperate, needy low. "Fuck, Sunshine," I manage. "I love it when you handle me like this."

She's lost, though. Lost in chasing her pleasure. Eyes rolled into the back of her head, she sinks on and off me in the freezing water until I don't feel the cold at all. There's nothing but her sheathing me inside her, taking every inch of my substantial cock and milking me for all I'm worth.

I let her keep control until her cries ring out over the water. Then I bring both hands to her hips and thrust, jolting her off my cock and slamming her back down. She clamps tight around me, her pussy sucking at my dick until I see stars. Her pleasure unleashes me, and I ravage her, obsessed with how her breasts rise and fall in the water with every thrust.

I fuck her until she tightens and pauses, a low moan tumbling from her lips. Then they curl back into a vicious snarl as she draws in a breath, then two, then three, rapid-fire. And then she explodes, arching high and hard against me as she thrusts her breasts into my face. Her pussy flutters in great big waves, dragging an orgasm from me that has me roaring my pleasure into the scant space between us.

Pleasure drags on as the rollercoaster of her bliss milks seed from me until I've got nothing left to give. After what seems like an hour of coming, she slumps against me, forehead pressed to mine. Her fingers slip from my nose ring as she groans in my ear, her breathing harsh and ragged.

"Nor, I..." She falls off with a laugh as her teeth start to chatter. Shimmying a little, she plants a string of tender kisses on the end of my muzzle. "That damn cold crept back in faster than I expected."

I was seconds from telling her that I'm fucking falling for her. But I can't have that conversation when my woman's freezing. Grinning, I reach down and pull my cock from her slippery, hot channel. I run my fingers through her folds, cleaning her even as she hisses. Then I carry her back to the rocky beach and tongue-bathe her dry until she's grabbing my horns and commanding me to put my tongue somewhere else.

~

"You gotta be shitting me." I stare into my nephew Alarion's bright blue eyes, shocked at how much he's changed since I was last home. He's bigger than ever, almost bigger than me, packed with muscle. The same dark spots litter his broad, thick horns.

The difference is how jittery and on edge he is. He was always a quiet, slow-to-anger calf. As we stand in the forest on my property, squared off like we're about to fight, the difference in him is stark.

He runs a hand through his chocolate waves, looking everywhere but at me.

"I don't wanna fight with you, Uncle Nor. The ophiotaurii are doing important work and—"

"That so?" I quirk a brow up. "'Cause I heard they were stealing cattle and sneaking out into the human world. What could possibly be so important about that?"

He grits his jaw so tight, I swear it'll crack. When he lifts his chin, I suspect I won't get anything out of him. So far, he's been short on detail around why he's even hanging out at the ophiotaurii den in the first place. That chimera breed is typically antisocial and solitary as a species. They pick a territory and don't venture out of it. It's weird how he even got mixed up with them. They're far more like their snakelike ancestors than their minotaur halves.

"I want you to come back to Ever with me," I say when he doesn't respond to my earlier comment.

Bright eyes narrow, and he shakes his head. "Naw, Nor. I'm a grown-ass male, and I don't need babysitting in that tiny little haven. I'm not leaving, and you and Daddy can't make me."

"Listen to yourself," I growl. "You sound like a petulant child. Is this really how you wanna play things? Just come back with me for a couple weeks. We'll hang out while I'm interviewing, and if you wanna return home after that, you can. I strongly suggest a change in perspective."

His brows knit together, his expression almost desperate, but it's there and gone so fast I wonder if I imagined it.

"Naw," he repeats. "I gotta go, Uncle Nor. They need me."

"Go, then," I say softly. "But consider my offer even if it's just for a short time. And consider that Bishop Rygold's gonna come out of his stone sleep in a day or two, and word has it he's gonna rain hells down on your crew for whatever the fuck they're doing."

"Wouldn't happen if we had a good keeper," he grumbles.

"We've never been able to keep a good one," I remind him. "Not everyone's cut out for these wide-open spaces and all the quiet. I think you gotta grow up here, and nobody's ever tested positive and come back home."

"I know." He turns from me, giving me a view of his broad back and long, powerful horns. "Good to see you. Travel safe."

I stand in utter silence as he stalks through the trees, crossing the dappled grove where my statues stand. He doesn't bother to look at them as he passes. It's disrespectful, and I'd shout about it, but all I've *done* this morning is shout at him.

Last night with Cath was perfect. Beyond perfect. This morning, not so much. This shit with Alarion started my day badly. I can't help my nephew if he doesn't want it, and apparently he and my brother aren't even on speaking terms.

I lift my comm watch to call my sibling and chat about the Alarion convo, but unfortunately, our call devolves into a one-sided screaming match with him shouting and me waiting for him to calm down enough to talk about it.

By the time I'm free to ring Rip Shorthorn, I've got a headache building behind my eyes.

Catherine's sleeping in, so hopefully I'll be done with this family maintenance craziness by the time she's up. I miss the days of my father being around to manage Alarion. They always had a special relationship, and when he died, it tore our family up.

Rip picks up on the first ring. "Longhorn, get somewhere private, if you would."

Fuuuuuuck.

I look to make sure nobody's around, although nobody would be, not out here.

"Listen," I start. "I spoke with Alarion just now and—"

Rip cuts in, "No offense, old friend, but your dumbass nephew ain't an issue I'd touch with a ten-foot pole. I'm calling about the Punishers."

I cross my arms and shift from one foot to the other, brows scrunching. "I'm listenin'."

Rip pauses for a moment, then clears his throat. "I'd deny this 'til my last breath if asked, but I'm finally considerin' retirement. I haven't fully decided, but if I do, I'll recommend the Punishers bring you home to take over, assuming you'd want that."

My mouth goes dry as a ball drops in the pit of my stomach.

Oh gods.

Double triple quadruple *fucking* shit.

"I..." I can't manage to find a single godsdamned word.

"I know I said I'd die before I retire," he continues, "but you know how grueling the pace of coaching is. I've got a new grandcalf on the way, and, honestly, I want more time with my grands."

"Keep me posted," is the only response I can manage. "I never let myself hope this role would open up, and I'm looking at other opportunities as we speak."

He's quiet for a moment. "Understood, Manorin. I'll let you know when I make my final decision, but, again, between us, I'm pretty well decided."

We chat for another moment, but when we sign off, I stand in the forest and stare across the winding gulch into the distance.

This is my dream. Has *been* my dream since I first left Pine Gulch.

But Catherine's never leaving Ever, and I'd never ask her to.

Not to mention this shit with Alarion is gonna come to a boiling point. If I was around more I could help my brother with him, maybe get him out from under the thumb of the Sidewinders and whatever the fuck they're doing.

And yet this opportunity's never coming back around, either. I've got one chance to take over my dream team, and this is probably it. Staring at the rolling hills, I close my eyes as sunshine warms my face. But all I can see in my mind is *my* Sunshine, my Catherine.

I can't keep this from her. It's a conversation I don't relish happening. I can't imagine taking a job with the Punishers and picking that over her, but I also can't imagine just saying no without looking at all the options and maybe finding some happy medium.

Grumbling at the way the gods are meddling in my life right now, I return to the Welcome Inn and our room. My Sunshine's just waking, smiling sleepily up at me from the tousled sheets.

Better rip this Band-Aid off.

She throws the sheets aside and spreads her legs wide for me, shooting me a sultry smile. "Morning, Nor. Want to wake me up with that big tongue?"

I sink onto the edge of the bed and take her hand. "We need to talk, Cath."

CHAPTER NINETEEN
CATHERINE

I shoot back against the pillows, clapping my thighs together as I drop Manorin's hand and sink against the headboard. Drawing the covers up over my chest, I level him with what's probably a horrified look. "We need to talk" has never preceded any good news.

He shakes his head. "I didn't come in to break your heart this morning, Sunshine."

I curl into a ball and stare at him. "Then what do we need to talk about?"

It's bad news, I can tell by the sorrowful look on his face. Even his horns seem droopy. I don't even think that's *possible*.

"Rip Shorthorn asked me to call him this morning," he starts. "I thought he wanted to discuss Alarion, but he wanted to tell me he's retiring, and he's going to recommend the Punishers offer me the head coach position upon his departure."

Oh *gods*. His dream job.

I suck in a deep breath and glance across the room to the only window. The roofs of the buildings across the street are barely visible, but I focus on what I can see as I fight to steady my voice and handle this logically. But we said no strings attached, and that's what this should be.

But how can it be, when I'm falling for him again? Because I am. I think I started to the moment he looked at me from the middle of the skyball field and smiled like I was the only thing he ever wanted to look at.

After a quiet moment, I force a smile and look at him. "You should take that job if it's formally offered. You've wanted this as long as I've known you."

"I can't take that job for two reasons," he says, lifting a finger. "Firstly, it hasn't officially been offered, and he's not even sure he wants to retire. Secondly, you and I haven't discussed it, and I'd never take a new job without discussing it with you in depth."

I shake my head. "You don't need to discuss this with me, Nor. We're just," I wave a hand awkwardly between us, "playing around, having fun. It's not serious."

He cocks his head to the side. "We both know that ain't really how it's working out though, don't we?" His expression is so assessing, so shrewd, I wonder if he can see right to the heart of me where those damn feelings are taking hold.

"I'm falling for you," he whispers, moving forward to hover his upper body over mine. "And I think you're feeling the same, Cath. Am I right?" He strokes big knuckles up my chest, then drags his fingers along my jawline.

In my mind, walls begin to snap up around my heart. I picture Wesley and the trust I had in him. He shattered it so completely, and I don't know if I can trust like that again.

"This'll work out how it's meant to, right?" It's all I can think to say as he reaches for my hand.

He gives a slow nod. "You didn't answer my question, Catherine." His crimson eyes focus on my mouth. "Am I wrong? If I am, you can tell me that, and I'll understand. I..." his voice trails off.

I can't find the words. If I admit them, a dam will break loose inside me, and I'll be overcome. So, I plaster a bright smile on my face. "We don't have to cover this now, Nor. Let's go to breakfast and the running of the bulls. I need a minute with this, okay?"

He sighs, his expression unreadable. After a moment, he rises from the bed. "Alright, but you know I wouldn't just *take* this role, right?"

"Okay," I agree as I slide off the bed and round him. "I'm going to shower and get ready, and then we can go, alright?"

He says nothing as I disappear into the bathroom. The moment I shut the door, I sink against it and to the floor as I try to collect my thoughts.

Manorin's quiet during breakfast. I try to enjoy Betty's famous roast beef breakfast sandwich, but Rip Shorthorn's sitting at the bar with Hadrian Alkazar—wining and dining him, no doubt—and Nor's a silent, frustrated-looking presence across the table from me.

Now that I've had a little time to sit with his big reveal, we should talk about it, but we obviously can't do that in public. Especially not with Rip sitting right there at the bar.

Nor looks over the table at me. "I'm kinda thinking we should head back to Ever, unless you want to stick around for the running of the bulls? And Amatheia might be disappointed if you don't sing karaoke. But..." He trails off. It's obvious he wants to talk about this too, but knows this isn't the right spot.

I fight back a frown. I want Annabelle and a quiet place to talk with Manorin.

"Can we go after breakfast?" It's all I can manage, but his quiet nod tells me he's feeling the same way. This whole situation, even this weekend, was always meant to be pure fun. The reality is, despite my best efforts, my long-dead feelings for him are back with a vengeance.

Knowing he's going to get the Pine Gulch job makes it feel

like I've already lost what I don't even have. I'm sick to my stomach over it, and I can't manage to eat, even though breakfast was my idea.

Eventually, Nor slaps money on the table and stands. He grabs my hand and pulls me to him, tucking a stray wave out of my face.

"Let's go pack," he says quietly, "and we're going to discuss this, Catherine. I won't have another meal where we don't talk."

I nod, glancing around at the overfull restaurant. Behind him, Alcazar and Rip Shorthorn are laughing over Bloody Marys.

I feel sick.

Rip Shorthorn's recruiting for Manorin to swoop in and take over a kick-ass team. Everything sucks, to use one of the triplets' phrases.

Nor sighs and pulls me toward the door. We remain silent all the way back to the room. But the moment he closes the door behind us, he hauls me up over his shoulder. Stalking to the bed, he lays me carefully against the pillows and climbs on top of me, sitting on his haunches. He reaches down and unties my wrap shirt, pulling it open to reveal my soft belly and breasts.

A rumble from deep in his chest stokes a fire inside me, even as misery does its best to douse it. He unbuttons his collared shirt and shucks it off his enormous shoulders, crimson eyes meeting mine. Tossing the shirt aside, he slides one arm under me and flips us, settling me splayed across him.

"That's better," he says with an appreciative smile. "When we fight, we should fight topless. Easier to make up."

"We're not fighting," I manage.

"We're not *not* fighting, either." One of his dark brows curls upward. "We're gonna get all of this out on the table now, Cath. We started this thing for the sex. We're adults; we knew what we were getting into. I won't speak for you, but it's not just sex for me. I'm in love with you. Again," he tacks on. "And based on how upset you seemed with the Rip Shorthorn news, I'm gonna guess you're feeling something like I am."

A muscle in his jaw works overtime as he glances away out the wall of windows. After a quiet moment, he looks back. "I don't want to assume that you're in love with me, but—"

"It's headed that way fast," I whisper.

A slow smile spreads over his face, lips curling to reveal his twin front fangs. "Cath, I..." His voice trails off as the grin grows wild and big. He slides both hands up my back and presses me to his chest. "Guess all that romancin' did you in, huh?"

I'm too worried about the Punishers job to say anything else.

When I remain quiet, he strokes my hair. "Nothing's set in stone, Cath, and I don't want to put expectations on you when we've been dating all of a week, but—"

"The Punishers is your dream job," I say miserably. "You've wanted to come back here your entire life. We can't ignore that."

"Yeah, and I've wanted *you* for just as long, you might remember."

"I don't want you to have to pick."

He grips the back of my neck. "You worried I won't pick you?"

I scoff. "No, I'm worried you'll pick me and be miserable because you could have been here..."

He sighs. "What'd I tell you about my priorities when we arrived, Sunshine?"

"I don't remember the order."

His low chuckle tells me he knows I'm lying. He lifts a finger. "You first. Extended family next. Job after that. I make my decisions based on that list of priorities."

"I'm trying to think about how I'd feel if you asked me to leave Annabelle," I admit. "Because I feel like that's what you'd be doing if you get the Punishers job and don't take it. You're giving up a centuries-long dream, Nor. It's not okay of me to ask you to do that."

He pulls me to his chest, wrapping his big arms around my entire body in a tight hug. His heart pounds loud and low, and I center on that, even as misery fills me. Maybe it's not misery. Maybe it's pure dread, knowing he'll be torn. I don't want that for him. He deserves the best of *everything.*

I don't feel any better by the time we get back home to Ever. Everything seems dim and muted under the weight of his impending offer. If I know anything it's that there isn't a better coach in the business. If Rip gave him a heads up, Nor's gonna get offered that job. I don't doubt it for a second.

When I broke things off with him all those years ago, I knew it was right at the time. But I've thought about him a lot since then. And now that we started up this no strings attached thing that immediately turned into feelings, I can't help but feel like us parting a second time just isn't *right.*

Not even Annabelle's friendly welcoming creaks and groans lift my spirits.

Manorin does his best to act normal, but I'm crushed regardless. He was right to tell me, I know that. But after last night, I was feeling so *good,* and now I feel like I've lost something I didn't know I had to have.

CHAPTER TWENTY

MANORIN

C atherine's been quiet since we returned to Ever. I don't know if she and Annabelle have talked, but even Annabelle seems quiet to me. Cath was busy all afternoon and evening catching up with the Hector triplets, who wanted to know all about our trip. It was hard dancing around the obvious misery in her manner.

She was slammed with guests all evening, but once they were taken care of, I pulled her into the kitchen and sat her on a barstool. After grabbing a water from the fridge, I set it in front of her. "Drink, Sunshine. You've been on your feet all day."

Her smile's half-hearted as she uncaps the bottle and sips delicately. I lean over the counter as the kitty cat timer flips head over tail and joins us, meowing softly. I pet the tiny cat on the head as I look at my Sunshine.

"The kitchen ain't the right place for this conversation, Cath, but we need to talk. I can't have you feeling some kind of way about this," I glance around to make sure nobody is nearby, "Punishers news."

She shrugs. "I honestly think I need to just sit with it a day.

That trip was a little more than I was planning for." It's on the tip of my tongue to suggest we go to her room and talk there, but she beats me to action. "Can we talk in the morning, Nor? I'm exhausted from getting caught up, and I need to get my thoughts together. I'm scattered at the moment."

I'm simultaneously frustrated not to have the important conversation and worried I don't have a good answer for her. Part of me feels uncertain, too. Back home, I said I was ready to drop everything for her—and I would, in a heartbeat—but I don't know if she feels pressured that I told her that. There's a lot of uncertainty, and I don't care for that.

She stands, water bottle in hand, and rounds the island. Popping onto her tiptoes, she kisses my muzzle inside the ring. I close my eyes to bask in the sensation of her so close, but before I can wrap an arm around her, she turns and heads for the archway toward the front of the inn.

When she's gone, I stand there for a while, considering what the right thing to do here is. Instinct tells me to go to her, but it also tells me not to push an important conversation when she's exhausted.

The timer mewls at me, nudging me with her tiny face.

"Sorry, sweetheart," I murmur, brushing her head with my fingertips. "I'm in a pickle with my Sunshine. Got any ideas about how to fix that?"

On cue, a cupboard flies open, and an unopened pack of sandpaper gets thrown out, landing on the countertop in front of me.

Laughing, I pick it up and shake it at the timer. "Shutters, hmm?"

The cat meows her assent as Annabelle rapid-fire opens and shuts the kitchen windows.

"I got you, sweet girl." This I can do to help Catherine. If I can take things off her to-do list, that's a start.

Heading for the front entry, I use my multitool to remove the closest shutter. Annabelle, helpful girl that she is, swings the second-floor shutters down for me. Placing each shutter on the white railing, I sand diligently until the shutters are ready for painting. It's awkward without a sawhorse to prop them on, but I do my best, and Annabelle creaks and groans the entire time.

It's like she's having an entire conversation with me, and somehow, I understand the vibes. She missed Catherine, and so she's nattering away like an excited child after a parent returns from a trip.

I chatter back to her about nothing in particular until I've got all the shutters sanded and primed. Patting Annabelle's siding, I laugh when she shimmies as if it tickles. The kitty cat timer sits on the railing and dings when I finish priming the last slat.

Exhaustion hits me as I drop my hand by my side. "I'm gonna hit the hay, Annabelle. You need anything else, pretty girl?"

She says nothing, but swings the front doors slowly open for me, inviting me back inside. The timer hops onto my open hand and rolls up my arm to my shoulder, tucking herself under my ear.

I head into the house and pause in the kitchen, setting the timer down on the countertop.

Making my way to my room, I read for hours, eventually falling into a fitful sleep in my chair. By the time I wake in the morning, I'm desperate to see my Sunshine. Glancing at my watch, I realize she'll be up shortly. A quick shower and fresh outfit later, I'm in the kitchen, stirring her coffee as I wait for her to show up.

The timer's busy trying to toss sugar cubes in my mug when Catherine appears by my side. She tsks as she grabs the cup of sugar cubes and shoves it to the far end of the counter.

"Annabelle, stop that, please. You already know how Nor like his coffee."

Sweet girl tosses a final sugar cube at me, but it bounces off my muzzle and lands on the counter. Picking it up, I toss it in my mouth as I wink at Catherine.

"Didn't say I hate sugar," I say, "just don't think the coffee needs it."

Catherine smiles up at me. "We had originally planned breakfast at the diner. Are you still down for that?"

I nod. "You wanna talk there?"

She shrugs. "There's a nice little booth to the back where we should have plenty of privacy, and I'm starving."

I put my hand on her arm, rubbing her soft skin as I admire the frilly sleeves of her form-fitting shirt.

She sinks closer to me, pressing her body to mine as she gazes up into my eyes. Pulling her flush with my chest, I sink a hand into her hair and hold her, her heartbeat steadying me. I've got a busy day ahead, but she centers me. Around us, Annabelle creaks and groans, but it sounds happy to me. The kitty cat timer pops up onto my shoulder and tucks herself under my ear with a tinny purr against my fur.

The moment stretches into long minutes where I simply hold her, this woman who's captured me so completely in mere days.

Eventually, the timer lets off a small ding next to my ear.

I reach up and grab her, setting her back down onto the counter. "Thank you, sweet thing. You're right, we've got a breakfast date."

Cath sighs as she pulls away from me and poofs her gray waves. I lean against the counter and stare, because I will never, ever get enough of looking at her.

"Mine," I whisper, my voice ragged as I move to pull her back into my arms.

Catherine's eyes flash golden for a moment, but she dances out of my reach. "Nor, you've got a jam-packed schedule today, and my stomach is rumbling."

"You know how to get me moving," I grouse. She knows her comfort is always top of mind for me. Can't do a thing until she's fed and full. Everything else comes after that.

I blow the kitty cat timer a kiss and tickle one of the cabinet doors on the way out. We pause by the front door and Catherine takes in the shutters, staring for a long moment before looking up at me.

"I can't believe she actually let you tackle this project. I've been trying for ages and she just wouldn't let me take the shutters down."

I wink. "She needed a man's touch, Sunshine. Like any good woman, sometimes she just wants that masculine energy. I'm sure you can empathize…"

Catherine loops her hand through my arm with a laugh as we head up Sycamore toward Main Street and the Galloping Green Bean.

As we near the diner doors, a deep voice shouts my name. Expecting one of the leadership monsters, or maybe a fan, I turn with a smile.

A gigantic green troll wearing aviator sunglasses jogs across Main Street toward us, wearing a big ole shit-eating smile. I refuse to lose the smile as he reaches out to shake my hand.

"Longhorn, good to see ya; it's been a while." Gil Stoneswallow's amber brows rise mischievously. "Think last time we met was that game in Brazil where I crushed the Hellions, right?"

I resist the urge to ask him what the fuck he's doing in Ever when I still have another two weeks of my trial period. There wasn't supposed to be overlap between us.

He removes his glasses, amber eyes dropping lasciviously down Catherine's lush figure. "I was coming to chat with Manorin, but who might you be?"

I'm about to verbally bitch-slap him for being rude when Arkan trots toward us and claps the troll on the back, interrupting what's about to be a tirade from me.

"Gil, you're here early." He glances at Catherine and me. "We weren't expecting your trial to start for another two weeks."

I glance at Catherine, who has a frown on her beautiful features. "Cath, this is Gil Stoneswallow from the Sao Paulo Silents."

She forces half a smile but doesn't reach for his hand. Instead, she glances at the big troll. "We weren't expecting you, Coach Stoneswallow. But I'm on the decision committee, so I'm sure we'll be meeting soon."

Stoneswallow's eyes drop to her hand tucked into the crook of my arm, and I do grin for real at that.

Looking to Arkan, I decide to let him handle this. It was his plan to bring Gil here, and he can deal with the brash, assholish young troll. "Keeper, this shouldn't change our schedule for today, but I assume you and Gil need to catch up. I'm taking Cath to breakfast, but let me know if you need me to amend any of the schedule for the next week."

Arkan nods, but he looks irritated as hells. Gil starts talking as I turn Catherine and grab the Green Bean's front door, pulling it open for her.

I'm a quietly seething mass until we're seated in a booth inside the Galloping Green Bean. Alba seats us and waits expectantly, and Cath looks up at her with a half smile.

"Give us five, friend?"

As Alba clip-clops away, I rub both hands over my eyes and down my snout in irritation, tugging at my nose ring. The pull centers me when I need to think. After a moment, I glance at Catherine.

"That was awkward," she says. "We were purposeful in not overlapping the two of you. How's that going to work with the exhibition game?"

"I don't know, but the nerve to show up early and unannounced. That kid's such an asshole," I hiss. "I hate him for Ever, and I hate the idea of him trying to build something here. He wouldn't know a good program from a hole in the damn ground." My nostrils flare. "Not to mention I was about to deck him for looking at you that way when Arkan trotted up."

"You'd have had to deck him after I did," she says with a wry laugh. "Arkan saved him by appearing."

We sit in uncomfortable silence for a moment. I lay a big arm along the back of the booth, looking across the table at her. "He staying with us?"

She shakes her head. "Thankfully, no. He opted for the wraith motel, last I heard. Although, I suppose his plans could change."

"The gods are smiling on us if he doesn't," I say. "The idea of him under Annabelle's roof makes me want to rip something in half."

She pokes at the menu on the tabletop. "Annabelle has strong opinions. If I don't like someone, or if she doesn't, she runs them off."

Manorin laughs, crimson eyes going wide. "Really? I'm surprised that's allowed to happen."

Cath shrugs, leaning over the booth to grin at me. "Well, she and I are in lockstep, and I'd rather a bad review than deal with a shit customer."

"Heard." I glance around, sucking at my teeth before returning to her with a frustrated look. Reaching across the table, I pull both of her hands into mine. "Why does it feel like everything suddenly got a lot harder? I'm sorry for that, Sunshine."

"We'll figure it out," she says. "It'll work out one way or another."

I sit back and cock my head to the side, staring quietly at her. "That belief in something working out is a very minotaur-like approach, Sunshine. I was serious last night and this morning when I shared my feelings. That hasn't changed."

She strokes my palm with the fingers of one hand. "I know. Me too. I just don't want you giving things up, Nor. Never." Her expression goes fierce. "Never, ever."

CHAPTER TWENTY-ONE

CATHERINE

L ater that afternoon, I'm in the kitchen baking pies to leave on the buffet when Manorin ducks into the kitchen.

"Hey, Sunshine, I've got Alkazar coming in so I can wine and dine him a little bit. Mind if I allow him into the kitchen for a little chat before I take him to dinner?"

My brows travel skyward. "Hadrian Alkazar? He's here?!"

He grins. "After we got back, I suggested he should come take a peek at Ever. Nice little haven, got a lot of promise. He could be the biggest of stars here versus trying to join a well-established team and maybe being the littlest fish in a new pond."

I snort out a laugh. "Alkazar's not going to be the littlest fish anywhere."

Manorin grins. "Well, he looks to me for guidance. I'm still his coach. And I think Ever could be a good fit based on what's important to him." His smile falls a little.

I wonder if he's thinking what I'm thinking, that Ever would be a good fit for himself too, depending on what thing is most important to him.

I am that thing, but I can't shake a terrible feeling about him giving up something important. To the point that I've wondered if I need to figure out how to dismantle Annabelle and move her. If that's even possible? I have no idea...but I'm actually considering it.

"Alright," he says cautiously, "I'm gonna pick him up at the portal station. Then I'll bring him back here for a quick chat. Need anything while I'm out?"

I shake my head. "All good here, thanks."

There's a tense, silent moment between us that threatens to stretch long. But Manorin gives me a final, cautious look, then turns to go. I slump onto one of the bar stools, but no sooner have I sat than Morgan Hector sashays into the kitchen with a wicked smile.

"Oh, Catherine, *Catherine*. You're gonna tell me everything, and you're gonna tell me right now."

I stare at my young friend. "What are you doing here?"

She points to the back door. "Manorin comm'd me that there's a tear in the screen from the last time Iggy flew through with the hellhound pups. He asked me to come by and fix that and," she reaches into her back pocket and pulls out a small slip of paper, "like six other little things? Apparently, they need doing."

My mouth drops open. He's fixing things around *my* inn just because they need to be done? The shutters were enough of a surprise but now this? I'm not even sure how to make sense of the emotions welling inside me.

"Cath?" Morgan's auburn brows form a vee, and she crosses the kitchen to me. "You okay? You look like you've seen a ghost."

The whole story spills out of me then. How Manorin and I had a wonderful time in Pine Gulch, the conversation with Rip Shorthorn, my desire for him to have what he wants, and my worry that he'll pick his home haven over me because he really *should*.

Because that's really it. I told him in no uncertain terms that I'd never leave Annabelle under any circumstances. I said that before we'd even been on a date.

But now? Now I'm less sure.

She listens in supportive silence until I'm done, and when I am, she smiles at me. "This is all gonna work out, Cath; I'm predicting it now."

"You don't have that power," I say with a sigh. "There's only one witch I know who does, and she hates your mother-in-law too much to live in the haven system."

Morgan wraps her arms around me, pulling me into a tight hug that steals my breath. "It's gonna be *fine*, Catherine, better than fine. He's *amazing*. A smart, driven, thoughtful gentleman, and you seem absolutely besotted with him. I have to believe it's your time for love, friend."

"That's what he says," I manage. "But if this were Abe, and his dream job was about to be offered to him, would you not feel guilty?"

Morgan steps back and barks out a laugh. "Hell no. He got me. What else could he possibly need?" She winks as I manage a laugh. "Not that we don't talk about possible jobs, and, anyhow, I wanted to chat with you about that, but we can table that for later."

Logically everything she's saying is true, and I know that. I've seen this situation in others' relationships many times over my long life. But I've never been in it myself, and it's terribly discomfiting.

Annabelle slings a bag of chocolate truffles out of the cupboard. The kitty cat timer hops over from the far edge of the island, nudging the bag toward Morgan and me.

When it gets close, she picks it up and examines its corner. "Aww, you're a little bit bent at the base. Shall I fix you?"

A happy little meow is her "please."

She closes her eyes, and I watch in amazement as the dings

and dents in the timer's base pop out and buff away. When she's done, she sets the cat down, good as new.

"Your magic is a wonder, Morgan." I smile. "I'd love for you to take care of the list Manorin gave you, if you don't mind. Also, can I see it?"

She smiles at me as she sets the slip of paper on the island. That done, she turns toward the back door.

I unfold the paper and recognize Nor's handwriting. It's as sharply angled and scribbly as ever. He's listed a solid six or eight things I've been meaning to ask Morgan about, but they were never huge and never seemed to bother Annabelle.

I don't get time to examine my thoughts about that, though, because a guest appears in the doorway with a question about restaurant recommendations, given the Green Bean's current wait time.

Half an hour later, I'm running around like a crazy person changing sheets and cleaning. I've got four check-outs and five check-ins this afternoon, and I am absolutely bonkers. Morgan called her sisters and their mates, and everyone's pitching in changing sheets, cleaning bathrooms, washing laundry and all the other myriad things that go into owning a bed and breakfast.

Even Betmal and Amatheia have joined us. Ama's washing sheets, and she and Betmal are remaking all the beds and helping to clean.

And it is exhausting. For the first time in a long time, I'm not having fun running Annabelle as a business. If I'm honest, I don't think she's having that much fun, either. The downstairs pipes over the check-in desk groan loudly every time the front door opens. I make a mental note to revisit temporary housing options with Arkan at my earliest convenience. Annabelle and I can't keep up with this pace.

When Manorin shows back up with Alkazar, everything stops as the triplets ooh and ahh over him. Manorin takes me to the side, stroking my cheek as he watches Betmal and Ama haul a pile of sheets upstairs, Wren right behind them with a basket of cleaning supplies.

"I hate that I can't help you right now."

"Kitchen's nice and clean, though," I say with a wink. "There's a nice big bowl of apples. Do what you need to do, Nor. I've got plenty of help, and we're nearly done. I do usually manage this on my own, you know."

He frowns. "But I don't want you to have to unless you're thoroughly enjoying yourself."

I snort out a laugh at that. Fun isn't what I'd call it.

I push Manorin toward the kitchen, smiling brightly at Alkazar, the handsome star skyball player. "There's tea and lemonade in the fridge, and I left fresh pie on the countertop. Help yourselves, alright?"

Alkazar smiles, white fangs flashing as he runs a hand tentatively through his dark hair. "Thank you, Miss Catherine. I've heard so much about the Annabelle and you over the years. It's lovely to finally meet her in person, and see you again, of course."

Gods, he's adorable.

"You too." I wink at him. "Maybe we'll see a lot more of you soon!"

He blushes, his cheeks going dark purple as he nods, then turns to follow Manorin to the kitchen.

It takes us another hour to get the inn in shape. The triplets and their mates leave, and it's finally quiet. I head for the back of the house, forgetting for a moment that Manorin and Alkazar are in the kitchen. Their deep voices stop me, and I halt, not wanting to disturb them.

"It's a lot to consider, son," Manorin says in a deep, comforting tone. "Gil's here, so I imagine you'll meet up with him too. He's got talent as a coach, I'll give him that, but his attitude's poor, and, ultimately, that'll reflect in the team's behavior.

You're a good kid, talented and easy to coach, but part of what you have to decide is if you're okay being aligned with a coach like that, if you come here, and he's offered this role. He's got a reputation now, and it'll only get worse unless he fundamentally changes."

"Yeah." Alkazar sighs. "You know it's always been my dream to play with the Punishers, but I don't have a huge desire to work with Rip Shorthorn. I love working with you, but I definitely don't want to stay at Hearth HQ. It's too dark and moody for me. I want friendly people, open sky, low-key, even if the skyball's wild and crazy."

I should stop listening, I really should, but I'm rapt waiting for Manorin's answer. Will he tell Alkazar about Rip's retirement? Somehow, I don't think he will. It's not his secret, and he's a vault when it comes to keeping secrets.

"Follow your heart, son," he finally says. "Take all the meetings, learn as much as you can, visit every haven that courts you. But make the decision for yourself; don't let other folks sway you. When I came here, even though we had a scheduled kickoff meeting, I came early and walked around to get a feel for Ever. I formed my opinion before the sales pitch started. Do that and trust your gut. You'll land where you're meant to be."

He pauses, and I hold my breath.

"Things work out exactly as they're supposed to."

I release the breath and step into the kitchen with a wave. "Sorry to interrupt, boys, I'm just grabbing something from the fridge, and I'll be outta your horns."

Manorin smirks as I cross to the fridge and grab the extra lemonade pitcher for the front buffet. He waves at me as he smiles. "I was just telling Catherine here the very same thing, as a matter of fact."

Alkazar spins on his seat, his expression earnest as purple eyes flick to mine. "Oh? Are you stuck with a big decision too, then?"

Oh, that bratty minotaur male. I set the lemonade down and give Alkazar an encouraging smile. "Just a matter of the heart. I think we make our fate, but Manorin's advice still holds true. Your heart will tell you when you've found the right place for you." I flick my gaze to Manorin's, but I can't read his expression.

"Well," Alkazar rises from the barstool and dips his head respectfully at me as he grabs Manorin's hand to shake, "I'm a little late for a meeting with Gil Stoneswallow, so I'm gonna go do that. See you around, Coach."

"Have fun, kid." That's all Manorin says, and he doesn't watch as the young skyball prodigy leaves the kitchen.

Silence stretches long between us as I smile at Manorin.

He rises from the barstool and rounds the island to lean against it. Putting a finger under my chin, he pushes up until I'm staring straight into those beautiful, dark eyes. The moments grow into a full minute, maybe two, maybe forty for all I know. I can't tell anymore because there's just Manorin's quiet dominance. After an eternity passes, he glances at the front of the inn, then back to me.

"Cath, there's something between us, something momentous. I know it. You know it. We admitted as much in Pine Gulch. But you've also got walls up around your heart because of my love for the Gulch. I'd never blame you for that, but are you gonna let them down and let me in? Because we both know you haven't done that, not really, not yet."

His words hurt, but he's not wrong.

"I want us to have our cake and eat it too," I admit.

He snorts and pulls me into his arms, grabbing my ass with both big hands. "I've got the cake, Cath, and I love eating it." He jerks his head toward the front of the house. "Let me take you to bed, pretty girl. Let me do something about that worried wrinkle between your beautiful brows."

When he puts it that way, I can't deny him. Calling my

power, I tug at his agency, leeching it from him as his gaze goes hazy.

He rumbles happily. "That's it, Sunshine. Take what you want…"

I slip from his embrace and grab his hand, pulling him up off the barstool. "As you wish, Mister Longhorn."

As he throws me over his shoulder and I command him to take me to my room, I realize I didn't really answer his question. I'm not even sure how to. I don't want him to feel like he's settling.

I just don't know what, exactly, to do about it.

CHAPTER TWENTY-TWO
MANORIN

"Gods, this town could be mine like *that*."

Gil Fucking Stoneswallow snaps his fingers as he flops into the seat opposite me at Higher Grounds.

"I will absolutely rule this place," he muses as he looks around at the busy coffee shop.

I sigh. "I'm waiting for someone, Gil, so that seat's taken."

He smiles and uses both forearms to lean onto the table with a wicked grin. "Arkan, I know. I saw him on the way here. He's gonna tell you about an idea I had, a coach-off, if you will. We're gonna host a game here in Ever, me against you."

I refuse to let shock show on my face. Instead, I sit back in my chair, steepling my fingers. "I'm coming to the end of my trial period. If that's what Arkan and the leadership team want to do with the rest of it, that's fine by me. We'd already planned an exhibition game, but I suppose we'll repurpose that?"

"I'll get Alkazar, of course. I bet he'll stick around for it." Gil says with a sneer. "You might coach him now, but it won't take much for me to get him."

He doesn't know shit about Alkazar—that much is clear—

because that kid is big and quiet, but he's also smart as a whip, and he sees right through assholes to the gross, gooey center. Off the skyball pitch, he gets underestimated a lot, but for being such a young, soft-spoken male, but he doesn't suffer fools.

Higher Grounds' door opens, and Arkan steps in, looking around until he sees us. His friendly smile becomes forced when he notices Gil sitting at the table. I stand to greet him like a fucking professional, and Gil remains in the seat I told him was taken.

When Arkan joins us, I smile. "Good to see ya this morning, Keeper. Gil was just leaving, as he's on your bench."

Gil snorts and stands just as Arkan opens his mouth to say something. Arkan shoots him an irritated look that Gil doesn't appear to notice.

"See ya, Boss," is all Gil says before he gives Arkan a mock salute and turns for the door.

I don't bother to watch him go, but I do level Arkan with a look as he settles down onto the curved centaur bench across from me. "If you hire that asshole instead of me, I'm gonna be offended, kid."

"He's worse than I thought," Arkan muses. "This morning, we had a check-in because he's asking the players to do practices, which, as you know, isn't really their thing. And I mentioned the exhibition game, which he somehow turned into a coach-off thing, and now it's his idea, and he's already bringing new life to our tired program." He gives me a displeased look. "His words, not mine." His expression's wry as he stares at me.

I pick up my black coffee and take a sip as I look at the young keeper. "You don't have to hire me, although I hope you will, but please don't hire him. Keep lookin'. If you end up not wanting me for this role, I can hand you a short list of qualified, excellent coaches. I don't know if any of them are looking, but…"

Arkan snorts. "It's not gonna be Gil if I have anything to say about it." He winks at me. "Plus, Catherine's got a pretty big say in it." His smile falls. "She's seemed a little morose since you returned from Pine Gulch. It's not my way to meddle super deep in monsters' business, but do I need to check in on her? Seems to me it might be between you two."

I suck at my teeth, staring around at the coffee shop. I can't share what Rip told me; it's not my secret to tell.

Returning my focus to Arkan, I opt for as much of the truth as I can share. "I'm being courted by another team on the down-low. I told her because I didn't want to hide it, but as you might imagine, it upset her. She really loves skyball," I tack on, unsure how much, if anything, she's shared with Arkan about our arrangement.

Arkan nods, glittering eyes scanning my face. "And you *have* to consider this other role?"

I'm straying close to dangerous territory.

"It's an excellent offer," is all I say.

"Well." Arkan grins at me. "I guess we'll just have to make you a better one, then. Let me know what you need to keep you here, Manorin, and if I can make it happen for you, I will."

I consider that as we talk through final logistics of the coach-off event. Catherine's with the Hector triplets all day, painting signs for the team and distributing them around downtown. Arkan and I talk through glamouring downtown to really bring the feeling of game day to Main Street and Shifter Hollow.

But my mind's never far from my Sunshine. If they give me this job, I'm taking it, and I need to remind her of that in no uncertain terms. Because, when I think about going home to the Gulch and coaching, I feel a mix of excitement and dread. I could come see her relatively easily, but it wouldn't be the same. A coach has to live in the haven they coach in.

My dream of going back home doesn't feel like it fits me

anymore. Losing a chance with her would devastate me more than anything else.

By the time Arkan and I finish our meeting and finalize the details, I'm ready to stampede through the door to get back to the Annabelle and level set with Cath.

When we leave the shop, Arkan's mate, Hana, stands outside. Her face lights up with a smile when she sees me. "Are you by chance headed back to the Annabelle?"

I nod, and she reaches down, slipping her hand through my elbow. "I'm gonna walk with you. Mate, I'll find you after, alright?"

I look between them. "Why does this feel like some sort of intervention?"

Arkan grins. "Okay, bye!" Turning, he clip-clops off toward Main Street.

Hana smiles over at me. "Mmm, not an intervention. More of a 'please don't leave us with that asshole, and please do make Catherine the happiest female alive by staying.'"

I laugh as we cross Main and head up Sycamore. Looking up at the young centaur, I give her a bemused look. "You know, this is a conversation for me to have with Catherine before I have it with the rest of town."

"I know," Hana says lightly. "I'm just here to reiterate that Ever loves you, the leadership team came around very quickly, and we're all in on a skyball program with you. But frankly," she looks around, "I told Arkan if he even thinks about hiring that asshat, I'm gonna divorce him."

"Harsh words from a species who usually mate for life." I grin up at her.

"I would rather be single," she says with a snort. "Being the Keeper's mate keeps me busy, so I can't play full-time. But I'd like to be considered for a backup, and I'd like to come to the practices."

And here's where things get a little tricky.

"I don't know if I can agree to that, Hana," I admit. "Even second-strings are full-time folks. They come to every practice, every meeting, every game."

"I'd have to be an exception to that rule," she says easily. "I'm just saying, if you're down to the dregs, and you need a girl to step in, let it be me!"

I snort out a laugh, the ring in my nose quivering. "The dregs. Gods help me, I hope we don't have any dregs on the team after I'm done recruiting."

Hana smiles as we continue past the Community Garden and take a right toward the Annabelle. "You haven't asked for my opinion, Manorin, but anyone with eyes can see the draw between you and Catherine. I'm as bossy as my husband is, maybe worse, so I say go for it, ya know? Get that love over the finish line, to use sports terms."

I groan. "Hana, that was the worst analogy I've ever heard. Stick to regular words, please."

She winks at me as we arrive at the Annabelle, who waggles her primed shutters. I take my leave of Hana and jog up the front steps, calling for Catherine.

Annabelle waves the stair runner, indicating I should head upstairs. Instinct tells me to follow her lead, and I do all the way to the third-floor attic that Catherine occupies.

When I knock, quiet footsteps let me know she's inside.

It shocks me how nerves fill me every time I get to see her. A few hours apart are enough to make me crave her presence.

She swings the door open with a paint brush in one hand, and I grip the frame as her scent wraps around me like a blanket and drags me toward her. She's drenching the air in pheromones. They practically drip like honey from her, reducing me to pure sensation and emotion as I stare deep into those gray eyes.

"I'm here to beg for the job," I manage, pushing into the room far enough to pull her curvaceous body against mine.

She spins and takes my hand, pulling me into the room as I stare in awe. Two entire walls are covered in paintings of Ever. Stacks of canvases lie everywhere, and open paint cans sit in a corner. A partially finished painting of the view from my property back home sits on an easel.

She leads me across the wood plank floor and runs her fingers over the dry paint. "You don't need to beg for the job, Nor. Come here. I was just reminiscing about the horses and your view, and I had to paint it. I had planned to gift it to you when, well—whenever, really. It's yours no matter what happens."

I slide one hand along her jaw to cradle the back of her head. "Offer me the job, Catherine, so I can take it and put your unease to rest." I back her against the bed and hover my mouth over hers. "Ask me now."

She stares up at me, gray eyes gone wide as her pretty bow mouth drops open.

"Ask me," I command.

"Manorin." She covers my hand with hers, pressing her cheek into my palm. "Shouldn't we take this slowly? You might not wa—"

I silence her with a press of my muzzle to her mouth. I've never wished more to be able to kiss her, but I'll settle for nipping softly at those beautiful lips.

I nip and bite at her mouth before moving to her neck and biting my way softly down it and along her collarbone. "Mine," I growl. "I need you to be mine, Cath. Mine, after so long."

"This is complicated," she says with a soft moan as I close my lips over her shoulder.

"It's not," I say. "I'll always love the Gulch, that's true, but I'll never want it like I want you."

She pushes away just far enough to look up into my eyes. "Can't we find a happy middle ground somewhere, Nor?"

"Don't care about that," I grumble as I press her down onto

the bed and climb over top of her, rocking my hips against her body. "I want you all in on this love, Sunshine. Because I'm all in on it. I don't want any part of you to hold back from me. I want you to love me the way you want to. Tell me you will."

Gray eyes flash with gold as she reaches up and slides her forefinger through my nose ring, holding me captive. "We have to be at Town Hall in an hour for a meeting about the proposed town expansion, and I need you before then."

"Whatever my Sunshine wants, she gets." I run a hand under her and turn her on her belly. "On your knees, female. I'm gonna mount you first, and then you're gonna ride me. I need you coming at least four or five times before you leave this bed."

She smiles up at me and flips onto her knees, casting me a wicked look over her shoulder as her eyes begin to gleam gold.

"Take what you want, Nor. Because all of this? It's yours."

"Perfect," I murmur as I dip low and rub my muzzle all over her ass. "Mine, Catherine. Repeat it after me."

"Yours, Nor. Always." Her voice is muffled as she lifts her ass high, rubbing it all over my face.

Heat shreds my sanity as I pull her pants down and off her legs, tossing them to the floor. Beautiful pink lace hides her pussy from me, and I press it to the side to lick her. The first taste of my woman fully banishes rational thought from my brain. I'm reduced to fire and need as I lap at her pussy lips, wetting her to prepare her for me. She soaks my tongue with honey as I gradually lose my godsdamned mind.

When she starts panting softly, I pull the panties down and throw them to the floor. I shift forward over top of her, notching myself at her entrance. Slipping slowly inside, I thrust with light, shallow moves, just enough to tease her.

And me.

Because the way her wet heat grips me has a desperate sound rumbling from my throat.

"Harder," she commands, her tone breathy and laced with need.

"You'll get that when I'm ready," I correct as I watch my cock disappear inside her slippery channel.

A little growl is the first hint at my woman's frustration. Catherine grips the sheets and uses them as leverage to push backward, impaling herself until nearly two thirds of my length is buried inside. She lets out a happy little mewl and rocks her hips as slick drips from her, covering me in that fucking scent I can't seem to get enough of.

"Sunshine," I warn, but she does it again. If I'm honest, I can't stop staring at where we connect, at the way her pussy gobbles up my cock like it can't get enough. Shifting up and back onto my heels, I watch as she takes what she wants from me. I'd intended to ravage her when I got here, but the way she takes charge has always been hot for me.

Her first orgasm surprises me, her channel clamping down and locking me inside her as fluttery waves pulsate against me. Cath arches and screams, thighs trembling. My eyes roll into my head as I allow myself to simply feel her, to experience her, the way she responds so beautifully to me.

As the orgasm fades, my need to dominate rises and I flip her onto her belly. With a quick thrust, I take her again, lifting one leg to drape it over my forearm. I grab her other knee with my left hand and push it out wide so I can watch every moment. I haven't come yet, and I won't until I drag at least one more orgasm from her.

Big breasts sway, their pink tips peaked and hard.

I meet her feral gaze. "Do you need my mouth, Sunshine? Do you want my tongue on those pretty rosy nipples?"

She shifts onto one elbow and runs a hand over her right breast, plucking the nipple until it stands tall.

It's all the invitation I need, so I lean forward and suck nearly her whole breast into my mouth, pulling hard as she whines and grips my left horn. Cath rolls her hips in time with me, and it's just moments before she comes again, thrusting fast and hard as orgasm builds in my sack.

When her orgasm stretches long, I can't hold back and I follow her into bliss. My roars of triumph echo off the ceiling beams as I take my woman a half dozen more times.

Even that won't fully sate her, not when her near depthless power needs so very much from me.

And that's just fine because there won't ever be a day when I'm not ready to fulfill every fucking need my Sunshine has.

～

Night stretches long as I hold Cath in my arms, stroking her naked back. To our left, a wall of windows lets faint moonlight in. Annabelle opens the center window with a soft, sad sigh. Somehow, despite not having the same obvious connection to her that Catherine does...I sense what she needs. My other girl needs attention that I've been promising.

Carefully, I tuck Catherine into the sheets, guiding her leg over a long body pillow I've noticed she uses. Gray waves are splayed over the pillow. Annabelle shuffles the blanket up and over Catherine, shimmying it until it's covering up to her chin. My woman looks so peaceful like this.

"I'm all yours, sweet girl," I quietly call to the windows as I grab jeans and slide them up my body. It's late and I'm gonna get dirty, so I opt to forego a shirt of any sort. Padding downstairs, I head toward the front door and out onto the porch. The shutters shimmy from their spots propped against Annabelle's white railing.

One of the porch boards pops up and rolls the closed can of paint toward my foot.

I laugh. Annabelle's insistent even when I've already made it clear I'm coming to help.

For the next few hours, I talk about Pine Gulch and my family, telling Annabelle little stories as I paint every shutter a brilliant white. Ever's quiet this late...not a single passerby in the street. It's a good thing, because this time with Annabelle is something I'll cherish.

As I brush a stroke onto the final shutter, Annabelle waves her front doors open wide, a soft rustling sound emitting from inside the building. I close the paint up and grab the brush, returning inside. A light flickers from the kitchen hallway, so I follow it to find the kitty cat timer propped up on the kitchen sink handle. It meows and hops up and down.

Annabelle might not have command of English, but she's communicative all the same. I turn the water on and wash the brush until it's free of paint, then sit it beside the kitchen to dry. The timer hops onto my forearm and rolls up toward my ear, nestling herself beneath it like she seems to enjoy.

I'd love to go snuggle Catherine, but I'm wide awake now. And somehow, a trip to the gym doesn't feel quite right. So instead, I make a steaming pot of coffee as the timer snores softly beneath my ear. Heading for the front porch once more, I ensconce myself in a rocking chair and sit in silence with Annabelle as the moon heads low and the sun slowly rises.

If I know one thing, it's this—Ever's starting to feel a lot like home.

CHAPTER TWENTY-THREE
CATHERINE

The next week passes in a blur with the Annabelle full to the brim with travelers coming to town for the coach-off. Apparently, Gil took it upon himself to take out ads in several haven newspapers to let monsters know to come to Ever for the game.

It's not ideal because we didn't prepare for a sudden influx of hundreds of monsters, and nothing's ready. We even had a scheduled meeting to vote on the new Ever team name and scrapped it because dealing with Gil is taking all of Arkan's free time...and then some.

The only silver lining is that it's highlighted just how important growing Ever's infrastructure is. Jezbelah, the manager of the wraith motel, has comm'd me several times about taking his overflow guests, but I have no room at all. I've heard a few monsters mention opening their homes to family and friends from other havens simply because there's nowhere else for them to stay. This morning, I saw a group of minotaur in the Community Garden in an efficient tent camp.

"Gil Stoneswallow is the worst idea I've ever had," Arkan grumbles as he helps me carry trays of breakfast quiche into the buffet in the dining room. We have to move half-finished exhibition game flyers to make room for the food. He doesn't even look to see if anyone's around to overhear the gripe.

"Lesson learned," I offer quietly as a shorthorn minotaur walks past the arched entryway and waves at me, headed for the front door. Looking back up at Arkan, I smile. "Let's get through this coach-off, and then we can reconvene about who we're offering the job to."

Arkan frowns. "Gods, is there even any doubt it's Manorin at this point? Although," he gives me an assessing look, "I'm not a hundred percent sure he'll take it. Are you?"

I shake my head. "I think he will. But we have to make our offer very attractive."

Arkan's typical smile finally returns. "Can I physically dangle you in front of him with a stack of cash and maybe a cute little home on the outskirts of town?"

Around us, Annabelle groans, the pipes shrieking at Arkan's suggestion. A terrible, tinny cat meow echoes from the kitchen.

Arkan's dark brows curl up. "Point taken, Annabelle. I rescind my comment."

I bark out a laugh as I set the quiche down on the buffet with a pair of serving forks.

"Speak of the devil." Arkan looks over my shoulder and breaks into a huge smile.

Manorin comes up behind me and bends low, pressing a half kiss to my shoulder. I risk a look up at Arkan, who's smiling down at us, black lips curling up at the corners.

Manorin slides a hand over my belly and curls his fingers around one of my soft rolls. "I managed to get a couple guys from the academy team back home to come join my side for the coach-off tomorrow, but it's gonna be a shit show with the rest of what I'm working with."

Arkan's smile turns wry. "Well, if it's any consolation, Ohken already told Gil to fuck off and refuses to play under his command. You can probably steal him, and he might demolish Gil for you on principle alone."

Laughing again, I shake my head. "That young troll has a lot to learn about leadership."

Manorin grumbles at my back, "Gil Stoneswallow wouldn't know leadership if it bit him in the ass. But he's got Alkazar, and that kid alone is deadly enough. Plus, he's trying to get recruited, so he'll give it his all."

"Well, Hana's gonna kick ass for you," Arkan says. "She's really damn good, as you know."

"I need a whole team of Hanas," Manorin says, sighing. He rubs my stomach softly, going quiet as he snuffles against the back of my head.

I sink against him and rub the arm around my belly as he lets out another beleaguered sigh.

"I've got to head to the stadium for practice. Depending on how that goes, I might be back late." He spins me in his arms. "Late dinner at Herschel's? I'll make us a reservation."

I rub his big chest, loving how solid he is beneath my hands. "Sounds great, but I'll call Herschel. You just focus on kicking Gil's ass, alright?"

He grins at me, dark brows arching high. I call my power, swirling gold into my irises to tease him, despite Arkan at my back. Manorin's lips twitch, nostrils flaring.

"Okay then, I'm gonna get out of your horns," Arkan says as he clip-clops toward the front door.

When I turn to say goodbye, he winks at me. "Don't forget to *dangle*, Cath."

Laughter erupts from me as Manorin looks between us.

"Dangle *what?*"

"Me," I manage with a laugh. "He wants me to dangle in front of you to convince you to stay here."

Manorin's smile goes more thoughtful. "I've gotta be offered the job, first, and I'd never want to assume it's a given."

I pop onto my tiptoes and grip him by the nose ring, ensuring he has to look at me. "The triplets and I are going around with Betmal, Ama, Iggy and the hellhound pups later today to pass out the rest of the signs. I didn't make any for Gil's team, so hear me on this, Coach: I am one hundred percent in your corner, okay?"

And I always will be.

CHAPTER TWENTY-FOUR
MANORIN

The day of the coach-off game, Ever's slammed. Every restaurant has lines out the door, and Main Street is flooded with monsters from dozens of other havens, thanks to Gil's meddling. Arkan glamoured downtown so everything is awash in the Misfits' green and gold hues. Flags hang from every possible surface and matching fireworks whiz pop off at random intervals.

It's honestly pretty damn festive and I love that. Not to mention, I'm relieved to see just how into skyball Ever got when given the chance.

Catherine and I sit in the Community Garden at the singular table, eating a delicious picnic she packed for us this morning. I had intended to take her out to breakfast before heading to the arena to meet the team and prep, but then Ohken paid us an early morning visit, demanding to be on my team to "crush the smirk off that fucking asshole's face."

My Sunshine elegantly bites into a cracker with jam-covered cheese, chewing thoughtfully. The jam covers a little of her top lip, so I reach over and brush it away, smiling.

"Come sit on my lap, Sunshine," I say, patting my thigh. "Let me lick that off you."

She opens her mouth to speak, but the sound of a throat clearing interrupts her.

When I turn, Hadrian Alkazar stands at the garden gate, thumbs tucked in the leather belt around his waist. His tail lashes slowly from side to side as he looks at me.

Catherine turns to look, then rests her hand over mine. "We'll pick this up later, okay? I think your busy day's about to start, Nor."

I frown as she stands and rounds the table, pressing a kiss to the end of my snout.

"Find you later," I promise as she plays with one of my ears, rubbing the inside of it as I resist the urge to demand she use it like a handle.

"You'd better." Her tone's light as she saturates the air between us with that gingerbread scent.

She turns to go, passing Alkazar, who inclines his head respectfully. When she's gone, he joins me at the table and sits, eyeing the feast in front of me.

"I'm sorry to interrupt you, Coach, but I needed to speak with you, and this is the only time we'll have before I leave after the game."

I sit forward and rest my forearms on the bench, clasping my hands together as I eye the young prodigy. "What's goin' on, kid?"

He sighs and looks into the distance, squinting.

It's bad news.

Fuck. "You picked a team. Who?"

He returns his gaze to me, his expression cautious. "Punishers. My family used to visit Pine Gulch every summer when I was a kid, and I love it there. My best friend lives there now. I've been leaning toward it, and even though I don't love the coach, I think I could still learn a lot from him."

I hold back a few choice words because I'd have really liked to get him here. "It's a good choice," I offer instead. "Ever'd be a good spot for you too. Were you torn at all?"

He looks around at the Community Garden but shakes his head. "Not really, Coach. I'm supposed to visit a couple more havens, but in my heart of hearts, it's always been the Gulch for me, if they'd have me."

I hold back a sigh. It's a major loss for Ever. And now I'm in a bad mood. The Punishers will be practically unstoppable with Alkazar on the team.

I smile at him. "You look like there's more. Spit it out, kid."

He sits up straighter. "I'm not gonna finish my last year at the academy. I'm moving over break."

Fuck. Fuck me. That's not great news. He's a huge part of my first string, although no team should rely wholly on one player. But it's a loss for the HQ team for sure.

"I know that's not what you want to hear." He sighs. "I didn't want to share this news prior to the game, but better to rip the Band-Aid off." He laughs a little. "That's a saying one of the humans here taught me."

I reach across the table to shake his hand. He takes mine and shakes vigorously, dark eyes glittering.

"Congratulations, kid. I can't wait to see what the Punishers do with you on the front lines."

He winks. "Well, and I mean this in the most respectful way possible, Coach, but I hope I kick your ass, wherever you land." He looks around at the Community Garden again. "This is a beautiful little haven. Diverse, comfy, kind, feels like very little interference from HQ. But I miss the wide-open spaces. I need to look out my window and see…nothing. Sunset and wheat fields."

His words rip a hole in my heart. He's saying the same thing I've always felt about home. Yet when I think about leaving

Catherine and Annabelle behind, the hole grows bigger until I'm nearly choked with anxiety over it.

Alkazar stands and claps me on the shoulder. "I'm gonna head to the stadium. I see I interrupted your breakfast, but can I help you clean this up?"

I stand and start grabbing food, putting it back in the picnic basket. "I've got it, kid. Head over and get your head in the game."

He laughs. "You sure you don't want me to throw it a little? Gil Stoneswallow is a grade-A jackass."

I level him with a serious look. "Never tone yourself down for anyone, Hadrian. Not your Coach, not your team, not your family, not your future mate. Be you, and the right ones will stick by your side. If you learn only one thing from your time with me, let that be it."

"Heard, Coach," he says softly, shuffling the big leathery wings at his back. "You look really happy with her, by the way." His blush grows darker. "I hope that's okay to say. We don't usually get into matters of the heart." He rubs at his chest where his own heart will be silent until he finds a mate.

"I am," I confirm, a grin overtaking me. "I'm... She's everything I could ever want."

I lose track of enough words to explain what Cath means to me, but Hadrian flares his wings with a little chuckle. He smiles at me for another moment, then pushes off the ground and beats up into the sky, flying toward the skyball stadium.

When I think about him moving to Pine Gulch, everything inside me clenches with frustration. That desire to be around the people I grew up with, in the spaces I grew up in. I want it so badly, I can taste it. But a stronger part of me knows I can't lose my Sunshine. I lost her once, and it killed me. It's my biggest regret in life.

I refuse to have that regret twice. Even if I don't get the Ever job, I'm moving.

But I need to set all of that aside right now and focus on fucking Gil Stoneswallow up.

~

Six hours later, I'm standing in the middle of the skyball field with my team at my back, staring at Gil Stoneswallow as he raises the roof with both hands, trying to get the crowd to scream louder. It's already loud as fuck in here. The stadium's packed, every seat filled. I didn't anticipate this. This was only meant to be an exhibition game, not this public fucking spectacle Gil's turned it into. If Hearth HQ wasn't hearing through the grapevine about my coming here, they'll know now.

Not that it matters, because after this, I'm resigning and moving.

I'm already in a bad mood, but as the ref tells us to split to our sides, I hear Gil tell one of the guys he brought in to play dirty. It takes everything in me not to cause a scene. Instead, I return to the bench and approach Hana and Ohken. Popping a squat, I look between them.

"Gil's told his team to play dirty. I know Alkazar and the other gargoyle well enough to guarantee they won't do that no matter what Stoneswallow says. But keep an eye out for everyone else. You two are my defense. Try not to let anyone get hurt, alright?"

"That motherfucker," Hana hisses, crossing her arms. "I hate him so much." She immediately blanches. "I suppose I shouldn't be saying that, as we're technically interviewing him."

Ohken lets out an irritated growl. "If you hire that asshole, I'm taking my mate, and we're moving." I sense he's at least partially kidding, but I level him with a concerned look.

Standing, I clap my hands together, gathering the rest of the team's attention.

"Do your best out there, folks, and that's all I can ask. Keep an eye out for any bullshit. We're keeping everything legal here today, alright?"

Nods and murmurs of assent reach me. I've got a solid team, and I called in some favors, bringing a couple of the Protector Academy players in.

Yet, forty minutes later, I'm staring at three benched monsters with injuries and a scoreboard with a big fat zero under my team's colors. Hana stands by my side, chest heaving as we watch yet another play where the ref seems to ignore the fact that Gil's players are playing dirty as fuck. She scoffs as one of the other team's players trips Ohken, who stumbles to the ground with a big thump.

Alkazar frowns as the centaur canters off, waving his hands victoriously in the air.

Hadrian pauses and reaches a hand out for Ohken, helping him up. They exchange words I can't hear, and Ohken nods, then turns for the bench. He's bleeding from both knees and a gash above his lip.

Fuck.

I catch the ref's eyes and crook my finger for him to come over.

The big pixie male blushes but jogs toward me as Stoneswallow watches us. I meet the ref on the field, crossing my arms as I dip low. "The fuck is going on here? I've got four injured players and not a single flag thrown in the first half."

The ref looks up, red dusting his cheeks. "Are you accusing me of not doing my job?"

I scowl. This isn't a real game, so there's no ruling party for me to take this behavior up with, not that it would stop me from reporting him. This dipshit doesn't matter.

"You're either blind or willfully ignorant. Which is it, hmm?"

The crowd starts chanting for the game to begin again, but all I can think about is this clusterfuck.

The ref blusters. "What in the...I would never!"

"I'm glad to hear that," I bark out. "If you don't throw a flag next time one of these motherfuckers tries something, I'll see to it that your coaching card's not renewed. I can do it, too. Good buddy of mine runs the renewal program."

The pixie stands, gobsmacked, as blue wings flutter wildly at his back. "You...wouldn't."

I snort. "Watch me."

Point made, I stalk back to my team where Hana's patching up Ohken's injuries, wrapping his knee in a thick white bandage. He glares down the field at the ref.

The game starts again with the crowd going wild. If I can say just one positive thing about this game—it's clear the Evertons are thrilled about having skyball. They're a fantastic crowd and it's about the only thing keeping my players going when the ref ignores foul play after foul play.

We rally in the second half and manage to lose by a single point to Gil's team. The crowd floods the field after the game's done, but all I want is to make sure my folks are taken care of and then bury myself in my woman and forget this day. I can take a loss but a dirty loss sucks.

I comm her as we trudge toward the locker room. "Sunshine, meet me in the locker room, alright?"

"Be there shortly," she chirps. Despite our loss, she doesn't sound as disappointed as I feel in that damn game.

"Longhorn."

I freeze as the players continue on past me toward the locker room.

When I turn, Rip Shorthorn stands at the entrance to the lower hallways, a wry look on his wrinkled face. "You got a second, old friend?"

My mouth goes dry, but I return to him and shake his proffered hand. "Didn't expect you here, Rip."

He shrugs and offers a soft smile. "Wanted to see Alkazar

play one more time. It's such a pleasure to watch that kid. He's a damn pro through and through." He winks at me. "Pretty excited I got him for the Gulch. Not an offensive line in the business that can beat mine now."

I groan. "Don't rub it in."

He sucks at his teeth and looks at the field, seeming to consider something. When he turns back to me, I know what he'll say before he says it.

"I've officially resigned, Manorin. It'll go public next week, and Alkazar knows. I was up front with him and told him I wanted you for the role. Town leadership's putting together an offer for you. It'll be generous. I told them whatever they were thinking...double it to get you."

He looks at me as I stand there, dread filling me.

Realization drifts through his eyes. "Oh. You don't know that you'll take the job, do you?"

"No," is all I can manage. "It's complicated here."

He lifts his chin slightly, eyes scanning my face. "That pretty little succubus got something to do with it?"

I nod, running both hands through my hair. "She has everything to do with it."

He gives me an understanding smile as he slips his big hands into his pockets. "Well, I can't give you any advice you don't already know, old friend. You'll get a beyond attractive offer from us in the next day or so. I imagine Ever's gonna make you one too. You'll make the right decision...I know you will."

That said, he turns and disappears toward the stands where other monsters are still leaving.

I turn and sink against the wall, groaning. It's shitty poor timing for my career aspirations to finally align and be so at odds with my personal life. I'd bet a thousand bucks Hadrian took that job assuming I was headed there.

Irritated, I cast that aside. I've got to take care of my team because that game kicked our asses.

CHAPTER TWENTY-FIVE
CATHERINE

Normally, I adore skyball. And while the crowd was insane over the game, I recognize poor sportsmanship when I see it. I can't imagine how frustrated Manorin likely is. When he asked me to come to the locker room, I sensed it in his tone.

I pass Gil Stoneswallow with a gaggle of female monsters surrounding him, peppering him with questions. He catches my eye and waves, but all I can manage is a quick purse of the lips as I skirt past the group. I run right into another monster in my haste to get out of Gil's view.

"Oh my word, my apologies," I manage as I bounce off the bigger-bodied male and try to right myself.

"No worries, Catherine."

My mouth drops open as I look up into Rip Shorthorn's ruggedly handsome face. He winks. "Quite a game, huh?"

"What are you doing here?" I blurt out. But I already know.

"Came to see Hadrian play." He gives me a cagey look. We both know that's not entirely true.

Oh shit. Oh shiiiit.

I clear my throat. "Alkazar played a professional game. He's a good kid."

Rip smiles. "He is." He glances behind me toward the busy hallway. "Well, I'm goin', Catherine. Have a good one."

"You too," I manage as he strides past me. My chest heaves with tight anxiety. He was here for Nor, I know he was. Which means he's retiring and making sure Nor gets offered that job.

Anxiety piles on until I have to suck in great gaping breaths to fill my lungs. I tuck my Ever Misfits sign under my arm and lean against the wall as I think about workarounds and alternatives and any possible future that would easily allow us to both have our dreams.

Heading into the depths of the stadium, I find the locker room assigned to Manorin's team. His deep voice echoes from the inside.

Pushing the door open, I find Ohken standing there leaning against the wall with an ice pack strapped to one big thigh. He shoots me a quick smile as I enter the space, sliding my arm around his waist. He puts an arm around my shoulder as we look into the packed locker room. Every player is here, staring at Manorin at the front of the room.

Manorin stands there with a half smile on his face, both hands slung low in the pockets of his athletic shorts. His whistle hangs between both pecs, glinting in the room's low light as he looks around, capturing each player's attention.

"I am incredibly *proud* of each of you," he says. "That was a rough game, and not because of this team. You persevered through a metric assload of bullshit from the other team. You could have stooped to their level and you didn't." He pauses, looking around. "It's rare that I'm proud of a loss, but I'm proud of that one. I don't wanna win if that's what we have to do to secure it."

Murmurs of assent rise from the group.

He nods. "Most of you aren't full-timers, either, and it means a lot to me that you gave it your all today regardless of your skyball dreams. Thank you, from the bottom of my heart." He looks at Ohken and dips his head respectfully.

A beat of silence becomes two, then three.

The players stare raptly at Manorin.

He smiles, removing his hands from his pockets and lifting them. "Another huge thanks to my academy friends for coming to support. I don't know what'll happen tomorrow or the next day, but this opportunity to be part of the Ever Misfits has been an absolute highlight for me. Thank you, Evertons, for being so welcoming. Hope you keep me around." He winks, and shouting and whooping rises from the crowd.

The happy noises echo off the ceiling as the players stand and one by one greet Manorin with hugs and handshakes. They begin to dissipate after that, and I stand by the door, watching as he does the post-game wrap-up.

It irks me for the other team that Gil didn't seem to do anything like this. I don't use a lot of curse words, but that male is an absolute dickhead.

As the players filter out, Manorin comes to me and pulls me into his arms, resting his forehead against mine. "What a shit-show," he murmurs, his nose ring jiggling against my chin.

He slides his hand up the front of my throat and grips it lightly, a deep sigh leaving him. "Missed you the entire time."

I brush my fingertips along his tapered ears. "Well, the good news is that if anybody here *wanted* to hire Gil, I'm pretty sure he ruined any chance of being Ever's pick."

I mean the comment in a lighthearted tone, but Manorin grumbles anyhow. "The day I miss out on a job opportunity to a jackass like that is the day I've truly lost my mojo."

I can't think of anything to say to that. I want to mention that I saw Rip Shorthorn, but I don't know—

"Shorthorn's here," Manorin says softly, parting from me but pulling me toward one of the benches. He straddles it and sits me across from him, pulling my thighs over his and holding me steady against him. "Offered me the Punishers job. He's officially retiring soon."

Dread fills me so fast, I choke on it, sputtering as I attempt to drum up an answer that sounds supportive. I knew when I saw him, but to hear Nor say it…

"I know," Manorin says with a heavy sigh. "I think part of me was pretty sure he was kidding when he mentioned retiring." Crimson eyes come to mine.

"Do you have an offer?" It's all I can manage.

"Forthcoming," he says with a grumble.

I roll my shoulders, trying to center myself as I consider what this means. Can I ask him to stay for me? Should I? Could I forgive myself if I asked him to do that, knowing he wants to be in Pine Gulch?

He strokes my hair over my shoulder. "I'm not taking that job, Sunshine. I can't lose you. I won't. Not this time."

Hope fills me right along with the dread and upset. "This is your dream job, Nor."

"It's not the job, really," he says. "That program's rock solid and built. What originally interested me about Ever was building from the ground up. The main thing attracting me to PG at this point is just that it's home." His eyes go soft at the edges. "But it won't feel like home to me without you. I love you to the ends of this world, Catherine. I'm staying right here with you."

I press myself against him, brushing his snout with my nose as I stare up into those dark eyes. "I love you too, harder and faster and deeper than I could have imagined loving someone."

He beams at me. "Good. 'Cause you're stuck with me, Sunshine. And you better give me the Ever job because I'm not ready to be retired."

I laugh. We both know he's got that job locked and loaded.

But as he dips me backward and kisses down the front of my neck, discomfort niggles its way through my mind.

He's giving something up to be with me, something he's wanted for his entire life.

I just can't have that, not at all.

I have to find a way to fix this for him.

I want his dreams to come true. I know I'm one of them, but it's not enough. Not for me. I will fix this...somehow.

His comm watch rings just as he tugs my tee down and closes his mouth over my peaked nipple.

Manorin growls and rights us, staring at the blue leather band around his sizable wrist. His brother's name hovers above it, flashing incessantly as he groans and wipes a big hand over his face.

"We aren't catching a break today, Sunshine."

When he directs the comm watch to answer, his brother launches right into a story about his nephew, Alarion, and some trouble with the gargoyle sheriff. I don't follow the entire thing because his brother speaks in shrieking, run-on sentences that don't make any sense to me. But Manorin seems to follow, his expression darkening by the minute.

By the end of the call, he's tense and tight in my arms.

"I'll be there in a bit, brother. Calm down."

"Just get home!" his brother shouts. "Before Rygold kills Alarion!"

"He's not gonna kill Alarion," Manorin rumbles, "but I'm on my way."

The brother hangs up without saying goodbye, and Manorin sighs. "Gonna have to rain-check that dinner, Cath. I'm so sorry."

I tickle my fingers along his jawline, admiring the strength of it. "Crazy as Alarion's antics seem to be, he's family. I'll be here when you get back."

He smiles, even though there's tension in it. "Because you love me?"

That pulls a smile to my face. "Because I love you."

I have to find a way to fix things for him. I want to keep him, and I don't want him to give up a single thing for our happiness.

Even as I think that, an idea starts to form in my mind, bits and pieces of info swirling into a slowly forming picture. When I get home, I'm calling Betmal. He might be just the monster for what I need.

CHAPTER TWENTY-SIX

MANORIN

"Thanks, Uncle Nor," Alarion says quietly as we cross the Grand Portal Station from the Pine Gulch portal.

I sling an arm around my nephew's shoulders, crushing him to me as I focus on just getting home. What an absolute shit show of a morning.

"Ever's a great little spot, kid. And I think it'll do you good to be away from the Sidewinders crew for a bit."

He sighs as the Ever portal comes into view at the far end of the station. "I thought those dudes were my friends, Uncle Nor. They've been like family to me since Mama died, and I needed that. But they were just using me, it turns out. I was just a pawn to them, something to use to,"—he lets out an angry growl, shaking his head as he runs a big hand along his right horn—"it doesn't matter."

I didn't expect to have to bust into the Sidewinders clubhouse this morning and practically trash the whole thing to get Alarion out. I also didn't expect Bishop Rygold to swoop in after me and drag half the ophiotaurii out by the horns to toss 'em in the PG jailhouse.

But that's what we did, and I'd do it again if I had to.

"I'm surprised Rygold let you take me," he says, halting in front of the final portal.

I turn to him and level him with a serious look. "He knew you were on the verge of makin' the type of mistakes a male can't come back from, Alarion. There reaches a point of no return, and you were there, kid."

His chocolate brows furrow, then the frustrated expression falls, and he looks pained. I wait to see if he wants to expand on his thoughts—we've been talking all morning—but he falls silent.

"We got a lot of conversations ahead of us, kid, but things are gonna be fine. I'm here for you, okay?"

He nods as we head for the portal.

As I step out into Ever's portal station on the other side, I wipe a hand over my face. At my side, Alarion's golden eyes are wide as he takes in the Ever portal station. He's never left Pine Gulch, and it took me the better part of the morning to convince him to come back to Ever with me.

My brother, Walter, declined to join us, but I know Alarion's relieved to be out of PG and the crowd he'd gotten into there. Of course, I'll have to make sure he doesn't bring any of that bullshit with him to Ever. Thank the gods there aren't cattle here *to* rustle.

I drop him at Hel Motel with an Ever welcome book and a promise to take him to breakfast in the morning. Jezbelah, the wraith manager, offers to take Alarion to his room.

My nephew turns to go and I note the slump of his shoulders and the near droop of his horns.

"Everything's gonna be fine, son," I say to his retreating back.

He pauses and turns to look at me over his shoulder. "Thanks Uncle Nor. I'll meet you at the diner in the morning, if that's alright?"

"Comm me any time, even if it's just to talk." Striding

forward, I clap him on the shoulder, then grip the muscle hard as I stare into pale blue eyes. "Love you, kid. I mean it when I say this town is a good place for a fresh start."

He huffs quietly, the gold ring in his nose shimmying. "That what you're doin' here?"

His question pulls a smile to my face.

"Yeah." The smile grows into a broad grin when I think about Annabelle and my Sunshine. "That's exactly what I'm doin' and I'm glad you're here to bear witness to it. Maybe we'll even get your ornery father out this way sometime soon."

Alarion chuckles and shakes his head. "Don't think you'll ever get Dad outta the Gulch, but I guess we'll see." His expression goes thoughtful. "Maybe he'll visit."

We fall quiet as Jezbelah pokes his head around the corner, waving to Alarion.

"Arrrrreee you commmmingggg?"

Alarion hikes his bag high on his shoulder and disappears into the darkness of the wraith motel's opulent first floor hall. I watch him go, sending up a quick prayer to the minotaur gods and goddesses for peace and happiness to come to my nephew.

Then I head for the Annabelle. I've barely talked to my Sunshine in the last two days, and I'm anxious to get to her. I walk Main Street, considering the formal offers of employment in my inbox from both Pine Gulch and the town of Ever. Despite dealing with Alarion, I thought about the offers situation a lot while I was home.

In a way, going home was a good thing, because everywhere I turned, I saw PG in a new light—little views I wanted to show Cath, things like that—and not experiencing it with her made it all a little bittersweet. Home wasn't home for the first time.

There was never any doubt for me that I'd pick her, but going back reminded me that it never *was* the same after she and I split. Home always held a little bit of heartbreak because she never saw it with me. Never saw the land I bought us or the statues I erected to honor longhorn ancestors.

Which, I think, is why I didn't get back home that much to begin with. I love Pine Gulch. But Catherine has my heart and soul.

Friendly Evertons wave at me as I walk up the street. The sun'll be setting soon, and all I want is to hold her in my arms in her room.

When the Annabelle comes into view and I moo to greet her, all the shutters wave in frantic excitement. Her pretty pink siding ripples in great waves as all the windows on the front of the house open and shut in a rapid melody. She reminds me of a dog spinning in circles when its owner returns home.

"Darling," I murmur, stroking the front doors as she opens them for me. "Where's my Sunshine?"

Catherine emerges from behind the check-in counter, wearing a simple shirt dress that hits mid-thigh. I sigh and lean against the door frame as she walks toward me, nails painted a viciously bright red.

"Damn, Sunshine. You keep wearing outfits like this, and you might give me a heart attack." I eat up her long legs, staring at thick thighs and a soft belly I love to kiss. The dress's fabric clings to her heavy breasts, highlighting every luscious, over-sized curve.

"I have something for you. Come upstairs with me?" She waves a hand toward the stairs as Annabelle ripples the carpet runner to direct us.

I take her hand and spin her around, running an appreciative palm over the soft globes of her ass, then up her belly and over a breast. Trailing my knuckles along her nipple, I grin when it peaks and hardens beneath the velvety fabric. She drenches the air in pheromones, her body calling mine in the most primal of ways.

"Two days is two more than I ever want to be parted from you," I manage as she tugs me toward the stairs.

She smiles, the expression genuine and welcoming and so tender.

I shoo her toward the stairs but pause at the bottom. "Go on up, Sunshine. I'll be behind you. Just wanna enjoy the view a bit."

She winks over her shoulder and sashays up the steps, every footfall giving me a better view up her skirt. By the time she reaches the top, I'm adjusting my aching cock and staring at the bottommost swell of her luscious ass.

"I missed you like crazy, woman." I grip the banister and the railing and lean forward, staring at her like a male starved. I suppose I *have* been starved all these years, trying to find someone that feels as right as Catherine.

"I missed you more," she says in a playfully challenging tone, her eyes swirling with gold. "I said I have a present for you, and I'm absolutely desperate to deliver it. So please come to my room, Mister Longhorn."

"Better be you sitting on my face," I growl as I stalk up after her.

She tosses her gray waves over her shoulder and winks back at me. "Oh, it'll end there, Manorin. I've no doubt about that."

Speeding up, I swoop her into my arms and carry her up the final few stairs, down the long hall and up the next set to her room. Annabelle, that darling girl, swings the door open for us so I can sail through.

I head for the bed, and Catherine laughs as I drop her into it and fall on top of her, bracketing her between my arms so I can stare. "You look so fucking pretty in this bed," I muse as I lift one hand to run it over her breast, pinching the nipple until it peaks high. "Look at you, Cath. You smell needy, woman. Tell me how you pleased yourself while I was gone."

She lifts her chin in playful defiance. "I didn't. I saved all that pleasure and desire for your return. I was quite busy with my gift."

I bend low and nuzzle at her breasts, wanting to rip the dress from her but not wanting to ruin it if it's a favorite of hers.

"Get naked, woman."

"Not yet, Nor. The present, remember?"

I sigh and sit up, pulling her upright with me. Slipping both hands into her hair, I bring my forehead to hers and close my eyes, breathing her in. That sweet, sugary gingerbread scent is home. Her heart beats slowly, steadily as I consider the path that led me back to her after so long apart.

She's quiet, stroking my ears and the side of my neck before moving to my horns. As she touches them, I shudder and sink harder against her.

"How was it being home?" Her tone is curious but cautious.

"Miserable without you," I admit. "I want you to get to know PG, but on our terms. Not because I ripped you away from everything you love."

Around us, Annabelle lets out a miserable-sounding groan, the pipes in the floor creaking as she shudders and shrieks.

"Easy, sweetheart," I caution her. "I would *never*. Age brought me the wisdom to know my place is here with my girls, building something new with you both."

Catherine squirms out of my grip and backs across the room, beckoning me with a crook of the finger. I slide off the bed and follow, thinking about how I want to press her to the window and sit her on my muzzle to do naughty, naughty things.

"I scent your need, mate," she whispers, "but I promise you'll want to see this."

Shock and pride course through me in equal measure, forcing me to halt in place.

"You called me mate," I manage.

She plants both hands on her hips, a dark brow quirking upward. "Are you not?"

I'm across the room before I consciously think about moving, hauling her into my arms and pressing her to the far wall. It's covered with a large velvet curtain, and she—

"Stop, Nor," she commands, eyes swirling with gold. "Or I'll be forced to stop you. I want to give you my damn present."

"You called me mate," I practically whine. "I need to touch you, Cath, to show you how much it means to me that you called me that."

Annabelle creaks and groans, and Cath cocks her head to the side. Like every time she and the inn communicate, it amazes me how they seem to have their own language. "Okay, darling girl. You first." She looks quizzically at me. "Annabelle has something for you too."

Surprised, I lean against the closest wall and wait to see what happens.

A creak across the room draws my attention. A giant ceiling beam creaks, and then a tiny door opens, and something drops onto the floor, disappearing behind the bed. Cath and I watch as the whitewashed floorboards ripple, tumbling something small toward us. A second item drops out of the hole in the beam, and the kitty cat timer meows as she gets tumbled to meet up with the first thing.

Annabelle tosses both items to me with a quick flip of the closest floorboard. I catch them easily, the timer leaping up onto my shoulder and tucking under my ear with a happy purr. Cath presses closer as I open my hand to reveal whatever Annabelle brought me.

It's a heart. A wooden heart. It's made of dozens of small pieces that look like Annabelle's siding. They're every shade of pale pink and a few white, too. The heart fills my palm but weighs almost nothing.

But I can't find my breath as shock and love courses through me in equal measure.

"Oh Annabelle..." Catherine's hand trembles as she lifts it to cover her mouth. Her eyes fill with tears as I struggle to pull breath into my lungs.

"Annabelle," I manage, my voice wavering as I lift the heart to my chest.

Tears stream down Catherine's face as they well in my eyes. I press a hand to the wall, clutching the heart to my chest. "This is a gift beyond measure." I curl my fingers into the wooden wall as Annabelle rumbles and flutters everything around us.

I risk a look at Catherine, who's wiping tears away. "Did you two plan this?" It's all I can manage as she shakes her head.

"I had no idea," she says, her voice shaky as she swipes at the still falling tears.

"We love you," I say to the inn. "Forever and always, Annabelle. You're my best girl, right?"

The timer mewls in my ear, rubbing against the underside of it.

Catherine dabs at her eyes. "Okay, my turn! I can't wait any longer."

I hold Annabelle's heart to mine as Catherine backs into my arms. With her free hand, she grabs the velvet curtain and shoves it aside to reveal an incredible painting of my view back home at the Pine Gulch property.

"I painted this for you." She takes our joined hands and places them on the intricate strokes. "Pine Gulch will always be a part of us, and I want you to feel that every minute of every day. It means the world to me that you're building something with me in Ever, but I don't want that to mean you're giving *anything* up, Nor."

She rests her head against my chest and looks up at me. "This isn't all, though."

I'm too overwhelmed by the incredible painting to fully

process it when she moves her hand from mine and electricity begins to crackle in the air. She grabs a paint brush from a nearby jar of water and dips it in black paint, then begins to paint a circle on the wall. It's on the tip of my tongue to tell her not to ruin her incredible painting, but her magic stands all my hair on end, halting the words.

I've seen her succubus power to beguile many times over the years, but this is different.

This is *that* magic—the magic that built the system that protects monsterkind from the outside human world.

My heart speeds up at the surprise of it.

Catherine's paintbrush shimmers and morphs, almost seeming to become one with the painting, flattening and turning three-dimensional once more. The art itself begins to shimmer and writhe, the entire wall twisting and curling and snapping as electricity rends the air. She remains with her back to my chest, painting and swirling as tiny green sparks fly from the tip of her brush, skirting along the painting, following the lines of her strokes until—SNAP!

With a great crack, the paintbrush becomes a flat part of the painting, and it's as if I'm staring at Pine Gulch itself.

Catherine spins in my arms. "This is a little something from me to you, mate. C'mon." She turns again, takes my hand, and steps forward, disappearing into the brushstrokes.

CHAPTER TWENTY-SEVEN

CATHERINE

I step through the newly created portal, my shoes crunching on the tiny pebbles littering the rocky surface just before the cliff.

This view—our view—is perfection, and I couldn't have lived with myself if I stole one of Manorin's greatest dreams from him. Not even if he swore up and down every day that the dream didn't fit him without me in it.

He gasps, pulling me against his big body. His chest heaves, his warm breath tickling the side of my neck. Big fingers curl into my belly and hold me tightly against him.

"Catherine...I...I'm at a loss for words."

I spin in his arms, putting a finger through his ring and guiding his focus to me.

His black pupils overtake the crimson of his irises—he loves to be tugged around by his nose ring. "You belong to me, and as much as it's your job to make me happy, it's mine to do the same for you." I slide a hand up his shirt, over miles of abs to rest over his rapidly beating heart. "I could never let you give this up, Manorin, not for anything, not even me. So I made us this portal. We can come and go any time we want, but eventually Evenia will find out about i—"

He silences me by bending down and nuzzling my mouth with his big lips, the closest thing he has to a kiss. He nips at my chin and bends lower, licking a hot path down the front of my neck then back up beneath my ear.

"You're breaking a million rules, Sunshine. Will there be consequences for that?"

"Mmm." I lean to the side, giving him an easier path to bite and nibble his way along my skin. "Not for me, there won't. I'd like to see Evenia try." It's laughable, really.

I'm not going to bring up the portal, but I suspect she'll find out. It's mine and Manorin's, and I'll never tell another soul about it. Still, I know she built safeguards into the system when we originally created it.

"I want us to build here," I say quietly. "I want us to build the property you always dreamed of, and we can come here anytime we want, Nor." I wave around us. "You have Annabelle's heart and the timer, so she's with us still. It'll be perfect. We can have our cake and eat it too."

He sinks to the ground and pulls me into his lap, my back to his chest. "Thank you, mate," he whispers into my ear. "You two are my gifts, and I'm not entirely sure I deserve them."

I shrug and smile at him over my shoulder. "I suppose you'll have to work really *really* hard to make sure you do deserve us, then." I wink. *"Really fucking hard*, Nor."

He chuckles into my ear, nipping at my sensitive skin. "I'm really fucking hard right now, Sunshine. Shall I start focusing on being worthy?"

Before I can answer, he rips off a piece of clothing and tosses it on the ground in front of us. In a swift move, he pushes me forward onto my knees and flips my skirt up, burying his big snout between my thighs and licking.

"Right there," I encourage him as he licks a delicious path up my pussy.

A possessive, deep rumble is my mate's only answer.

And it's the only answer I'll ever need.

~

Two months later

I've truly come to love our weekends in Pine Gulch. This haven is homey and charming in such unique ways from Ever. The downtown area has her own entire sassy personality, and it reminds me so much of being home with Annabelle. Some weekends we arrive via the portal I created. Other times, we come through the official portal station so as not to arouse suspicion.

It took about a month for a local troll builder to build our new place to Manorin's specifications. It's stunning.

"Can't beat that view, hmm, Sunshine?" Manorin crosses the dark stone kitchen floor as we stare out the giant singular piece of glass that forms an entire wall of this floor of our underground house.

The wooden ceiling beams creak and groan.

"She's happy we're here."

On cue, the string of bells over our staircase entryway rings.

"Annabelle misses you," I say, winking at Manorin. "I'm beginning to think she loves you more than me."

"Never," he scoffs, setting a coffee down in front of me. "But she does love me a whole, whole lot, and there's a lotta me to love."

I turn to look at the pretty wooden heart he mounted over

the expansive glass window. Annabelle's never out of mind here, even if all of her can't be with us physically. The timer comes with us on every trip, though.

Stepping to the huge glass wall, I stare out at the cliff face around us, marveling at how nearly the entire home is built underground. The only thing up above us is a huge greenhouse with our portal hidden at one end. When we want to sneak here, it's easy enough to do.

No harm, no foul.

The round communication disk on our wall lights up, Evenia's name hovering above it—speaking of foul. I knew this was coming, but I'm ready for it. I've been planning out how this whole entire thing will go. With the help of a few friends, of course. Some of whom are standing at the ready to help me deal with her. I press a button on my comm watch to send a quick message.

Manorin glances at it, then me, before crossing the kitchen to lift the comm disk from its holder. He lets it ring as he returns and sets it down in front of me.

"Want me to stay?"

I smile at him. "Sit wherever you like, my heart."

He stalks to the end of our dining table and sits with his coffee, one hand behind his head as he stares with glittering crimson eyes.

Gods, he's so handsome.

I sigh as I press the button to answer Evenia.

A hologram of the dark-haired vampire who runs the haven system snaps into place. She looks absolutely livid, dark brows formed into a harsh vee as she stares at me.

"How *could* you, Catherine?"

I take a sip of my coffee, determined to make her spell out my infractions. I suspected she had a way to be notified of new portals to the system after the same thing happened during last year's skyball tournament.

"I'm afraid you'll have to be a little clearer, Evenia," I say sweetly, smiling as if it's any old regular day.

"You painted a godsdamned portal into existence somewhere, and that poses a threat to our fucking security. Take it down, at once."

"I won't." I smile again. "There's no threat, and I won't paint another one, but I need this one."

"Absolutely not," she hisses. "You'll take it down, or el—"

I let my smile fall. "Or else *what*, Evenia?" My words drip with acid as I spit them at her. "You'll give someone else a portable portal generator and direct them to toss me into a dark hole somewhere?"

Her mouth drops open. "Of course not." The quietness of her words tells me everything I need to know.

I lift my chin. "I know for a fact that you gave the portal generator to King Caralorn in Ever. He then used that portal to mount an attack against his niece, Amatheia, which was thwarted. But she very nearly got dumped right into the open ocean into a new mer clan that wasn't made aware she was coming. She'd have been killed if she'd fallen out of the sky right into their kingdom. You knew all of that, and you did it anyway."

Her protective white eyelid flashes over her irises. "I was keeping the peace."

I lift a brow. "You orchestrated an attack *within* a haven, Evenia. You know the rules about that because you wrote them with me, all those centuries ago."

She snorts. "You're breaking a rule right now, Catherine, creating portals you're not allowed to create."

"Ah." I lift a finger to correct her. "The difference is that the law clearly states I cannot create new haven portals without going through the planning process. I didn't do that. This portal's personal, starting inside a locked room at the Annabelle

Inn and ending in my home in Pine Gulch. No one else will ever see it or know of its existence."

"Pot or kettle," she says with a dismissive wave. "We're at an impasse then, Catherine. I suppose I could allow you to—"

I rise to loom over her hologram. "You still rule because I allow it to be so, Evenia. You have remained in power this long only because I do not want that role for myself. The true mother of the haven system is me, and if I wanted to, say, paint a dark hole and trap you inside it for the rest of your very long days, I could. Do you understand?"

I lean closer to the hologram and point a red-nailed finger at her. "You have ruled only because of your role in the system's creation. But the reality is that we no longer need you, and you've broken the trust of monsters everywhere with your actions against Amatheia of House Zeniphon. As of today, you are relieved of duty. Formal paperwork will follow. I believe Betmal's got it drawn up and sitting at the ready with the same lawyer who drew up your separation papers."

She bristles. "The absolute *nerve* to have conversations about me behind my back."

I set my coffee cup down, letting my smile fall. "As it turns out, Morgan and Lou Hector have a lot of interest in running things. Being that Morgan's mate is your son, and he's already been a beloved keeper for centuries, I don't think we'll have any problems when they take over your role. And Lou's a blue witch, the only one who's ever agreed to live within the haven system. If she makes it safer for blue witches to not worry about being pressed into service as your watchdogs, more blues will come into the system. The havens will be safer than they've ever been." I grin. "There's literally no downside. Plus the girls will have my guidance and Betmal's. He and I have discussed this, of course."

Evenia's mouth drops open. "A coup, Catherine? After all these years we've worked together?"

"A coup, bitch." I bat my eyelashes at her as I pull a victorious smile to my lips. "I have long waited for the day where you'd fuck up and a good replacement was available. Today's that day."

"And what?" Her expression goes bored. "Can I assume you want to throw me into Belcastle as well?"

"Not Belcastle, no," a male voice rings out behind Evenia, and she spins, mouth dropping open. "Betmal?" She's aghast as my friend appears in the comm disk space behind her.

I don't recognize this version of Betmal. He stands with his arms by his sides looking like he's about to pounce, the white eyelids covering his crimson iris. He bears both fangs.

"You tried to hurt my mate, to take her from me, to *scare* her." He flicks his fingers, and dark claws slide out long from the tips. Slowly, one at a time, he unfurls his giant shadow wings until they shroud Evenia in darkness.

"Well," I say with a chuckle, "looks like you've got your hands full, Evenia." I glance at Betmal, who's glaring at his former mate with hatred in his eyes. "Have fun, my friend."

"Oh, I will," he purrs cruelly. After a moment, white eyes flick to mine. "Catch up over lunch next week, darling?"

"Let's," I say as I click off. The beginnings of a shriek are all I hear as I direct the comm disk to end the call.

Slow clapping echoes from the far end of our long breakfast table. Manorin smirks at me as I rise and walk down the length of the table to join him. He flares his nostrils and grabs his giant coffee mug in both huge hands, the kitty cat timer nestled under one of his tapered, fuzzy ears.

"That was magnificent, Cath," he says quietly. "Absolutely fucking breathtaking."

I shoot him a smug smile and grab his coffee cup, taking a sip of the Azuro dark roast.

He pats the table in front of him. "Come sit here, sweet girl, and let your mate feast."

I hand him the coffee mug, which he sets aside. The kitty cat timer slides down his neck and chest to the table and rolls away.

Nor grabs my shirt, ripping it down the middle and pulling me to the edge of the table. "Mine," he growls as he bends low over my chest, pulling a taut nipple into his mouth.

"Yours at last." I reach up and grab ahold of one of his beautiful long horns as I lose myself to the pleasure of his masterful tongue.

CHAPTER TWENTY-EIGHT
MANORIN

Staring deeply into Catherine's beautiful gray eyes, I get lost as I snap my hips, balls slapping against the backs of her thick thighs as I fill her. Like always, the sensation of her sweet pussy taking all of me, every long inch, has my eyes rolling into my head.

"Nobody ever took me like you," I grunt out, forcing my gaze back to her.

I have her pressed against the giant plate-glass wall in our kitchen, the entire valley visible behind her. She's pinned by my hips as I hold her up with one hand, her arms above her head with my other.

Catherine moans and rocks her hips, pussy clenching around my length, milking precum from me as I struggle against the rising orgasm.

"God*damn*, Sunshine," I manage, pulling out and slamming back in hard enough to shake the glass. "You fit me so fucking well."

Her soft moans rise into desperate panting, her breasts heaving against me as her pussy begins to flutter.

"That's it," I croon, fucking her deep and hard and slow.

"Tighten up for me, my Sunshine. When you explode, I want you coating this fat cock with your sweet honey."

Her cheeks turn pink, the shade traveling down her neck to her chest as her thighs begin trembling. Her pants morph to deep gasps as she writhes and tightens against me.

I'm losing my fucking mind, barely holding on to an orgasm that's about to obliterate my brain.

When bliss hits, I roar as my head falls back, balls tightening and pumping hot seed down my shaft. I lash her womb with cum, filling her until it drips down my thighs to puddle on the floor. White-hot ecstasy electrifies my muscles as her pussy massages and squeezes my length. She screams my name over and over, and it throws me deeper, harder into another orgasm that locks my muscles and blackens my vision. There's nothing, *nothing*, but the female taking everything I have to give.

My cock kicks inside her as orgasm fades. Catherine slumps against my chest, burying her face in the soft fur as I back to the dining room table and fall on top of it with her riding me. I sit up enough to arrange her thighs carefully on either side of me, slipping a hand between her soft ass cheeks to rub my cum into her skin.

The slippery feel of it has me hardening again. "How many times can I fuck you today before you're ready to eat something?" I laugh as I slip a finger, then two, into her ass, pumping carefully as she looks up at me from my chest, resting her chin on her forearms.

Her eyes roll backward as my fingers delve deeper, stroking her G-spot from the other side. "Don't know. We have yet to reach the limit." She smiles, mouth dropping open as I rock my hips, my cock hardening again.

"You're going to tire this old man out," I say playfully.

She gives me a sassy look. "I don't think so. And, in any case, that's why I took a younger male for a mate. I've got a few centuries on you, Nor."

"Less talking, more fucking." I flip us and straddle her, bringing a leg out to the side so I can stare at her pretty, well used pussy. She's dripping cum and honey, coated in my sticky white essence. Reaching down, I rub it into her clit and along her pussy lips, loving how puffy they are.

Hours later, she's had enough of me to sate her for an hour or two. We're not due home to Annabelle until later tonight, and we're up in the greenhouse putzing around with our plants as we share a bottle of wine.

The greenhouse windows flap open and shut rapidly, announcing someone's arrival. Through the milky glass, I see a tan truck with a giant black and tan logo on the side.

Winking at Catherine, I head for the door. "Fish and Wildlife," I shout over my shoulder.

When I open the door, Furyon stalks toward us with a book under one arm. The big dark elf grins as Catherine joins me in the doorway, slipping her arm around my waist.

He smiles from her to me and back again, offering the book to her. "Normally, the sheriff'd be the one to officially welcome you to Pine Gulch, but seeing as he's once again pissed and gone to stone-sleep it off, I thought I might do the honors."

He thumps the hardcover book. The front says, *Welcome to Pine Gulch, where the land kisses the sky.*

"We just got in a shipment of the new welcome books, designed by Betmal and Amatheia from Ever, if I'm right?"

Catherine nods and opens the book, smiling at Betmal and Amatheia's signatures on the first page. "Gods, they truly are a team. This is stunning." She flips through the pages, laughing when she comes to a table of contents. "Wait, this is new. Scavenger hunt around town?"

Furyon grins and crosses his arms, smiling at the book. "A little something we like to do here in the Gulch, helps new folks get acquainted. The scavenger hunt is a good excuse to visit every business and make a few friends when you're new."

Catherine beams up at us. "Well, I'm new. I guess I'd better start this next time we come to town."

Furyon smiles at her, pale eyes flashing. "Welcome to Pine Gulch, little lady. Holler if you need anything, anything at all."

I grunt and grab his shoulders, spinning him and shoving him toward his truck.

"Whatever she needs, I'm handling, Furyon. Get your ass back to town."

He winks at us and hops back in the truck, heading off down the barely-there dirt road we recently built.

Catherine sinks against me, rubbing her face against my chest. "He wasn't flirting, mate; he was just being nice."

I don't deign to answer that. Instead, I grab the welcome book and set it down just inside the door. After swooping Catherine into my arms, I head for the stairs.

"Let me take you back to bed, woman, and show you just how nice this big mate of yours can be."

She presses her forehead to mine. "Forever and ever, Manorin. Forever and ever."

$\sim$

"Ou sure about this, Sunshine?" We stare at the book of mating tattoo designs. Some are intricate bands; some are simple. They all serve the purpose of magically binding minotaurs to their mates.

Today's trip to High Moon Ink, the shifter tattoo parlor in downtown PG, was all Catherine's idea. I've been wanting to ask her, but even after everything between us, I worried it'd feel like pushing her. So I didn't bring it up.

She woke up this morning and declared that we were going to get tatted up, and I don't think I've ever gotten harder faster in my life.

But now that we're here, I'm unexpectedly nervous. She

wasn't ready when I asked her all those centuries ago. I probably wasn't either, but it crushed me either way. My asking her to get the tat was the beginning of the end for us, really. I had sky-high expectations of our future, but I was brash and overconfident.

"That one." Cath points to a thin braided design. "That's the one."

I stare, trying to imagine the beautiful braid around her throat. Emotion wells up in my chest as I pull her to it, burying my muzzle in her hair.

"And, yes, I'm sure." She rests her head against my pecs and looks up at me. "I want you, Manorin Albert Longhorn."

I laugh as I bend down and nuzzle her ear. "Don't ruin a beautiful confession of love with my middle name, Sunshine."

She chuckles and rubs her cheek against me. "I think it's a cute middle name."

I pinch her side until she squirms. "It's awful, and that's why you're the only person I've ever told it to."

She spins in my arms, batting her lashes. "Alarion and Walter know it, I'm sure."

Her mention of my brother and nephew sends me spiraling. "I wonder how Alarion's getting on back home."

Cath smiles. "Oh, he's plenty busy with the construction project for the new road. Betmal's keeping an eye on him for us."

That eases my mind a little. Alarion hasn't caused any trouble in Ever, but I know he's missing the monsters he used to consider friends, even if it seemed like they were using him. He's still never been super clear with me on what went down that got him to agree to leave with me. I may never get the truth out of him.

"You two ready?" a deep voice breaks through my thoughts.

Cath and I turn as a giant shifter male enters the room carrying a tray with the ink and his tattoo gun. He's as tall as I am, huge for a wolf, with a shock of unruly blond waves that no amount of gel holds back. Tattoos start under his jaw and crawl all the way into his shirt.

"Ready, Cairn," my Sunshine says, sliding onto the chair and pulling her gray waves into a claw clip.

The shifter smiles at her. "You pick a design?"

"This one." I point to the page, and Cairn glances over. He gives me a clipped nod, then starts prepping his gun.

I cross the room to hover over Cath, but she looks unruffled by this entire thing. "You nervous, Sunshine?"

She beams up at me. "Not at all, Nor. Are you?"

I resist the urge to touch her, to remind myself that she's here and mine, and she's about to become mine in a very permanent fucking way. Pride and love fill me, banishing those dark, painful places that were empty when I lost her.

"No, Sunshine," I murmur, reaching out to tuck long gray bangs back behind her ear. I stare at her creamy, delicate skin as I fantasize about what she'll look like with a permanent Longhorn collar.

"You look pleased as punch," she says, chuckling as Cairn leans over.

He winks at her. "If you two are done flirtin', it's time to get started, pretty lady."

She never looks away from me as she replies to him, "Get goin', sir."

Cairn moves quickly, and Catherine never flinches. Not even when he's tattooing the side of her neck. I'm sure that spot's sensitive as hells, but she smiles the whole time. Now and again, gold flashes through her gaze as she looks at me.

When Cairn's done, he holds a mirror up for her to see. She turns from side to side, admiring the shining silver braid that encircles her delicate throat. The skin is raw and red, but she runs her fingers along it, and the magic gleams bright as she touches it.

She looks up at me. "Will I feel you with me always?"

Cairn hops out of his seat and departs, smart man that he is. I sink onto his still-warm chair, straddling it as I hang over the back and grab her hand. Pulling it to my cheek, I nuzzle her palm, loving how *mine* she smells.

"Yes." I reach into my pocket with my free hand, pulling out a bright silver nose ring inlaid with black pegasite and tiny red diamonds. Handing it to her, I smile. "Mark me as yours, Sunshine."

She takes the ring and leans forward, her breasts brushing against my chest as she unlocks my nose ring and gently removes it.

"You're teasing me," I murmur as she slips the new silver ring through and clicks it shut.

My Sunshine shimmies her breasts against me, sending white-hot heat shredding through my core as lust rises. The magic-imbued silver ring in my nose prompts a sensation like a warm hug around my entire body. Even when we're far apart, I'll always feel her with me, as if she were in my arms.

"Welcome to the Longhorn family, Miss Evrien," I say with a smirk.

She runs her fingers along her new tattoo again, a dark gray brow rising. "Isn't that Mrs. Evrien-Longhorn?"

I chuckle. "It's whatever the fuck you want, woman. Let me take my wife home now, please. I am in desperate need of you and a bed."

"Don't forget to put healing cream on the tat for the next two days, though," Cairn shouts from the front. "I'm trying not to hear y'all, but shifter hearing is horribly excellent. Manorin, come and pay your fucking bill and get outta here, would you?"

Catherine and I share a laugh as I help her up. We barely make it outta Cairn's shop because I can't stop staring at that silver band around her soft throat.

As we pass other monsters in the street, whispers rise about my new silver nose ring and her tat. When we walk past Betty's Bar, Furyon's in the middle of the street chewing on a piece of wheat as he smirks at us.

He slips both hands into his jeans pockets as we stop in front of him. "Don't think you newlyweds are gettin' outta downtown without a celebratory drink. Get inside Betty's, and let me buy you a round."

Catherine's bright laughter fills my soul with joy as we follow the dark elf into the saloon. *Joy* is what lies in our future, thank the gods and goddesses.

Viya will bring us the cool, healing wash of water.

Ratek, the gentle wind to ruffle our hair and kiss our cheeks.

Vejoom will steady the earth beneath our feet.

And Firbell will grant us the fire of determination and love.

And she and I deserve every minute of that.

CHAPTER TWENTY-NINE

CATHERINE

"Put the puppies down, Ig!" Alo shouts as he tries to wrangle his six—no, today he's seven—year old into a chair. Fifteen other seven-year-olds run in various states of disarray around us. Alo's been trying to wrangle them to stop their game of hide and seek and come eat cake. Oh, I think it's been about fifteen minutes, and he's no closer to getting anyone to come sit.

Nor sits at the long table set up behind Annabelle, one big arm laid over the back. The female hellhound puppy lies on his chest, her head nestled between his pecs as she stares up at him.

"That puppy loves you," Miriam says as she sits next to him and strokes the pup between the ears.

Nor glances over at me. "Sunshine, I think we mighta gotten ourselves a dog."

I shake my head as I laugh. Manorin draws love to himself. I don't know what it is about him. Annabelle loved him right away. This little pup does too. Iggy sat on him the day they met. Nor is a magnet.

On cue, the tattoo around my throat pings, sending a phantom hug sensation down my spine. Across the table from me, Nor shivers. The pup nestles up higher and sticks her head along his jawline, her snout just under his ear.

Where the kitty cat timer is because of course. Yet another being madly in love with Manorin.

I'm not jealous. I want all the love for him.

"Catherine!" Iggy flies out of a shrub and zips toward me, wrapping himself around me like a blanket as his shrieking laughter rises. Pixie wings flutter around us as hands claw at him and their laughter goes wild and crazy.

"Kevin! Get off Catherine!" someone shouts, but I can't tell who because I'm wearing a gargoyle and a pixie as hats.

Alo un-Velcros his son from my head, and Iggy goes limp but winks at me.

"Just needed a hug. Love you, Miss Catherine."

Tears fill my eyes. At six—no, seven—Iggy's starting to really lean into emotion and connection. It'll come more naturally to him as he gets older.

Minnie joins us and sits at my feet, staring up at Iggy with bright, happy eyes.

"Love you too, Ignatius," I say softly.

He's already gone, though, zipping over the table to land on one of Nor's horns. The pixie kiddo, Kevin, joins him as they each pick a horn and swing around, effectively turning Nor into a jungle gym.

The hellhound pup on his chest lets out a warning growl, and Minnie rushes under the table. Hopping up, she snaps at Iggy's shirt and drags him away.

Alo, Miriam and I watch as Iggy spins in place and presses his face to Minnie's, whispering sweet nothings to her.

The hellhound pup nuzzles against Nor's jawline again, blowing out a big sigh that rustles his ear hair. The timer starts purring, and then everything goes back to normal.

Alo throws his hands in the air. "It's almost time for the parade. Are we giving up on the cake or what?"

Behind him, Annabelle lets out a horrible groan as if she's telling him to chill.

He shrugs and drops into a seat. Picking up a fork, he spears a piece of cake and takes a bite. "Stick this fork in *me* 'cause I'm done. Is it bedtime yet?"

Miriam snorts out a laugh and opens her mouth for a bite of his cake.

I drop onto Nor's big thigh and stroke the hellhound pup. "So, what are you naming her?"

Crimson eyes drop to the pup, and he rubs her fuzzy butt with a thoughtful expression. "How about Ember?"

"Nooooooo!" Iggy swoops back into view, alighting on one of Nor's horns as Minnie growls out a warning from somewhere in the rose bushes. "That's a dumb name. Name her something badass like Cerberusa!"

Nor looks up. "Cerberusa? I gotta say that doesn't roll off the tongue, kiddo."

Iggy shrugs and leaps off Nor's horn, gliding back toward the rose bushes. Giggles erupt as the bushes sway. I make a mental note to have Wren come by later and boost the flowers back up. They're taking a beating from this very long game of hide and seek.

A half hour later, Iggy swoops into the kitchen where I've begun cleaning up from the party.

"Catherine!" His voice is about fifteen decibels higher than it needs to be. "Dad says we're late, and we're going to miss the parade if we don't go now! Do you have your sign?! I've got Minnie, and the puppies aren't following that well. Can you help me? We have to go right nowwwww!"

Laughing, I swoop down and pick up a puppy. Manorin enters the kitchen and scratches Minnie under the chin.

"Hey, Coach!" Iggy shrieks, diving toward Manorin and landing on one of my mate's beautiful long horns. "Get the puppies, would ya? Especially Cerberusa since she seems to like you."

With a smirk, Nor drops to one knee and gathers the other two puppies as Minnie rubs her face along his thigh.

I smile up at him, laughing as the kitty cat timer flips from the island to his shoulder, tucking under his ear, which seems to be her favorite spot.

"Why does everyone love you so much?" I muse as I stare up into his handsome face.

He winks at me. "Something about the horns and size. I'm a badass, I'm big, and monsters feel safe."

I laugh at his explanation, but it's so true. There's not a monster in town who isn't obsessed with our new skyball coach. And today's a big reveal—we've got a lot of new Evertons, including some new skyball players, so we're hosting a welcome parade and party.

"Let's goooooo," Iggy shrieks, yanking on Manorin's horn. "We're gonna be late, and Dad said I would be in so much trouble if I was late since we're in the parade."

Nor rubs the kitchen archway lovingly with his cheek as we head out of the kitchen and toward the front of the inn. Minnie trails us out onto the porch, and the pups all howl loudly. Annabelle waggles newly painted white shutters at us and we wave goodbye back.

We manage to make it to Sycamore Street in front of the diner, where we're all due to meet. Arkan's there, shouting directions as he tries to corral everyone. "Alright, Misfits, you go first, come right up here."

"Enforcers, honey," Hana says with a wink. "The new name is the Ever Enforcers. We literally finished the rebrand yesterday."

"Fuck," he mutters. "One of these days I'll get used to it."

Nor stalks to the group of players who make up our new

team. It's a scrappy, young team, but give us a year or two, and we'll be kicking the Punishers' asses.

"Alright, Enforcers, join me here. Who's got the sign?"

Twin gargoyle brothers, recently graduated from the Protector Academy, unfurl a sign painted in green and gold announcing the team's new name.

"Logo looks good, right?" Morgan joins me, holding Abe's hand as they stare at the new logo.

"It's pretty badass," I say with a laugh. "Sorry to kick your prior logo to the curb, Abemet."

The tall vampire grins as he shrugs. "We've got bigger fish to fry these days, what with running the haven system and all."

Ah yes, my little coup. Morgan, Abe and Lou have only been in charge for a few short months, but in that time, they've done incredible work.

We share a smile as Arkan and Nor manage to get the gathered monsters in some sort of order. When Nor turns to me, holding a hand out, I join him. We'll be right after the skyball team and before town leadership. Behind us, hundreds of monsters are gathered on the sidewalks lining Main Street.

Arkan raises both hands. "Alright Mis—shit, Enforcers, go ahead—and remember, we're stopping on the lawn *between* the gazebo and Town Hall! Go on!"

Whoops rise up as the team heads for Main and hooks a left, cheering and shouting. Raucous cries and cheers rise from Main, along with plenty of clapping and shouts of the new team name. Nor and I go next, Iggy still hanging on to Nor's horn like a handle.

It takes us a solid fifteen minutes to make our way down Main. I recognize many of the gathered monsters but I *don't* recognize just as many. The current construction at the end of Main Street and the new cross street, Pine—a nod to Nor's home—brought with it an influx of new Evertons.

Miriam's Sweets Shop sprays candy out over the crowd in an

arch. Young monsters dart into the street to grab the candies, which turn into bugs and snakes and slither around trying to escape grabby little hands.

I laugh as monsters shout Nor's name, screaming and cheering as the new team makes its way down the street. By the time we get to Town Hall, I've got several pieces of candy in my hair and had to put Cerberusa down so she could wriggle off to find Minnie.

Turning just past the gazebo, which is creaking and groaning with excitement, I watch as Ever leadership makes their way along the last bit of the parade route.

There's Shepherd with Thea up on his shoulders, his hands on her knees. They're both laughing hysterically, and as the joyful gargoyle looks up at his mate, my heart grows two sizes. Wren and Ohken come next, Wren tossing beautifully cut flowers at the onlookers. Some explode into bits, raining petals down. But others expand and grow as big as umbrellas, twirling and dancing over the crowd. Alo, Miriam and Iggy come next with the hellhounds stalking behind them.

There used to be terrified whispers when the townsfolk saw Minnie, but that's all changed, especially with the puppies. They dart into the crowd, stealing bits of candy with excited yowls. It's not until Minnie sneezes fitfully at them that they fall into line again behind Alo.

Morgan and Abe come next, holding hands as she waves at the crowd, shouting and pumping everyone up. He's as austere as ever, the slightest of smiles on his angular features.

The Shifter Hollow crowd follows. There's Richard and Lola, who strums wildly on an electric guitar, the notes echoing off the buildings and reverberating until the street shakes. She's wearing her crown, and something about that brings tears to my eyes.

Betmal and Amatheia walk with Connall, Dirk and Lou. The blue witch spins two blue spears over her head, playing with the crowd as I marvel how much her magic has grown in the short time since she discovered it. Dirk disappears on a gust of wind, ruffling hair and wings of those in the sidelines before popping into view again. Connall grins as he trails his mates.

The crowd joins behind the official parade, the party already kicking off.

I look up at Nor. "They're not gonna make it all the way to Town Hall, mate."

He laughs, waggling his brows at me. "Never, *Ever*, Sunshine."

I smile so big, it hurts my cheeks as the Evertons advance toward us, spreading out on the lawn as Arkan tries to get everyone into the right spots. Above us, Iggy zooms in great big circles, screeching hysterically.

When there's a momentary lull in the sound, Ig whistles down at the crowd. Most of the monsters look up as he flaps above the group, beaming at the Evertons.

"Welcome to Ever," he shouts, his voice just audible over the crowd. "Where Ever-yone is welcome! Population 852? Pfft." He winks at the crowd. "Someone needs to update the sign!"

I glance at Arkan, who's smiling at the young gargoyle.

Nor elbows me playfully. "I'm pretty good with paint. Think I should offer to update it?"

I slap his big chest. "Maybe another day, mate. But after this, when we get home, you're gonna be busy."

His nostrils flare as sunshine glints off the new silver ring in his nose. The inlaid black pegasite and tiny red diamonds are a clear sign that he's taken.

He drags his knuckles along my jawline. "I'm at your command, sweet girl."

Beaming at the idea of that, I return my focus to the party. To my people. To my town. I laugh with joy as I turn my face to the sky, admiring the bright green ward that protects my family and my home.

Ever-yone welcome, indeed.

THE END

This might be the end, but it's not over. Because your love for Ever has filled me with a joy I never expected when I first started noodling in this world. When I told Mr Fury Mack I was writing something called Getting It On With Gargoyles, he encouraged me. He knew what we all now know—Ever is a beautiful, magical place and WE NEED TO FIND THAT DAMN MAP.

SIGN UP FOR MY NEWSLETTER TO READ THE FREEBIE EPILOGUE. THERE ARE MAZES INVOLVED ;)

++

If you preordered the book box then you'll be getting a first spoiler look at WHAT'S NEXT. I don't have the preorder up yet but I likely will by release day!!! STAY TUNED and all I have to say about it is "Giddyup"

BOOKS BY ANNA FURY (MY OTHER PEN NAME)

DARK FANTASY SHIFTER OMEGAVERSE

Temple Maze Series

NOIRE | JET | TENEBRIS

DYSTOPIAN OMEGAVERSE

Alpha Compound Series

THE ALPHA AWAKENS | WAKE UP, ALPHA | WIDE AWAKE | SLEEPWALK | AWAKE AT LAST

Northern Rejects Series

ROCK HARD REJECT | HEARTLESS HEATHEN | PRETTY LITTLE SINNER

Scan the QR code to access all my books, socials, current deals and more!

@annafuryauthor
liinks.co/annafuryauthor

ABOUT THE AUTHOR

Hazel Mack is the sweet alter-ego of Anna Fury, a North Carolina native fluent in snark and sarcasm, tiki decor, and an aficionado of phallic plants. Visit her on Instagram for a glimpse of the sexiest wiener wallpaper you've ever seen. #ifyouknowyouknow

She writes any time she has a free minute—walking the dogs, in the shower, ON THE TOILET. The voices in her head wait for no one. When she's not furiously hen-pecking at her computer, she loves to hike and bike and get out in nature.

She currently lives in Raleigh, North Carolina, with her Mr. Right, a tiny tornado, and two sassy dogs. Hazel LOVES to connect with readers, so visit her on social or email her at author@annafury.com.